# I DON'T
# LIKE
# WHERE
# THIS
# IS GOING

# I DON'T LIKE WHERE THIS IS GOING

### A Wylie Coyote Novel

■ ■ ■

## John Dufresne

W. W. NORTON & COMPANY

*Independent Publishers Since 1923*

NEW YORK • LONDON

For information about permission to reproduce selections from this book,
write to Permissions, W. W. Norton & Company, Inc.,
500 Fifth Avenue, New York, NY 10110

For information about special discounts for bulk purchases, please contact
W. W. Norton Special Sales at specialsales@wwnorton.com or 800-233-4830

Manufacturing by RR Donnelly Harrisonburg
Book design by Ellen Cipriano
Production manager: Louise Mattarelliano

Library of Congress Cataloging-in-Publication Data

Names: Dufresne, John, author.
Title: I don't like where this is going : a Wylie Coyote novel / John
Dufresne.
Description: New York, NY : W. W. Norton & Company, [2016]
Identifiers: LCCN 2015043955 | ISBN 9780393244687 (hardcover)
Subjects: | GSAFD: Suspense fiction.
Classification: LCC PS3554.U325 I3 2016 | DDC 813/.54—dc23 LC record
available at http://lccn.loc.gov/2015043955

W. W. Norton & Company, Inc.
500 Fifth Avenue, New York, N.Y. 10110
www.wwnorton.com

W. W. Norton & Company Ltd.
Castle House, 75/76 Wells Street, London W1T 3QT

1 2 3 4 5 6 7 8 9 0

*for Cindy*

I DON'T
LIKE
WHERE
THIS
IS GOING

# 1

THAT AFTERNOON, WHEN the unthinkable happened, my friend
Bay and I were enjoying cocktails in the atrium of the Luxor
Hotel in Las Vegas. Although, as Bay informed me, here on the
Strip, we're not technically in Vegas. We're in Paradise.

Bay Lettique is a nimble sleight-of-hand man and a masterful
illusionist who makes a respectable living playing Texas hold 'em.
That afternoon he wore a seersucker suit and looked very much
the crusading Southern attorney sent over from central casting,
an illusion of gentility he gladly cultivated. He wore his fine blond
hair modishly, one might even say rakishly, long. His eyes that
afternoon were blue, to match the suit, I suppose. Those eyes were
naturally brown, but Bay owned and wore a variety of tinted lenses,
sometimes a green eye and a brown eye at the same time. Said he
wanted to know who was paying attention. His nose was thin, his
chin cleft, and his cheeks dimpled.

I watched the lights of an inclinator as it ascended to the apex
of the thirty-story pyramid, and wondered about the four thousand rooms in the hotel and the eight thousand or so stories being
played out behind their closed doors. I was a therapist in exile, and

I thought, only half in jest, what a marvelous place this would be to set up shop. Right over there by the food court, maybe. I could help my clients who had just lost their life savings or their marriages, or who had behaved disgracefully, in ways so reprehensible they were paralyzed with shame and overcome with despair, help them shape their lives into narratives, so that their lives made some sense again, so they understood that the best story is a story of redemption, and that their personal story was only in its second act.

Bay plucked a yellow primrose out of the air and set it in his highball glass. I said, "Do you think that's wise?" And I reminded him of the several thousand video cameras in the hotel and how some uniformed security officer scarfing shrimp cocktail at his surveillance desk was certainly watching us right then, and if you really want to gamble in the casino, you might not want the house to observe your sleights of hand.

Bay says illusions work like dreams work, and like memories or fantasies do: you see quite clearly, right there in front of you, something that is not really present. He also says that a shared illusion is a collaborative creation of the performer, who passes his hand over the three of spades, and you, the observer, who now sees in its place the ace of hearts. You are unaware of what actually happened and are unaware of your unawareness.

On our first morning in town, I had gone for a walk in our new neighborhood, known by the oxymora Wild Haven at Desert Shores. I turned a corner a block from our house and saw an elderly man in a white boonie hat and a green short-sleeved jumpsuit clutching a trembling Chihuahua to his chest, trying to protect it from four large, terrifying, and snarling dogs. I yelled, threw up my hands, and made what I hoped were menacing but not provocative gestures. The dogs had the man pinned against a wall. I took out my phone. Two of the dogs snapped at the man's legs, another tore at his arm. The largest dog got hold of the Chihuahua and tugged. Before I could tell the 911 operator my location, because I didn't know it, a police squad car sped toward us and screeched to a stop. By now, three dogs were tearing at the man's face and neck. The merciless, coal-black dog grabbed the Chihuahua and whipped its limp body back and forth in its jaws with such ferocity that the little guy's punctured skin split and the Chihuahua deflated.

I ran toward the scene without any idea what I could or might do. The police officer fired his service revolver and killed the largest of the dogs. I stopped dead in my tracks. The other dogs leaped in alarm, and two of them ran. The cop fired three more shots. One dog fell, another wailed, bit at the bullet in his rump, and hobbled off on three legs. It took a second shot, this one into the skull, to subdue the dog still gnawing on the poor man's face. The paramedics arrived and set about their grim work. I sat on the sidewalk, spent. The cop wanted to know what I'd seen before he arrived. I told him. I asked about the victim. His lips and eyes are mush, the cop said. And some of the left ear is gone. He'll be okay if he survives the shock. Okay? I thought. The dogs, he said, are feral. Former pets, most of them, pets or fighting dogs, abandoned by losers, who are either skipping town or eluding Animal Control. The dogs roam the hills out west, out beyond the Beltway, come into town when they're starving. You got any animals, he said, keep them inside.

Las Vegas looks the way I imagine hell would look if Lucifer had exercised his clownish sense of humor—a colossal and garish wreck of ironic architecture abandoned on the low and level Mojave sands, a city of gleefully appalling desolation, full of discordant sound and unavailing fury, a city built on a foundation of pretense and delusion. Yet there are those who find it delightful. Bay is one, so when we decided it would be prudent to leave Everglades

County, Florida, for an extended vacation following a season of baleful unpleasantness, and while certain aggrieved parties settled themselves back into their respective cozy criminal routines and forgot about us, we came to Vegas. I brought my indoor cat, but left my gainfully employed sweetheart behind. Patience would be visiting soon and often. Bay leased a furnished two-story, four-bedroom, four-bath stucco house with a barrel-tile roof, attached garage, gas fireplace, and a pool, just off Lake Mead Boulevard. We bought a used Mitsubishi Mirage with just under a hundred thousand miles on it.

We were into our second drinks when Bay made the bowl of spicy nuts vanish. When I said I was still hungry, he showed me the bowl of snacks on his iPhone. I said, "Can I eat those?" He said, "It's easy to make things vanish, harder to bring them back." Bay had explained the law of conservation of energy to me when I asked him how he made objects disappear. He said the object doesn't vanish; it just becomes something else. And he lifted his brow and smiled. And then his phone played "Everybody Knows." He put the phone to his ear and said, "Talk to me, Mikey." Open Mike—Michael Lynch—was a sketchy but valuable friend of ours from back home in Melancholy, Florida. Mike knows where the bodies are buried, Bay says—and how deep. While Bay listened, he levitated the drink coaster and floated it around the coffee table. I shook my head like, *Why don't you ever listen to me?* and he smiled.

Mike doesn't know what it's like to be afraid. He can be wary, even cautious—he's not a fool, after all—but he lacks the involuntary visceral response the rest of us feel when threatened, the response that causes us to freeze or to hide and then to flee. Mike is not afraid of snakes or spiders or heights or intimacy or death or failure or men with weapons. He's not afraid of clowns or scalpels. He told me he had been struck by lightning when he was ten. Bolt went in through his head and out through his feet, taking his shoes with it. I wondered if he'd had his amygdala fried in the blast and with the withered limbic almond went the seeds of fear. He, himself, didn't care to know the reason. Fear's not the worst loss you can suffer, he said.

Bay took the phone from his ear, shook it over an unfolded napkin, and the spicy nuts fell out. He wiped the phone on his thigh, smiled at me, picked up a walnut, popped it in his mouth, and went back to his conversation. I raised my hands like, *Where's the bowl?* Bay says every illusion tells a story in three acts. Setup, buildup, payoff. Some folks call it the pledge, the turn, and the prestige. Bay prefers the verbs *lure, beguile,* and *reveal.* He also says that magic is taking an absurd amount of time and trouble learning a skill that gives the impression that something has happened that hasn't.

False twilight is general in Vegas hotels and casinos. What is it, I wondered, that the casinos don't want you to see? Bay said, no, it's the opposite; it's what they *want* you to see. In the dimness they can direct your attention, choreograph your gaze with lights. I looked across the atrium near the entrance to the casino, where a woman in a glittering gold bikini and knee-high gold lamé boots danced halfheartedly to techno Muzak beside a sleek silver luxury car on a slowly revolving turntable. Her mind, it seemed, was elsewhere, as were her grace and sense of rhythm. Behind her a banner on the wall read ALL YOU CAN EAT, ALL DAY $27.50!

A woman in a silver tweed pantsuit pushed her white toy poodle in a large three-wheeled, canopied baby stroller. She stopped by a statue of the great and victorious Ramesses II and lifted the dog to her shoulder. She held the dog like she would a burping baby, swaying side to side, rubbing its back, and whispering into its ear. In ancient Egypt mummified dogs were often buried alongside women, archers, and dwarves.

First I heard raised voices, and then I saw a young couple arguing. The man jabbed his finger in the woman's face. When she looked away, he took her chin in his hand, turned her head, and stared into her eyes. The woman was a tiny thing with short black hair. She wore a simple sleeveless black dress, a strand of pearls, and ballerina flats. Her belligerent beau with his Wayfarer shades and soul patch wore a Bluetooth earpiece below his porkpie hat, a blue linen sport coat, a white oxford shirt, thin green tie, khaki cargo shorts, and blue Crocs. Yes, I judge people by their appearance. And it's sort of my job as a therapist to examine one's disparate physical clues and puzzle the pieces together into meaning. Look close, pay attention, read the body and its language. So I was thinking *Abercrombie & Douche* at the moment. The woman tried to walk away, but the man grabbed her elbow. He said, "What did you just call me?" I leaned forward. Bay held up a finger and shook his head no.

I looked up wondering where the camera trained on the couple might be and caught a blurry shape of red and white up near the apex of the pyramid. At first I thought someone must have folded a bedspread over the balustrade, but then the shape moved away from the building and into the compassed void, where it appeared to hover a moment, floating on an updraft before descending. And then I saw arms and legs spread-eagled and realized that this spectacle was either a clever, if alarming, performance staged by the Luxor or it was some renegade BASE jumper or wingsuit flyer putting on an impromptu show, and at any rate, what seemed to be a free fall would momentarily resolve itself into a breathtaking swoop, the deployment of a small parachute, and a controlled landing.

I heard the thud of the body on the carpeted floor a moment after it struck and shivered to stillness. The lady with the pet dog screamed. Bay told Mike he'd call him back. I ran to the body as if to prove to myself that what I thought I had witnessed had not happened. The berated woman cried into her hipster's chest while he photographed the corpse with his smartphone, until a bald and goateed security guard tapped the hipster's shoulder and held out his hand. Blood leaked from beneath the dead woman's head and pooled beside the slack jaw, the shattered teeth, and the broken nose. Both amber eyes stared up from the topside of her face. One lower leg was bent forward at the knee. Her arms made a cross above her head as if she might have wanted to signal that she was drowning.

She wore a milagro on a silver chain around her neck. Milagros I knew about from my client Maria Z. They're religious charms used for healing purposes. Maria's charm was a pair of disquieting eyes, which she hoped would cure her glaucoma. The dead woman's milagro was in the shape of a young girl wearing a mantilla, a blouse, and a flared skirt. I wondered if the woman had had an ailing daughter or if her child had died, leaving her bereft and hopeless. Suddenly a swarm of security personnel descended like blowflies and drove us toward the down escalator to the lobby, and two uniformed guards covered the body with a white linen tablecloth.

When we reached the lobby, Bay told me to follow him. We walked to a bank of elevators. Two gentlemen and a bedraggled young woman got off. The men each had short blond crew cuts and were dressed alike: teal camp shirts, black slacks, white socks, and chukka boots. My parents dressed my twin Cameron and me alike until we were five. Twins, if these two *were* twins, dressed alike at thirty seemed troubling and unwholesome to me. We boarded the elevator behind a guest with an access card. The guest told us he was in town for the World of Concrete National Convention. "What's all the brouhaha?" he asked us.

We got off at the last stop on the fifth floor, which was about

as high as I wanted to go anyway. I was *not* getting on an inclinator going up. I'm terrified of heights. When I was a kid, I often
dreamed, as we all do, of falling from some great height, and in one
of those dreams, I did not wake up before hitting bottom, as we
all do, but fell to the source of the gravity, and it was Hell, which
was dark and cold, and I was alone and on my back screaming.
My screams woke Cameron, who shook me awake. I told him the
dream. He said we all get the Hell we deserve, and went back to
sleep.

Nevertheless, I was able to peek over the low balustrade and
look down onto the pedestrianless atrium. The cleanup was under
way. The woman's shrouded corpse was being wheeled away on
a gurney. Maintenance workers steam-cleaned the carpet. The
inelegant dancer shimmied her bony shoulders at the luxury car.

Bay said, "Was she pushed, do you think?"

I was certain she hadn't been. There was no scramble in the air
to right herself, no flailing of arms, just a single-minded commit-
ment to this exhilarating and gruesome task. She never wavered
from her fatal and empty embrace. I couldn't stop shaking, trying
to imagine the level of despair that could have provided her with
the courage to step off into nothingness.

Bay said, "Was she alive when she was pushed?"

On the way to our car, I asked a uniformed guard if he'd learned
the name of the victim yet.

"Excuse me?"

"The woman who leaped to her death. Just now. Upstairs."

"I'm sure I don't know what you're talking about, sir." His name
was Loomis, according to his badge. He was muscled and stocky,
had a brown buzz cut, brushy white mustache, and small, thin,
almost folded ears. His eyes were dark and round, like lacquered
buttons, and his nose, snubbed and funneled.

I said, "Would you like me to tell you what happened?"

Bay took my elbow and Loomis pointed our way to the door.

"Have a good evening, gentlemen," Loomis said.

I shook my arm free and looked Loomis over. I said, "Still biting your fingernails, Loomis? That's an impulse control disorder, a problematic attribute for a man in your profession. Do you recall when this compulsion began?"

Bay said, "Wylie!"

I told Loomis I was a professional. I could help. "I'll leave you my card."

Loomis laid a finger on my chest and said, "Listen to me and leave right now."

I said, "Denatonium benzoate. Ask your pharmacist."

Bay led me away and said, "What set you on tilt?"

"The lying."

As we walked to our car down East Reno Avenue, a slim young Asian gentleman wearing a blue shirt, a white sport coat, and a black bow tie, looking like Elvis in *King Creole*, stopped us and asked me what I would give him in exchange for a used pack of candy cigarettes. He was charming enough, but I told him I'd given up pretending to smoke. Bay admired the gabardine blazer, ran his hand along the sleeve, nodded, and whistled his approval.

"A paper clip," the fellow said. "A napkin. A dime. Anything."

I said, "Is this an art project?"

He smiled. I gave him a dime. He handed me the pack, bowed, and hurried on his way.

I have a habit, a bad habit according to my ex-wife, of saving useless objects. Postcards; matchbooks; pens; every letter I've ever received, from back when people wrote letters; pennies; and campaign buttons. I have a plastic crate full of things I've found on my walks around Melancholy—a rubber lizard, baby pictures, credit cards, motel keys, doctor bills, shopping lists, barrettes, and so on. But this pack of candy cigarettes I figured I'd toss, but before I did, I opened it and got stung on my index finger by the furious bee inside, and it wouldn't let go. I brushed it off. My finger throbbed. The stinger was still in the skin. I eased it out. "Who the fuck does this?" I said.

Bay said, "What?"

I told him what had just happened. I pointed my toe at the twitching insect on the sidewalk. I looked around, but the dude was gone.

Bay said, "I'll tell you who did it." He held up the little creep's wallet. Opened it.

I said, "You stole his wallet?" A handsome wallet of light brown leather with a red baseball stitch design.

"Because he stole yours," Bay said, and he produced my wallet from midair and handed it to me.

Bay looked at the thief's driver's license. "His name's Johnny Ng." He looked at the second driver's license. "Or Michael Ho." Bay took the money from the cash pocket and dropped the wallet down the storm drain. He handed me the cash. "For your pain and anguish."

I shook my head. "Buy more vodka for the house. What if I were allergic to bees? I'd be going into anaphylactic shock right now."

"I got something at the house that'll take the pain away."

Bay drove us toward home. I switched on the radio and scanned for local news. Lots of talk shows, Christian rock, and country stations. Nothing about the recent tragedy. We saw the Luxor hipster and his unfortunate girlfriend, his arm over her shoulders, as they passed by a shabby convenience store that seemed to be called MART BEER & WINE FILM T-SHIRT SOUVENIRS GRAND CANYON TOURS

ICE ATM MAPS INFORMATION HOOVER DAM TOURS PHONE CARDS. We saw a half dozen cops busting a shirtless man outside the boarded-up and derelict Key Largo Casino and Hotel as a TV camera crew filmed the arrest for a reality show.

DJANGO, MY OUTER-SPACE-BLACK KITTEN, was halfway up the eggshell-white living room drapes when I opened the front door. He froze, like maybe we wouldn't see him or his unblinking golden eyes. When I said his name in my stern voice, he climbed down backward, dropped onto the back of the sofa, and sped off to the kitchen. I followed him and iced down my finger. Bay called Beach Pizza and ordered a Hang Ten and a chopped antipasto. I made drinks. Scott Beaudry texted me asking if I could cover his noon-to-three hotline shift tomorrow. I could.

I didn't gamble. I didn't enjoy the spectacles that passed for entertainment in Vegas, so I had time on my hands. I read like crazy, took long walks, and volunteered at a crisis intervention center doing phone counseling and some short-term face-to-face work with walk-ins and runaways. I spoke with lots of abused wives, some potential suicides, and not a few destitute and homeless people, sometimes whole families of them. And in this way I got to put some of my clinical training to good use. Some callers needed to express their pain to a person otherwise uninvolved. Others were so confused they couldn't make sense of their emotional turmoil. Listening to their stories kept me sane and feeling useful.

The young woman who delivered our pizza said she wasn't allowed to step inside the house. I took the boxes from her, asked her if she was sure she didn't want to take a martini break. We could sit by the pool. She had a pierced nose and a tattoo of a gray fox on her upper arm. Her spirit animal, she said. Cunning, playful, and quick. Just like her. She smiled. She said, What's that humming? I said, You hear it, too? She said, You got a semi idling in the backyard? Bay pulled thirty dollars of pain-and-anguish money out of the air and handed it to her. Told her to keep the change. She told us that she once delivered ten Maui Wowee pizzas to Carrot Top's house and got a five-dollar tip. I kid you not! She told us her name was Kit and said good night.

Bay and I ate at the coffee table in the den. I turned on the TV news, hoping for a story on the Luxor. Bay fed me the news from home. According to Open Mike, Jack Malacoda, K Street lobbyist and prominent GOP fund-raiser, had been indicted by an Everglades County grand jury on charges of fraud, corruption, and conspiracy to bribe public officials. My cleaning lady, whose Easter sunrise wedding on the beach had been interrupted by a fusillade of gunfire and at which Bay and I made our last public appearance in Melancholy, was still in the hospital, recovering from multiple gunshot wounds, but was expected to recover. I tried Channel 8 and got an investigative report on the staggering suicide rate for military veterans in Nevada. More than double the national average.

You have a fifty percent higher risk of killing yourself if you live in or visit Las Vegas than you do anywhere else in the country. Just crossing the Clark County line—a visit to a brothel in Pahrump, in Nye County, say—makes you safer from your lethiferous self. I knew the grim statistics from my work at the Crisis Center. I also knew that sixty to eighty people go missing every weekend in Las Vegas—up to seventeen hundred in a month. Some number of those, of course, come here expressly to get lost. Some people don't arrive in Vegas and then kill themselves; they arrive in Vegas *to* kill themselves. I asked Bay if he'd ever felt the urge to take his own life. He hadn't, he said. I asked him if there were any circumstances under which he might consider it.

He said, "Alzheimer's."

I said, "Me, too. And ALS."

Bay said, "I'd do it in private. Try not to leave a mess. Pills."

My mother, Birutė, who as a child in Lithuania had escaped the Rainiai Massacre near Telšiai in 1941, killed herself with an overdose of fentanyl. My father found her beneath their bed, dressed for Mass, or for her coffin, clutching her amber rosary beads, photographs of her slaughtered parents and siblings on the floor beside her. Most suicides kill themselves without an audience and quite often in hotel or motel rooms, knowing that their bodies will be discovered by strangers, saving the loved ones additional trauma.

Django sat on the arm of the sofa and stared a hole in the pizza. The news segment on TV was about this guy at the Bellagio who hit eleven reds in a row in roulette and then let it all ride on black because black was overdue. He lost every penny. Bay said, "Roulette wheels don't have memories."

UNLESS YOU'RE A CELEBRITY in Vegas—and you're not—you're an anonymous and expendable commodity. The only thing about you that matters at all to anyone here is the money you will leave behind at casinos, restaurants, wedding chapels, massage parlors, and hotels. Gamblers lose more than six billion dollars every year in Vegas. Visitors spend thirty-five billion more. Greed is the gravity that keeps the city from flying apart and showering the galaxy with its gaudy shrapnel. There are wealthy people in Vegas, but you will never see them. You will see the many more who yearn to be wealthy, but will settle for pretending to be for a long weekend, and others who seem content to kill what little time they have left slumping for hours in front of machines that are more animated than they are. And you will see the working poor everywhere you look—the half million underpaid service workers whose business it is to see that your stay is both exhilarating and untroubled.

Django crept to the corner of the coffee table, stretched out his front leg until his paw was a breath away from the crust, and looked at me like, *I'm not touching it, Wylie; what's your problem?* When I think of public suicide, I associate it with sending a message, often a political one, like the self-immolating Tibetan monks in China these days. Other times the message is personal: *Look what you did to me!* I wondered what kind of message the Luxor jumper might have been sending, and to whom. Maybe her suicide was a protest against her perceived anonymity, and anywhere else it might have guaranteed her a moment of lamentable notoriety. But I'd have to wait till the morning to find out.

I WOKE WHEN DJANGO took the earplug out of my ear and licked my earlobe. My bee-stung finger throbbed. I got up. I heard Bay in his room talking in his sleep. I brewed coffee, fetched the paper from the driveway, and sat on the sofa. I turned on a news-radio station and the local news on the muted TV. Nothing in the paper. Nothing on the radio.

Then on TV, a shot of the Luxor. I turned up the volume. A police spokesman told the reporter, "We have no idea who she is at this time, and we don't know why she jumped." But the reporter, who must have bothered to ask at the reception desk, knew the woman's identity. She was Layla Davis from Memphis, Tennessee. She'd checked into the hotel earlier that day, ordered a meal from room service: Australian lobster tail, strawberry cheesecake, and bottled sparkling water. The reporter had also learned from the room service waiter that Ms. Davis's suitcase had not yet been unpacked when he delivered the meal. I went to the Internet to learn what I could about the late Layla Davis.

Not much. Layla Jean Davis worked on proton therapy research at St. Jude's Hospital in Memphis. She was single, lived in a one-bedroom condo on Mud Island, had done her graduate work at Indiana University, and volunteered at the Shelby County Animal Rescue Shelter. From her office window, she could have looked out at the world's sixth-largest pyramid three blocks away on the river. In her photo on the St. Jude's website, Layla looked to be in her early to mid-thirties. She wore square-framed wire-rim glasses, a powder-blue blouse under her white lab coat, and an unfelt smile. Her brown hair was cut short. Her hands were folded on her uncluttered desk. No mention of a child. Did any of her colleagues suspect her pain? Was she ill? Depressed? Was that affected smile meant to mask her hopelessness?

Saint Jude is the patron saint of lost causes. The pyramid out her window was not a funerary monument, but was, absurdly, a Bass Pro Shop. Memphis is named for the capital city of Egypt's Middle Kingdom, whose local god Ptah, the patron of craftsmen, created humans through the power of his heart and his speech. The name Layla comes from the Egyptian and means *night*. Layla had no Facebook page, no blog, no Twitter account that I could find. To whom would they ship her body? Was it still in the morgue?

Those ancient Egyptians believed that a person's actions during life were judged in a ceremony in which one's heart was weighed against a feather, which represented things as they ought to be. The weighing was conducted by the jackal-headed god Anubis, and recorded by Thoth, the god of writing. Balanced scales indicated a person of "true voice," who would then join Osiris in the Land of Vindication. Unbalanced scales revealed one to be of "diminished voice." The measured heart was tossed to Ammit, the Swallower of the Dead, and he of diminished voice would continue to exist, but without consciousness. What had Layla believed awaited her? Oblivion? Elysium? Deliverance? And with what certainty had she believed it? And what is belief but conjecture?

I tried to imagine her booking the room at the Luxor, having already decided against household toxins, drowning, and an overdose of prescription pills, having decided not to profane her own home. Buying the plane ticket. One-way, of course. No backing out now. How long had she been contemplating her violent death? Why had she decided to act, finally, on the day that she did? Why not the day before? What was the precipitating event? We can suffer any degree of pain, I choose to believe, no matter how lacerating, if we know it is going to end. But when we know that it cannot . . .

I pictured Layla sitting in her living room with her laptop and with a glass of fortifying white wine. Music on the Bose. Samuel Barber's Adagio for Strings, perhaps. When she made the reservation, entered her credit card information, and confirmed, did she think about someone she would never see again, someone who would be startled awake in the middle of the night by a caller bearing the terrible news?

Layla, like Icarus before her, in Breugel's painting, in Auden's poem, plunged to her death while someone else was drinking a Cosmo at Liquidity or pulling a handle on a slot machine or just folding an anemic poker hand. For all the tourists at the Luxor, hers was not an important failure. The casino ran as it had to, the robotic clangs and beeps and dings of the machines droned on, and the patrons had places to go, shows to see, and games to play.

Bay said good morning. I said, "Who does that? Commits random acts of violence?"

"What are you talking about?"

"The bee guy."

"The bee was a distraction."

"Her name was Layla."

"Who?"

"The suicide at the Luxor."

He said, "We didn't necessarily see a suicide. We saw a death."

I kept expecting to read more about Layla in the coming days, an obituary, surely, a solemn mention in a colleague's blog, an announcement of a memorial service, an acknowledgment by St. Jude's or by the crestfallen staff at the animal shelter. But I did not. The passing of Layla Davis played like notes from an unclappered bell.

# 2

Y OU DON'T PLUCK out people's eyes and then reproach them for
their blindness, John Milton almost said. When your civic
pride rests on the label "Sin City," and when your official advertising slogan encourages people to engage in behaviors so censurable
that they must be kept hidden from family, friends, and colleagues,
then you're asking for trouble, and you should anticipate and prepare for the exploitation of women and children and the rampant
abuse of substances legal and illegal. You should expect to attract
the lubricious, the sociopathic, the treacherous, and the perverse.

I know, I sound like an unctuous puritan, but this ridiculous
city was making me cranky. I called Patience after breakfast and
asked her to fly out here as soon as she could. I told her we'd take a
driving tour of the state, see the Great Basin, the country's largest
desert. It'll be fun. Mining towns, ghost towns, empty highways,
Area 51, red rock canyons, salt flats, cowboys, and Basques. Quiet.
Nevada's the opposite of Florida, I said. It's the most mountainous
state, the driest, the fastest-growing, the most urban, if you can
believe it, and, perhaps, the most empty. She said she'd see what
she could do.

Doctors at Sunrise Hospital had been rebuilding what was left of Ronald Conlin's face when he died on the operating table. Ronald was the man I'd seen attacked by dogs. When I walked the streets these days, I carried a can of pepper spray. I downloaded the photo of Layla I'd found on the Internet to my iPhone. I'd ask about her at the Crisis Center. Ronald moved to Vegas from Idaho after his wife had died. They'd been independent painting contractors, a husband-and-wife team, for forty-six years.

So I'd been in town just two weeks and had already witnessed two violent and improbable deaths. I had been fortunate enough not to have seen Mr. Conlin's mangled face, but I had seen Layla's, and I couldn't scrub the gruesome image from my mind, especially those adjacent eyes and the fine line of carmine blood leaking from her ear. What was less disturbing, but more bewildering, was the mystery of Loomis's lie and the puzzling silence of the media. Why wasn't everyone in town talking about the electrifying and tragic spectacle that was Layla's death?

ON THE BUS RIDE down to the Crisis Center, I glanced through a book on optical illusions that Bay had recommended, *Seeing Is Deceiving.* I pride myself on being observant, on seeing what other people don't see. I can look at a person, at his expressions, his gestures, his clothing, his home, and his possessions, and I can tell you what the person's thinking. That's why lawyers and cops have used my consultant services in the past. Bay calls me an intuitionist. My own therapist, Thalassa Xenakis, says I have robust mirror neurons. I look, I stare, I gaze, and I pay attention to what I see. But now that I'd been out of work awhile, I worried that I was losing my empirical mojo. And the book wasn't helping. I saw a spiral where there was none, a straight line that appeared wavy, parallel lines that seemed to be on a collision course. I stared at a blurry rectangle of color until it disappeared. I saw small gray blocks that weren't really there but were fabricated by my lying eyes.

Bay had once shown me an illusion on his iPad called the Lilac Chaser. You see twelve blurred lilac disks in a circle, like the numbers on a clock, around a small black cross on a gray background. As you stare at the arrangement, one of the disks briefly disappears, and then the next, and so on around the circle, and then you see a green disk coursing around the circle of lilac disks, and then all of the lilac disks disappear, one by one, in a clockwise sequence, and the green disk is alone, but not for long, and then there are a dozen each of lilac and green disks. What had changed? Not the picture I stared at. What had changed was the way I looked at it. I saw it differently. Was the picture making me do it? Was this unchanging image changing me?

Bay had a theory about all these visual shenanigans. Scientists know that there's a tenth-of-a-second delay between the moment that light hits the retina and the brain's translating that neural signal into visual perception. Bay believes that we've evolved to compensate for the delay by generating images of what will happen a tenth of a second into the future. Call it foresight. Call a tenth of a second the measure of an instant. Knowing the future helps us act judiciously in the present. How else, he says, could our ancestors have survived an attack by the stealthy saber-toothed tiger? How else could Miguel Cabrera hit a hundred-mile-per-hour fastball thrown from sixty feet six inches away when he has only a third of a second to react before the ball is past him? He would have to begin his swing before the ball is pitched, right? We live with premonitions of the future. You think the phone will ring, and it does. You see the doctor's needle by your arm, and you cringe because you already feel the flash of pain. We're always trying to perceive what the world will be like in the next instant. That's what the optical illusions do—switch on our image-generating future-receptors.

And I had my own theory. What we remember may not be what we actually saw. What we saw was not all that there was to be seen. What we see is influenced by what we feel. When I saw Layla fall from heaven, I was baffled and panicked. I know what I saw, but don't know what I missed.

No one at the Crisis Center recognized Layla from my photo. No one had even heard about her death. All the talk in the coffee room was about a knife fight at a karaoke bar between two Taiwanese gangs, Posse Galore and Bamboo Rats. I looked at yesterday's logbook and didn't find an entry for a suicide call. Three people died in the karaoke bar; five others had been slashed and stabbed and were clinging to life. I handled a call from one of our chronic callers, a guy the staff referred to as Elmer the Dog Lisperer. You always knew it was Elmer because all his *l*'s and *r*'s were *w*'s, and he always wanted to tell you about his dog. The Crisis Center kept a file on chronic callers, and we knew, somehow, that Elmer's real name was Tom, and he was a paramedic with Clark County Fire and Rescue. He'd been a constant caller for over five years.

I answered, "Crisis Center."

Elmer said, "I just fucked my German shepherd, Bwondi. She woved it."

"Is there a problem?"

"Why would there be a pwobwem?"

"Then why are you calling? Call back, please, when you're in crisis."

The next call came from a woman who had to choke back tears before she could speak. She told me her husband had beaten her. I asked her if she was all right and if she wanted me to have a medical team dispatched to her house. She didn't. No, it isn't the first time—but he always calms down and apologizes. I asked her if she feared for her life, and she sobbed. When she caught her breath, she told me the fight was over something stupid anyway. She'd brought the wrong brand of beer home from Vons. I asked her what she wanted to do about this. She said she wanted it not to happen anymore. I said, What can you do to make that so? She hesitated and said, Not be stupid anymore? I said, Excuse me? She said, When he finds out I'm pregnant he won't want to hurt the baby. I said, You're pregnant? She said, I will be soon, thanked me, and hung up.

The Crisis Center occupied a former funeral home with a drive-thru viewing window that had been converted into our coffee room. I spent most of my time in the hideous, bleak, and window-less phone room, where the peeling walls were twilight-gray, the dripping water pipes were exposed, the carpet soiled, and the flickering lights fluorescent and maddening. The ugliness was almost agonizing. Volunteers had pasted cartoons on the wall: a clown trying to kill himself with laughing gas; a suicidal slug wearing a salt-packet vest. I tried to keep my eyes closed. On the whiteboard, the staff had written their New Year's resolutions. Gretchen B. wrote that she was finally going to get her teeth straightened and her eyebrows tattooed.

I was on the phone for two and a half hours with a man who had a shotgun on his kitchen table and was considering putting the barrel against his throat and squeezing the trigger. He racked a round so I'd know he was serious. The caller ID was blocked, and I suspected he was calling on a disposable phone, so we couldn't trace his location very quickly. He told me his name was Konnor with a K. He catalogued his miseries starting with a cheating wife, estranged children, an asswipe boss, and bills he couldn't pay in a million years. At the top of his list was the emphysema that was slowly, inexorably taking him out anyway. He spoke in a monotone that suggested this was a story he'd told too many times already, and he was bored with it. I realized that in order to choose to live, Konnor would need some hope to cling to, even if all he had was what he saw as the shambles of his life. Clinging to the wreckage might keep him afloat long enough to get rescued. Then he said he was going down with the ship, like he had read my mind, and he thanked me for listening, thanked me for my concern and my efforts, said I shouldn't blame myself, and he hung up, and I listened to hear the blast of the shotgun, which I imagined would drown out every other sound in Las Vegas.

What I heard instead was a girl weeping in the conference room. My shift was over. I wanted a drink. I tried to imagine Konnor in his kitchen, staring at the shotgun, thinking about how he was going to be late for work if he didn't get his ass in gear. If I could picture the scene clearly, maybe it could happen.

I peeked into the conference room and saw a girl who looked to be about fourteen wearing one of the center's EVERY DAY I MAKE A DIFFERENCE T-shirts over her floral-print dress. The left side of her face was swollen and bruised. Helen Lozoraitis, our director, comforted her. A volunteer I hadn't met introduced himself. "I'm Gene. Woodling."

"Wylie."

"Like the coyote?"

"But not spelled that way."

Gene told me that the cops had just brought the girl in. They found her crying her eyes out in Angel Park. She told them she'd run away from a brothel.

I said, "What happens now?"

"We're trying to reach her mom in Kansas. Meantime, we'll take her to Refuge House."

The girl held her head between her knees and wept. Helen hugged her. We protect our money in this country with more vigilance than we do our children. I showed Gene Layla's photo, but he didn't recognize her. "All right," I said, "I'm out of here."

"Adios, Coyote."

THERE ARE, I HAD read, over three hundred Elvis impersonators in Las Vegas, so I was not surprised when one of them, a Hefty Presley, boarded the monorail with me at the Sahara Station. He unbuttoned his gold-lined cape and folded it on his lap when he sat. I took the seat across the aisle and asked him how he liked his job. He looked at me over his gold aviator shades and told me he was living a dream. Not everyone gets to wear a white jumpsuit with sequined comets to work every day. He told me he'd just played a real estate open house in Centennial Hills and was on his way to a bachelorette party in a banquet room at the South Point Hotel. I asked if he had a Colonel Parker impersonator doing his bookings. He laughed and said, "I'm going to use that."

At the Quad Station we were instructed to exit the monorail and proceed to the station. Service had been temporarily suspended. The exit to Las Vegas Boulevard was closed. I walked down Koval Lane and found out what the problem was a few minutes later. They were making a movie at Flamingo and the Strip. One vehicle seemed to have exploded, and the flames shot an implausible thirty feet in the air. I saw several cars on their sides and another wrapped around a light pole. The movie cops were holding the gawkers away from the shoot, and I imagined the hero calmly walking away from the mayhem he'd created, having saved our great and sovereign nation from ignominy.

I walked through the atrium at the Luxor and stopped beside

the spot where Layla had died. I stepped back and looked around. Anyone at the Starbucks yesterday could have witnessed the fall. And anyone over at the wedding chapel. I asked the barista at Starbucks if he'd been working yesterday.

He said, "Noon to six."

"Then you saw the woman who fell?"

He wiped his hands on his apron. "The who that what?"

"A young woman leaped to her death"—I pointed—"right there. At five-ten."

He shook his head. "I'd know about something like that if it happened."

"It did happen. I was here."

"If you say so."

I took the walkway to Mandalay Bay and passed a heavyset woman in large turquoise hair curlers and gray sweats, dragging her reluctant child by the arm, telling him he was so getting his flippers bleached. I was meeting Bay for a drink at the Border Grill. Suddenly there were fussy and excitable children everywhere, many of them tanned and dressed the way I imagined their parents thought that adults should dress—like characters in movie musicals, not like shoppers at Walmart. I heard a mother say, "Do your duck face, Crystal," and little Crystal raised her eyebrows and lifted her flamingo-pink lips up and out in a kind of half pout, half pucker. And then I saw the poster that explained it all: the Little Miss and Mr. Nevada Glitz Pageant was going on this week at the resort. It did not, however, explain *bleached flippers.*

I was escorted to a table adjacent to one occupied by a boy and girl, each around seven, I guessed, who were obviously pageant contestants and who were dining without parents or chaperones. I ordered a Bloody Mary made with bacon-infused vodka. Bay texted that he was stuck in traffic trying to exit the 15. The girl was blonde, wore a white taffeta dress, and called the boy *Colt*. She described the cupcake dress she was going to wear in the competition: "Short to here, off the shoulder, sleeveless, beaded organza. It's lemony yellow," she said. "I'll look good enough to eat."

Colt told Mylie—I'd been thinking *Lindsay*—she was a lock to win Grand Supreme. And then there was a snarky exchange about an eight-year-old princess from Longview, Texas, named Evah, who'd won the title last year and the year before that. A woman walked by with her leather purse draped over the stub of her missing forearm. Colt said he would forgo his customary black tux this year in favor of a black-and-white silk cowboy outfit with a thoroughly butch black Stetson. He told the waitress he'd like the rest of his crab nachos boxed, please and thank you.

Mylie checked her face in her compact mirror, liked what she saw, and asked Colt if he thought the two of them would eventually get married.

Colt shrugged. "I might end up being the girl that Mom's always wanted."

"Cool!"

"You could teach me your sassy walk."

I turned to watch Colt and Mylie leave the restaurant and wondered how I would find out tomorrow if they'd won and wondered as well if every pedophile in Clark County would be in the audience at the pageant. When I turned back, Bay was sitting across from me in his blue linen suit and his magnolia-white silk shirt. He was trying to quit smoking but had an electronic cigarette in his hand. He took a puff and put the e-cig in his jacket pocket. He asked me what I was drinking, and I let him have a sip. He nodded his approval. I said the person who came up with the idea to infuse vodka with bacon should win the Nobel Prize.

Bay said, "They gave the Nobel Peace Prize to Henry Kissinger, a murderer and a war criminal."

"I mean the James Beard Award."

Bay ordered lemonade. He didn't drink spirits before playing poker. He'd been finding the competition in Vegas more formidable than he'd been used to in South Florida. Everyone plays like they can afford to lose. He was ahead a few thousand, but his game had been inconsistent.

I told him about the movie shoot I'd happened on. He said it wasn't a movie. I said I saw it.

He said, "Two guys in a black Hummer pulled alongside a silver Lexus and opened fire. The passengers in the Lexus returned fire. Both cars then headed north on the Strip at considerable speed. The driver of the Lexus took a bullet, lost control of the car, slammed into a taxi, and then there was a whole chain-reaction pileup. The taxi exploded. Four people dead. The Hummer got away."

"How do you know this?"

"It's all over the news." He asked me if I'd learned anything about Layla.

I told him about St. Jude's and about my dead end online.

He said, "I know a PI in Memphis. I'll give her a call."

POKERTOX, A COSMETIC and dissembling procedure, may not have been anything new, but it was news to me. Botox for card players—an attempt to disguise the signs of facial tells. My thinking was if you needed an injection of potent neurotoxins to elevate your game, you must not have been very skillful to begin with, and you were unlikely to benefit greatly from the immobilizing therapy. You felt vulnerable and exposed, and you questioned your cleverness at the table. You were leaking critical information through your unconstrained countenance. You got the dermatologic fix. But what you didn't realize was that even with your face as vacant as the Bates Motel, you betray your weakness in other ways. The face is not our only expresser of emotions, but it is the easiest to mask. Just smile with your eyes.

The tell is in the behavior, not the expression. Is he holding his breath or breathing rapidly? Are his hands still or busy with the chips? Is he chatty or quiet? Rude or cordial? Is he slumped in his seat or leaning forward? Is he putting on a show? If he's rubbing his forehead, you know he's struggling with something. If he's steepling his hands, you know he's holding wired eights or better.

There were two Pokertoxics at Bay's table. The older one, Bart, had also plumped his lips with collagen. His hair was as thin and white as finely spun glass, but his eyebrows were black. He wore ironically large glasses with metal frames, but he seemed unable to blink. The other fellow was Clifford, and he didn't have much of a face to start with: weak chin, a small and slightly celestial nose, tiny spectral-blue eyes, just a trace of blond eyebrows, and meager lips. His was the idea of a face more than a face, a first draft of a face, a sketch.

When I suggested to Bay a while back that not playing every hand would make the game boring, he smiled and said he counted on people like me sitting down at his table and opening our wallets. "Poker's like baseball. The most intense moments happen between pitches when nothing seems to be going on. The fielders, the batter, and the base runners all have to consider the infinity of possibilities that might ensue with the next pitch and prepare themselves for each contingency. When there is no apparent drama on stage, the imagination fires on all cylinders."

Poker isn't gambling, Bay was fond of saying. But it is luck. And *good* luck is understanding that you can't control randomness—the cards can't tell the difference between Amarillo Slim and Slim Pickens—but you can control whom you sit next to, and whom you bluff, and whom you call. "When I see a dude pull out his card-guard coin with a four-leaf clover on it, it warms my heart, and I know I'm going to bleed him dry. Poker is applied math and behavioral psychology." Bay says you play poker as if you can see your opponents' cards, and you can—in their behavior.

I took a seat by the poker table, ordered a martini from a waitress named Sincere Lee, at least that's what her name tag claimed, was served a Manhattan, which I took with a smile—apparently I'll drink anything—tipped her, and watched Bay go to work. He won a small pot and then folded on three straight hands. The joker next to him wore a gray hoodie and white shades, chewed a toothpick, grunted once in a while, and laughed at other players' failures. Watching him, I could tell what he was like away from the table, an excruciating asshole on whom therapy would be wasted because he didn't think anything was wrong with him. When he walks into a room, he's already smirking. I took my drink and went for a walk before he pissed me off even more. Only later did it occur to me that maybe this miserable, narcissistic piece-of-shit persona of his was an act designed to rile his tablemates so they couldn't think straight. Me, I would have flipped out five minutes into the game.

I took a stroll through Slotsville. I'd once heard on the BBC that American casinos pump oxygen through their AC systems to keep the gamblers alert and eager, and to mitigate the asphyxiating effect of the lowering clouds of cigarette smoke—so much oxygen that if there were a substantial fire, a casino would explode like Krakatoa. I didn't know about that, but I did know that there was not enough oxygen for a woman I saw playing a Seven League slot machine. She had an oxygen tank attached to her mobility scooter, an oxygen cannula in her nose, a cigarette in her mouth; she had a drink in one hand, a cup of coins in the other; she hit the spin button with her elbow.

I thought a walk outside might clear my head and focus my thinking. As I approached the exit to West Hacienda, I saw a young man entering the casino with a ring-tailed lemur on his shoulder. He was stopped by a uniformed guard. The lemur wore a service-animal mesh vest, had her elegant tail draped over her shoulders like a shawl, and was eating a pomegranate. When the guard touched the young man's elbow, I worried that the lemur would sink her prosimian teeth into his fleshy face. Instead, she wailed like a slowly closing screen door. I wondered what would happen to her if she got loose in the city. Could she survive an attack by a pack of feral dogs? She could climb a tree, of course, if she could find one.

I walked east toward the university trying to attend to the confusion I felt about Layla, about her death, and about what I thought of as a conspiracy to deny that death, and in so doing, deny her life. What I knew was that Layla Davis was dead. What I didn't know was why she was dead. And if you don't have the why, you don't have the story, and if you don't have the story, you don't know the life. I wanted to know the story. And the story might also explain the covenant of silence.

I had wanted to know my brother's story and never did. Cam, so bright, so charming, so brilliant—a polyglot who spoke four languages at age ten, a musician who taught himself piano and violin and played Mozart's Sonata in F Minor after hearing it once when he was seven. Cam, the happiest child I've ever known, got his neurological wires crossed at puberty and became a wretched adult who spent the next twenty years trying to kill himself with prescription opiates, and who eventually succeeded in having one of his playmates bludgeon him to death.

I've treated many suicidal patients over the years. Some I was able to help. One of those was Donny L. Donny's is the saddest story I know. His ten-year-old son, Max, checked into Everglades General for a tonsillectomy and died of a bacterial infection he likely acquired at the hospital, a superbug, the papers called it. When Donny first came to see me, he looked like he had never slept. But he assured me he had—one nightmare at a time. He told me about Max with his head lowered and his eyes closed. Then he said, "Tell me why I should go on."

I said, "Your wife needs you."

But as it happened, she did not. She left him for his best friend, Royal Hunter. Royal's forsaken wife, Claire, blamed Donny for her own divorce. And then he was out of a job. He took a buyout from the *Journal-Gazette* that ended his seventeen-year career as an investigative reporter. He was now a citizen journalist, which is what the online news outlets call you when they don't pay you for your content. And he still had his aging parents to worry about.

His dad, Al, was eighty-three and running on empty. He had Parkinson's, diabetes, prostate cancer, high blood pressure, and arthritis. Gwen, Donny's mom, was blind and had suffered two strokes and one heart attack. Their house in Melancholy was a demoralizing disarray of clutter and filth, but they refused to engage a cleaning service on the pretense that none of the ladies in the Maid Brigade spoke English. They would not accept Meals on Wheels deliveries because they did not take handouts. They wouldn't allow the visiting nurses into the house, and they screamed bloody murder whenever Donny mentioned an assisted living facility.

Every Saturday morning Donny took his mother food-shopping at Winn-Dixie and then took his dad for lunch at Svensen's Buffeteria. And then he'd sit at the kitchen table while his parents napped in their separate bedrooms and do the sorting and the splitting of pills. He'd fill each of their morning and afternoon color-coded seven-day pill organizers with the appropriate meds and hope that they would remember to take them.

Then one Saturday morning, no one answered his knock, so he let himself in. He found his mother dead on her bedroom floor soaked in blood. Her left arm had been severed below the elbow. The severing machete lay on the unmade bed. He found his father sitting on the Barcalounger in the den with blood on his hands and face. He seemed bewildered. He said, "That is not your mother in there." Al spent his remaining days at the Florida State Hospital up in Chattahoochee.

Before our recent troubles sent me packing for Vegas, Donny and I had settled into a comfortable routine. No more sessions. Instead, we met for oysters and beers every other Wednesday at Slappy's Wonderland on the beach. The last time we got together, Donny's dad had just died in the prison infirmary. Donny blamed himself for not being a firmer parent to his mom and dad and forcing them to go to a continuing care facility, dragging them kicking and screaming if he had to. They would have gotten used to it, would have thrived in their consenescence, would not have had to live in filth, and would have thanked him. We both understood the fear underlying their resistance—the fear of slipping away unnoticed in a geriatric warehouse. They were holding on to what they had loved, to what had sustained them—their home, their past, and their independence. Donny found no solace in his understanding.

Why had Donny been able to go on when Cam and Layla could not? Cam had been variously diagnosed as bipolar, as borderline schizophrenic, as having delusional disorder symptoms and substance dependence. I could see that he was often anxious and more often depressed. He was unable to get outside himself. The pain demanded all of his attention. Donny had some interest in and curiosity about the world outside himself and that saved him, I think. He understood he was not alone. Had Layla been depressed? Anxious? Had she come to feel helpless? Maybe there were some clues among her personal affects. If I could only get to them.

I felt a buzzing in my pants, reached for my cell phone, and came away with a pink-eared mouse with a bell at the end of its tail. And then I grabbed the phone. Bay wanted to know where I was. I looked up. "The National Atomic Testing Museum."

"Wait there. I'll pick you up in ten."

On the drive back to the house, Bay said that he'd been disarmed by a waitress he'd met at the casino, and I thought, So that's today's theme—one-armed bandits. He told me to close my eyes for an experiment. He was going to ask me to inhale a fragrance. "Don't describe the smell," he said. "Just tell me what image pops into your head." I shut my eyes. He handed me a small bottle and told me to unscrew the cap. I sniffed and sneezed. I said, "Loomis. I see Loomis, the nail-biting security guard at the Luxor."

"Do you know why you saw Loomis?"

"No." I looked at the label on the cologne bottle. Prada's Infusion d'Homme.

"Sillage—the trail left in the wake of the wearer. When Loomis jabbed you in the chest, waves of that noxious scent rolled off his arm. It was like he soaked his jacket in it."

I sniffed again. Fatty, waxy, like a soapy musk. A smell I somehow hadn't noticed at the time of our altercation. But my olfactory neurons had. What we smell we remember, even if we don't remember smelling it.

Bay told me he was going to play a song on the CD player. He said, "Close your eyes and tell me what you see."

The resolute music throbbed out of the speakers, and I saw

Layla's broken body on the hideous carpet. "What the hell is that dreadful noise?"

"Techno Muzak. Donna Summer's 'I Will Go with You.' The tune the model with the luxury car was dancing to when Layla fell."

So now I knew what I hadn't remembered smelling or hearing. What hadn't I remembered seeing? And what trigger might bring that back?

Bay said he'd gotten a call from our friend Charlotte. Her Yorkie Henry had gallstones. An ultrasound confirmed it. He was on all kinds of meds and antibiotics and was scheduled for exploratory surgery. Charlotte had taken a waitressing job at the fish camp in Immokalee where we all spent our last evening together. I should tell you about her.

# 3

C HARLOTTE EDGE UNDERSTOOD that confession needed to be a part of her new life, and she was ready, if not eager, to disclose her sins when Bay, Patience, and I, three desperate fools, stumbled into what had been her quiet world on this past Easter Sunday morning. We were trying to steal her Lincoln Town Car. She objected. We explained our harrowing circumstances, and when Bay flashed a clever facsimile of an Eden Police Department badge, Charlotte handed him the keys and hopped into the passenger seat with her very agitated lapdog, Henry VIII. Bay drove us away from the mayhem on the beach and away from the local law enforcement authorities, who had unfinished business with the two of us, regarding a police department death squad, Ponzi scheming lawyers, several gruesome murders, corrupt public officials, and both the Italian and Russian mobs, but that's a story for another time. Patience and I sat in the backseat wishing we were anywhere else but here, like in Peru, I was thinking, visiting the Uros people on their floating reed islands in Lake Titicaca. Far away from here.

Charlotte closed her eyes and rubbed her temples. Henry whined and licked her face. She asked us if she was in trouble for what she had done . . . for what had happened . . . to Mr. Kurlansky. Bay's eyes met mine in the rearview mirror. He raised his brow and shook his head like, *What's going on?* Bay's not an actual cop, Patience said. Bay held up the badge and made it vanish. Charlotte bit her lip and wept. Patience leaned forward and told Charlotte that I was a therapist for real, an accomplished listener. Charlotte looked at me. I nodded. Patience touched Charlotte's shoulder. Henry settled himself on Charlotte's lap. Charlotte took a restorative breath and told three strangers the story that no one but Henry had ever heard until then, a story of her sustained emotional and physical abuse at the hands and fists of the brutal Mr. K., a story of assault and degradation, of years of vicious humiliation and exhausting pain, all of which ended quite suddenly with his fall from a seaside cliff on a moonless night in Mendocino. "One minute he was squeezing my shoulders, shaking me, threatening me, and the next he was gone."

I told Charlotte she had nothing to worry about.

Patience shouldn't have said, but said, "Some motherfuckers need killing."

Charlotte said, "I didn't—"

Bay said, "Amen."

Charlotte said she had no idea why she put up with it all those years, why she didn't leave. How had she allowed herself to become irretrievable and pathetic and imprisoned?

I said, "Why don't you begin with the day you met Kurlansky."

Patience handed Charlotte a tissue, arranged a lock of Charlotte's damp hair over her ear.

Charlotte told us that the story started before that. Way before. "First you need to understand the foulness I was coming from."

And as Bay drove on deep into the Everglades, and with Henry curled and snuffling on her lap, Charlotte told us the unexpurgated story of her once-shattered life, and of her eventual triumph over squalor and misery, over self-pity and malice, and as she spoke, the heaviness in her heart was lifted, and the scales of shame and secrecy fell from her eyes, and she glimpsed a resplendent future ahead.

We ended up at Fatty Goodenough's Fish Camp close to Immokalee, and we were famished. Our waitress wore a T-shirt that read PUBLIX EXPLOITS FARMWORKERS. We ordered and ate piles of gator tail, catfish, frog legs, and hush puppies and washed it all down with swamp water cocktails. Henry ate the scraps and drank water from his plastic bowl under our picnic table. We told Charlotte about the sunrise wedding we'd attended that morning and the gun battle that ended the ceremony. Charlotte thanked us, gathered herself, and asked if there was anything *we* were ashamed of.

Patience said, "Stealing a car."

"But I gave you the keys."

"Not this car," she said. "I was young and foolish and in love with a bad boy."

Bay said he once left a woman at the altar.

I said, "My twin brother lost himself in drug addiction, and I tried to help him, until I got too angry, and I stopped trying, and then he died."

And so we talked and smiled and told each other tall tales about close calls and lucky breaks, and we drank the heart right out of a fine Easter Sunday afternoon.


BAY PUFFED ON his vaporette between sips of coffee. Django sat in the chair between Bay and me at the kitchen table, waiting for one of us to turn his head and leave his breakfast plate unguarded. I told him I knew what he was up to. He closed his eyes so I'd disappear. Bay said he'd heard from his friend Julie at the Wade

Detective Agency in Memphis, and we'd had a bit of luck. Layla Davis was Julie's client.

Bay said, "Julie Wade called me after she got my text and after she'd called the Clark County coroner, Vegas Metro, and all the area hospitals. This was the first she'd heard about the death, and no one she called had anything to say to her on or off the record. Layla had hired Julie to find her sister Blythe, and Julie had traced Blythe to Vegas."

Bay wiped his fingers and opened his laptop. Django laid himself down on the keyboard. I lifted him off. Bay opened an attached file on Julie's e-mail and read. Layla was born and raised in Monroe, Louisiana. A beloved older brother, Kyle, was killed in a water-skiing accident when he was in high school, and the tragedy sent the family into a tailspin. The father, Alton, eventually quit his job at the paper mill, abandoned his wife and daughters, and found himself a more sanguine family in Carthage, Texas.

Layla was salutatorian of her graduating class at Neville High School and earned a scholarship to Centenary College. Her sister Blythe, seven years younger, got mixed up with rednecks and crystal meth, lost all of her friends, some of her memory, six of her teeth, twenty-three pounds, her muscle tone, the sharpness in her motor coordination, the luster and elasticity of her skin, and the will to live a productive and examined life. When their mother, Mary Grace, died of emphysema and the bank foreclosed on the house, Blythe moved to Memphis to live with Layla. She went through detox a second time, and it took. And then she did thirteen weeks in rehab and went to a meeting every day for ninety days, got her teeth reconstructed, and seemed to have begun her second act. But when life with a steady job, an orderly and unsullied home, a devoted sister, and trustworthy friends proved unsatisfy-ing, Blythe, like her daddy before her, vanished. That was a year and a half ago, and that's when Layla called Julie. Julie was certain that Layla was not suicidal. But then you never really know what's going on inside people, do you?

Bay said, "Julie would appreciate knowing anything we can find out about either sister. She was hired to find Blythe and get her the help she needed, and she wants to finish the job."

"Sounds like we're deputized."

"If Layla didn't kill herself, then someone else killed her."

"The plot thickens."

"Tell me something. Why have you been so preoccupied with her death?"

"Because Loomis told me not to be."

"He didn't say a word."

"Because the media has pretty much ignored it, and that means, or might mean, that something dire and volatile has happened right before our eyes."

"Or something unfortunate happened which, if people found out, would be bad for business."

"How did Julie trace Blythe to Vegas?"

"Lied to creditors and banks, probably. Slogged through arrest records and mug shots. That would tell her Blythe was back on the streets and back on drugs. Blythe's last known address was the Lucky Boy Motel on East Bonanza, but that was a year ago."

"When do we start?"

"We already have."

"What do we do next?"

"It would be nice to find her suitcase. Her phone. Whatever she carried with her."

Bay's phone tweeted, and he slipped it out of his pocket.

I said, "Who is it?"

"Little Bob." Little Bob was Bay's dad.

"Where's he at these days?"

"Flaubert, South Dakota. Twenty men in the town and three are sex offenders."

"What's he doing there?"

"He followed a woman home from Pierre. He only texts when he needs money." Bay opened the text message and shook his head.

"What?"

"He thinks he got that gal in trouble."

"How old is he now?"

"Old enough to know better."

"Seventy . . . ?"

"Four." Bay sent Little Bob a reply and set the phone on the table. "You never stop worrying about them."

Layla played viola, devoured the novels of Anthony Trollope and the stories of Alice Munro. She had a weakness for Gus's fried chicken, but then, as Julie noted, who doesn't? She loved the music of Tigran Mansurian, especially ". . . and then I was in time again." She kept a framed photo on her desk at work of her family in happier days at a picnic on the bayou, all five of them on lawn chairs, biting down on deviled eggs.

I said, "Why would she come all the way to Vegas to find her sister and then kill herself?"

"Maybe what she found was very bad news."

But now I was thinking that suicide seemed less likely. Suicide is not about ending a life but about ending the pain. Layla's pain would have been relieved with the knowledge of her sister's whereabouts. Hope is a universal analgesic.

While Bay drove me to the Crisis Center, rolling a silver dollar over his knuckles in one hand and steering the car with the other, I called the cops—Las Vegas Metro—and asked the woman who answered for information on Layla and/or Blythe Davis.

She said, "And they are?"

I explained that Layla had died quite violently at the Luxor the day before last—you might have seen it on the news, I said (she hadn't)—and Layla might have been here in town looking for her little sister who had an addiction problem and would likely have been familiar to the police.

She said, "Are you a lawyer?"

"I'm not."

"Reporter?"

"Nope."

"What are you?"

That sounded like a trick question.

She said, "What's your relationship to these women?"

"I'm a concerned citizen."

"I'm not authorized to provide information to the curious."

"Can I speak with your supervisor?"

"This isn't Kmart, sir."

"What if I had said I was a lawyer?"

She said, "Then I would have told you to send in a written request," and hung up.

KENNETH WHEELER, TWENTY-SIX, single, and a clerk at the Smarty's on South Durango, was last seen by his neighbors on Wednesday, parking his Celica in the condo's parking lot on West Sahara. Jimmy Hecker of Jacksonville, Florida, was staying a week with an uncle in Henderson. He stepped into a cab outside the Bellagio just before midnight on March 31 and had not been seen or heard from since. I was reading through the missing persons reports at the Crisis Center. The phones were quiet; the anemic coffee tasted slightly of cauliflower. Tejuana Figueras sent an e-mail to her aunt Kiki from her room at the Motel 6 on Dean Martin and then vanished—six weeks ago. And then an item from the morning newspaper: The remains of fifteen prostitutes were discovered in a mass grave in the Moapa Valley. The women, in some cases girls, had gone missing over the course of four years. Here's a voice mail I listened to: *My friend Anthony checked into the El Mirador last week, but he and none of his belongings are in his room. Anthony is mental! And without his meds he is a danger to himself and could be easily taken advantage of by others, and the cops don't give two shits. Help me find Anthony please!* And there was a number to call.

Gene Woodling saw what I was up to, sat down at the next phone, picked up the *Sun*, stared at the driver's license photos of the fifteen victims found in the Moapa Valley, and said, "I've thought a lot about the girls who die in Vegas." He stared up at the map of Clark County over our desks and said, "They were the prom queens, the cheerleaders, the soloists on their dance teams, the female leads in the drama club's production of *Our Town*. They come from Sioux Falls or Kamloops or Charlottesville or Walla Walla."

I asked Gene where he was from.

"Star City, Arkansas."

"And you knew a girl like this?" I said.

"Kiernan Carlisle." For a moment he took off his glasses, covered his eyes, and drifted away. "One day our beautiful girl realizes—because the evidence is all around her—that the very best life she can hope for in her humble hometown is a solid marriage to a handsome and dependable professional from a respectable family; a storybook home in a leafy neighborhood; a couple of captivating and dutiful children; membership at the country club; and a torrid, brief, regrettable, but unforgettable affair with the husband of a friend. But it's the image of herself at the country club having drinks under an umbrella on the patio with the rest of the ladies after a Tuesday afternoon doubles tennis match that depresses her. She sees herself in a sky-blue T-shirt that reads PLAY. WIN. LUNCH., a flouncy yellow Stella McCartney tennis skirt that's feeling a little tight, and a leopard-skin visor. What are her exquisite good looks and seductive charm good for if all she can look forward to is the depleted American Dream and the inevitable weight gain? Her depression turns to panic; the panic ignites her flight response, and she catches the first plane to Vegas."

I said, "You really have thought a lot about this."

He raised his eyebrows and held up a finger—not finished! "She checks into an unembellished motel—it's tiny but at least it's cleanish—freshens up, slips on her vampiest black stretch velvet dress and the red sling-back pumps, and sets off to find herself a local boyfriend at one of the flashier casinos. Boyfriends in Vegas are like fire ants at a picnic. She sits at the bar, orders a Cosmo, flips her hair, and waits. She knows she's going to change her name but she's not sure to what. Either Lacey, Jade, or Rhiannon. She takes a selfie with her phone and texts it to her friend Rita back home. *Digging the life*, she writes.

"The boyfriend she meets has single-karat diamond studs in both his ears, a black Movado watch, white K-Swiss Classics, and red ankle socks that match his red silk T-shirt. His cargo shorts are gold-stitched denim, his hair is roached; his eyes are blue and dreamy. He used to wear Oakleys, but now he wears Ray-Bans. He drives a Jag, or someday he will. His name is TJ or Markus or Fadeproof, and it's not long before he's taking Lacey shopping for threads and bling at the Palazzo and escorting her to all the best shows in town: Celine, Shania, Donny and Marie. He rents her a tastefully furnished apartment in Sunrise and buys her a shih tzu she names Bianca. They make love every night he's free. He's coy about his employment. He's in the entertainment business, he tells her, and squeezes her ass. She gets a facial, a body wrap, and a sugar scrub every Saturday at the spa at the Four Seasons. She's over the moon, she texts Rita: he says he has a friend who's dying to meet her.

"She'd do anything for Markus. She owes him, doesn't she? Soon she's giving the visiting radiologist from St. Louis the whole girlfriend experience; she's going down on the prosecuting attorney from Sacramento; getting nasty with the handsome and dependable professional from a respectable family with the wife and two kids and the country club membership."

I asked Gene if he had followed Kiernan to Vegas, if he had stopped looking for her.

He said, "How does she die? Let me count the ways," and tallied on his fingers. "Addiction. AIDS. Assault. Suicide. Betrayal. A misunderstanding. A miscalculation. Her john's a psychopath. She decides to go solo and Markus finds out."

I asked Gene if he knew a sympathetic cop, one who might share info about Layla. He did not. I asked him about the girl from yesterday, the one weeping in the conference room. He told me they'd taken her to Refuge House but she left.

He checked his watch, said he had a flash of lightning—a glass of Tanqueray—waiting for him at home. There was something subtly disharmonious about Gene that bothered me, but I couldn't put my finger on which of his anomalous behaviors or features it might be. Whenever he sneezed, he sneezed exactly three times. Not a character flaw, of course, and neither were his ubiquitous plaid slacks and his Birkenstock nubuck clogs. He carried his right shoulder lower than his left. He wore aviator-style glasses with tinted lenses that were annoyingly crooked on his thin face. He had a graceless gait. His uncoordinated arms were alarmingly out of sync with his ungainly legs, resulting in a rather dissonant visual rhythm—two competing melodies making for one discordant marching song. Watching Gene walk was like trying to enjoy a dubbed movie—the lips are saying one thing, the voice another.

Before Gene left, he handed me a file folder, labeled *Abrel D'Arville*. "Another unsolved mystery," he said.

Every weekday during his sixteen-plus years of marriage, save two weeks every July, Abrel D'Arville kissed his wife DeFonda goodbye at seven-thirty and drove to work at a small regional office of a large national insurance company, and every weekday evening at five-thirty, DeFonda met Abrel at the front door with a kiss and a smile. She'd take his briefcase and bring it to his office while he changed out of his gray suit, white shirt, and pebbled black Florsheims, and into his khakis, polo shirt, and Cordovan loafers. They'd enjoy a casserole dinner, and, if the weather was pleasant, a stroll through the neighborhood.

The D'Arvilles were childless, petless, and serenely resigned to their cloistered solitude. As DeFonda described it, they lived in a suburban world of their own making that had not otherwise existed for decades except in old movies and TV reruns, the kind of world where a gentleman wore a suit to a cocktail party, stored his cigarettes in a monogrammed case, sat, leaning toward the conversation, in an upholstered chair, while his wife, in her strapless satin dress, sat on the arm of the chair and every now and then rubbed the back of her husband's neck. When hubby raised his empty cocktail glass, she knew enough to refill his drink. Abrel didn't drink, didn't smoke, and didn't gamble, but sometimes, at home, he pretended he did.

And then Abrel disappeared. This was around the time that severed feet were turning up all along the Gypsum Wash, so the police took immediate interest when DeFonda called to report him missing. Investigators were puzzled when they learned the large national insurance firm did not have a small regional office within two hundred miles of Las Vegas and did not have any Abrel D'Arville in its employ. That's impossible, DeFonda said. I've called his office a thousand times. The local phone number she gave the cops was no longer in service.

Yes, we had our little differences, DeFonda told the detectives. I was pie; he was cake. I was water; he was milk. I was fresh air; he was AC. I was romance; he was true crime. No, she said, she didn't know anyone who would want to harm her husband. We weren't close to many people. We had acquaintances, not any friends familiar enough to get worked up about some imagined insult.

There were no federal or state income tax records for Abrel D'Arville. No area bank accounts in that name. There was no birth record for Abrel D'Arville in Moab, Utah, where he claimed to have been born. There were no sisters in Boulder. DeFonda wondered, if that was the case, then whom had she been speaking with every Christmas Eve over the years? When Abrel's photo appeared in the *Sun* and on local TV stations, he was identified by multiple callers and online commenters as the man who spent his mornings at Sunset Park, sitting in his fold-out camp chair, reading a book under a mesquite tree. A waitress at Knockout Lunch in Henderson said he came in every day at twelve-thirty—you could set your watch by him—and ordered chicken and waffles, a side salad with ranch dressing, a slice of chocolate cake, and a glass of whole milk.

Three days after Abrel went missing, the body of a man was found in a shallow grave in the desert west of the city. The victim's spinal cord had been severed, and he may have been buried alive. The labels on his clothing had been removed. The dogs that had unearthed the body had done some damage to the lower extremities. Police found no matching dental records.

The victim was identified by his clothing, the gray suit, the white shirt, his mongrammed initials ACD on the left cuff of the shirt, and by the pale but distinctive Lichtenburg figure on his left arm, a fractal fernlike scar left by a lightning strike two weeks earlier. The body belonged to Abrel D'Arville, but Abrel D'Arville didn't exist. A mystery was solved; another was posed. Who killed the man who would be Abrel D'Arville, and why? Where did the man called Abrel get his money? Who was he? DeFonda said, Can you be married to a man who does not exist?

I asked Petra, the available desk clerk at the Luxor, to ring up Layla Davis's room. I told Petra she had beautiful eyes. She smiled and looked up from the computer screen. She'd been told that a thousand times, I knew. I asked her what color she called them. She said, Hazel. I said I had hazel eyes and they looked nothing like hers. I'd call yours chartreuse, maybe. She said they turned yellow when she wore green. She also told me that Layla Davis was not registered at the hotel. I said I knew she'd checked in Friday. Not according to our records, Petra said. She clicked her elegant magenta fingernail on the computer mouse and shifted her weight from one leg to the other. Are you sure you have the right hotel? I didn't ask Petra about the recent suicide because I didn't want her to lie to me. I asked where I could find the Lost and Found. She directed me to a computer and said there would be a form to fill out.

I couldn't describe the items Layla had left, of course. I wrote that the lost items were last seen in her room. I didn't know the room number. I went back to the reception desk and asked a young man if I could speak to his supervisor. A Mr. A. Jones asked how he might help me.

I explained that my sister Layla Davis left behind some items, and I was hoping to locate them in a real Lost and Found, not a virtual one. He said he'd see what he could do. And he clicked his pen and let it hover over a notepad. I told him she'd checked out in a hurry. Top floor. Not sure which room. He asked for an ID, and he noted the difference in our last names. I said Layla was married. Hubby was a reprobate. It was a long story. He said, I really can't help you unless I have proof of your relationship. Then I showed him Layla's photo and asked if there was any possibility he might look through the top floor's security camera files for the last few days. I'm just so worried about her, I said. He said that would not happen, even if he wanted it to. I said, Why wouldn't you want to? He said, Not my circus, not my monkeys. And then he told me there were no cameras in the hotel corridors. When I expressed disbelief, he said the only thing that needed protection was the money on the casino floor.

I knew that somewhere in this hotel, in some locked store-room, no doubt, might be everything that Layla had brought with her—the suitcase, clothing, toiletries, the clueful cell phone, a suicide note, perhaps. Answers! I needed a passkey. I walked up to a shampoo porter who was buffing the lobby floor and asked him how I could get a job in housecleaning. He said, Vienen cuando eres mexicano.

Bay texted me a video of himself standing on the porch of Chicago Joe's where he'd eaten lunch. He said he'd be at the Bellini Bar at the Venetian until five. And then he lifted up off the ground a foot or so, and then he vanished. He asked me how things were going at the Luxor. Bay always knows where I am or at least where my phone is. He's got an app that can find me. So later I met him at the bar. He was drinking a blueberry lime rickey. I ordered an espresso martini.

I said, "At first I was curious, now I'm pissed. The silence. The cover-up. Must mean something."

"Means business as usual around here."

I told Bay about Petra's denial, about A. Jones's disinterest, and about the hotel's documented denial that Layla had ever been there. "They're like the Soviets airbrushing undesirable enemies of the state from the propaganda photos, hoping the world will forget the former comrade's existence."

"Nikolai Yezhov."

"Who?"

"It worked. Chief of the Secret Police under Stalin."

"Or was he?" I told Bay I thought he was right. We didn't see a suicide.

Our waiter, Nevin, shook the cocktail shaker over his right shoulder and poured my drink with artful nonchalance. He patted his modified canary-yellow Skrillex hairdo and asked if that would be all for now. It would.

I told Bay about Tristina M., a client of mine, who was twenty-one when she jumped off the Cypress Avenue Bridge and hit the foredeck of a passing Bimini yacht. She had come to me for help, and I had failed her. Tristina lived with her elderly grandmother, the only family she had. She dated a man, Ron Someone, who punched and slapped her in private, insulted her in public, who neglected her but was insanely jealous and controlling. She couldn't or wouldn't leave him. When I asked her what she got out of this malignant relationship, she said she got the chance to love someone. When I asked why she had come to therapy, she said to make herself worthy of Ron. Not in so many words, but that was the gist. She jumped, but he pushed. Her grandmother died a month later. I may be the only person alive who remembers Tristina, thinks about her. I still see Ron around Melancholy. He has a wife and two adorable daughters and a steady job at Home Depot. He grew up. Good for him. Tristina did not. I want to make sure Layla's not forgotten. Maybe I think this . . . this investigation is my shot at redemption.

"You're so Catholic."

"Lapsed."

"The most dangerous kind," Bay said. "Maybe we did see a suicide."

"I could live with that, but I have to be sure."

Bay smiled. "You're going to get us in trouble, you know that."

"Maybe Blythe can be saved. Layla didn't give up on her sister. We shouldn't give up on her." What I was thinking was how I gave up on Cam and how you don't need a god to know that you must atone for your sins. "So now it's also a rescue mission."

"And here's something else for you to worry about. We've got sixty thousand honeybees in the eaves of our house."

"The hum!"

Bay drew a deck of cards out of his cargo vest pocket—he was dressed, apparently, as a fly fisherman for this evening's round of poker, all the better to distract his opponents—and shuffled them.

I said, "How did you find them?"

"I saw the honey melting down the wall out back."

"Did you call the landlord?"

He nodded. "I had Arthur, the bee guy, out for an assessment." Bay spread the cards in front of him on the bar. "He told me that all honeybees in Las Vegas are Africanized."

"That's not good."

"One sting won't kill you, but fifteen might." Bay told me to pick a card, any card.

I slid one card halfway out of the deck, slipped it back in, and chose another. He flipped the spread deck over, so I could see they were ordinary playing cards. He turned my card over: a joker. The little jester in motley clothes and belled shoes held a fool's scepter and strutted across the back of a flying honeybee. Bay said, "The TV reporter."

"Who?"

"He knows about her death—he found out who she was. Call him."

"Do you remember his name?"

Bay found the Channel 14 website and showed me a photo of Elwood Wingo. He said the bee removers would be by in the morning. "Arthur likes his coffee black. And you can take the car home. I'm playing through the night."

AT HOME I GOOGLED Kiernan Carlisle and found her 2008 obituary. I learned that she was "a loving sister, daughter, aunt, and friend to all that knew her," that she was "unique, special, intelligent, and compassionate," and that she was "taken too early." I was not told how she was taken. I found out how in a related article from the *Lincoln Ledger* out of Star City. She had been strangled in her own condominium in Las Vegas. Police were investigating. A neighbor who knew Kiernan "about as well as anyone can know an exotic dancer," and who requested anonymity, said, "I'm going to get me a gun permit tomorrow."

THE BEES HUMMED like a Tesla coil. I made a small pile of Kitty Yums for Django by the kitchen table. He ran across the kitchen and slid into them. Back on the Internet I learned that jumping from a high place was only the seventh most effective way to kill yourself, just after stepping in front of a train and just before exsanguination. I read my book (*To the Wedding*) till I couldn't keep my eyes open. I got into bed, put on my sleep mask, stuffed in my earplugs, and stretched out under the covers. Django hopped up on my chest, stuck his wet, cold nose under mine to see if I was breathing. I've had insomnia since I was a kid. Cam, up on the top bunk, slept like the dead. My frustrated father once whispered in my ear, "Why won't you sleep, honey?" I said I didn't want to sleep because I didn't want to be alone. And nothing has changed.

# 4

WHAT WOULD SLEEP be without a monster lurking in the dark? I was wrong, of course, to think I ever slept alone. Every night the people I unconsciously contrived visited me in dreams, and last night's dreams were uniformly distressing. In one, I made several annoyingly shy toddlers weep by asking them hideously avuncular questions like, *What is your favorite subject in school?* and, *What do you want to be when you grow up?* My words were met with mute disdain, but I wanted them to like me so badly that I felt compelled to impart some palliative wisdom that they might groove on. Children, I said, be bright in your lavish youth because time darkens everything. And that's when one sobbing boy bit his lip, shut his eyes, and told me I was stealing his childhood.

I woke when I heard the bee wranglers setting up their ladders and estimating the gallons of honey they'd harvest from this job. I tried to remember which Renaissance artist it was who first proffered the artistic and philosophical advice I'd inflicted on the children in the dream. After I'd dressed, I e-mailed Elwood Wingo, the TV reporter, explaining who I was and why I wanted to speak with him. He answered immediately and told me to meet him at a certain food truck parked on Fremont at noon. Bay came home from his long and successful night at the tables with breakfast burritos, Bloody Marys, and a lovely young woman named Mercedes Benz. I made coffee and set the table. "Your name," I said.

"My father had a droll sense of humor," Mercedes told me.

I passed on the Bloody Mary.

"He was so droll my mother left him and joined a cult."

I said, "Which?"

"Branch Davidians. She took me with her."

"Waco."

"We had been disfellowshipped by that time. When Koresh started raising the dead, Mom packed our bag. We took the bus to Colorado City, Arizona, and Mom married an FLDS Mormon with three other wives and two mentally retarded sons. One of the wives was fourteen."

"How old were you?"

"Twelve."

Django brushed up against Mercedes's leg. I refreshed our coffees. She lifted Django to her lap, and he allowed her to scratch him under the chin.

I said, "Were you worried you'd be next at the altar?"

"Yes, but by then my whimsical father had come to rescue me, and we moved here to Vegas. I went to school for the first time."

Django looked deeply into Mercedes's eyes and bit her finger. She said, "He's a naughty boy."

One of the bee wranglers whooped. He'd located the queen. In ancient Egypt, a man like Arthur was called the Sealer of Honey. The harvesting of honey began in Lower Egypt in first dynasty, and the pharaoh was called the Bee King, and Osiris was worshipped in the Mansion of the Bee. Mercedes tapped Django's nose and told him, "No!" He sprang from her lap and shot off for the living room, but slid into the cabinet beneath the sink making his turn. He just lay there like he'd meant to do it, dignity intact. Mercedes said her mom was still in Colorado City and had four other children whom Mercedes had never met. Her dad, she said, was a nomad. He called every few months. Last call came from Alberta. He keeps drifting farther north. The cold seems to comfort him.

Mercedes worked as a waitress at Yardbird Southern Table at the Venetian and shared an apartment in Spring Valley with another waitress. She took creative writing classes at UNLV. I said I'd clean up. Bay said we should all meet for dinner. Seven-thirty at Emeril's at the Grand. They bade me farewell and headed off to bed. I hoped Django wasn't in Bay's room bothering them. I called for him. He wasn't answering. I took out a can of sardines. Nothing like the sound of the can leaving the drawer to get Django's attention. Before I even snapped the tab on the sardines, there he was purring like mad and rolling on his back at my feet. I gave him a treat instead.

ELWOOD RECOMMENDED THE EGG burger and the duck-fat garlic fries. And the lobster mac and cheese. *To die for.* And the zucchini fritters. *Ambrosial.* And the bacon-fried rice. I ordered the burger, the shitake flan, and a bottled water; Elwood, the burger, fries, and a Diet Dr Pepper. He excused himself, answered a call on his cell, walked to the row of six empty newspaper vending machines, and leaned back against the *Las Vegas Weekly.* He put a finger in his unoccupied ear. Elwood was a large young man with small hands, long ears, orthopedic shoes, and snaggled bottom teeth. The sign on the grim-looking hotel/casino at the corner read $2 BLACKJACK $1 CRAPS. This unsightly stretch of the Fremont East District was sun-bleached and deserted except for the occasional solitary pedestrian slouching his way toward Binion's Horseshoe. Elwood apologized for the interruption—his handyman had run into a problem with the porch repair.

We carried our food to the shaded Eighth Street bus stop shelter, sat on the uncomfortable metal seats, and ate our lunches off our laps. The burger was so damn good I wanted to put a runny fried egg on top of everything. Elwood flashed his eyebrows and smiled. "Told you."

When he remarked that he and I seemed to be the only people interested in getting to the bottom of Layla Davis's death, I told him what Julie Wade had learned about Layla's sister Blythe. He guessed that Blythe would have been, or might still be, involved in prostitution.

He said, "There are thirty thousand very busy prostitutes in Vegas, where prostitution is illegal but only a misdemeanor." He wiped his lips with the napkin. "I figure hundred and eighty thousand blow jobs a day in Clark County. Makes you burst with civic pride." He thought we were unlikely to find out much more about Layla. Unless.

"Unless what?"

"Unless Blythe is still alive."

"And we can find her."

"Do you have a photo?"

I didn't, but I would have Bay check with Julie Wade. I told Elwood that the hotel cameras that I was told did not exist must have captured the activity on the thirtieth floor when Layla was disposed of. Elwood said he'd already checked on that, and the cameras, *he* was told, were not working that day. They couldn't even get their lies straight. A green and yellow Google Maps Street View car drove by snapping photos with its roof-mounted camera. Elwood said, "Now we'll always be those two unhealthy guys guzzling fast food and waiting for the Boulder Highway Express."

And then he said, "It's my job to investigate Layla's death. Why are you doing it?"

"You can't just sit by."

"Of course you can. We do it all the time."

"Because I was a witness. I saw those eyes and that broken face, and I can't forget. And because an acquaintance, a Memphis PI, the Julie I just mentioned, was hired to find her, and my friend Bay and I are doing what we can to help. Because I think she was killed, and someone's getting away with murder."

"Justice is a game of chance."

He told me he grew up in Manhattan on the Upper East Side, and had gone to prep schools and to Princeton. When he told his parents he wanted to be a reporter, not an academic, they laughed. But they weren't laughing now. His dad, Dr. Ned Wingo, was a Freudian analyst who rode motorcycles and fancied himself a swinger. Ned called Elwood on occasion to ask for his advice with younger women, whom he just couldn't figure out. Elwood's mom, Lainey Roth Wingo, was an atypical Jewish mother who wrote YA novels and did not like to be disturbed by rambling phone calls from her only child, whom she had fictively killed off in her break-out novel, *Rap City in Blue* (peanuts/anaphylaxis). The parents were not divorced but lived apart except for the month of August, when Ned migrated to Provincetown with all the other analysts, and Lainey joined him. They brought along their current girlfriends.

Elwood answered his phone, told whoever it was that he'd be there in five minutes, and invited me along to a breaking story. "A body's been found in the lot behind Lamps Plus on South Maryland." Elwood drove a Fiat 500 in which he'd installed a workstation in the passenger-side front seat—swivel desktop, computer, police scanner, and wireless printer. I climbed in back and shoved the camera bag and food wrappers to the side.

He said the on-air reports were essentially eye candy for the easily distracted. His real journalism happened on his station-sponsored blog, where he could go into depth on a story. We arrived at Lamps Plus. It helped that Elwood knew the detective leading the crime scene investigation. He and Detective Lou Scaturro belonged to the Bocce Club of Las Vegas.

I said, "You play bocce, Elwood?"

"For the Knights of Cabria. Lou plays for the Sons of It'ly," Elwood shook hands with Detective Scaturro and introduced us. "What do we have here, Lou?"

What we had was the body of a young woman, which had been discovered that morning by a homeless guy out Dumpster-diving. The body had been wrapped in the distressing green, gold, and black pleated polyester bedspread that was now folded next to the corpse. The girl, Detective Scaturro told us, had been garroted with an electrical cord, which was still coiled around her neck. He unzipped the body bag and held it open. A cluster of red dots rimmed the girl's eyes. Her lips were swollen. Elwood squatted to get a closer look. Her shaggy hair was black; she wore a nose ring on her left nostril and smelled like melting plastic. Her left arm was crosshatched with razor cuts. Detective Scaturro resealed the bag and nodded to the EMTs, who lifted the body onto a gurney. He said, "She hasn't been dead long."

Detective Scaturro had a high forehead and a thick brush of russet hair. His eyes were forest-green, his chin modest and dimpled. The wrinkles around the eyes suggested easy and eager smiles. I knew from his guileless face that Scaturro was married and had a flock of boisterous kids. I knew he speculated in real estate. I knew he drank modestly, favored grappa, and had never even considered smoking cigarettes. I knew he kept no untoward secrets and told no unnecessary lies. And when I say *knew*, I mean, of course, *imagined*.

Most body dumps are tough to unravel, but this one would not be. Detective Scaturro said, "Miss Doe was murdered elsewhere."

"And I know where," Elwood said. "I recognize the bedspread. Check the Starlite Motel on South Las Vegas Boulevard."

Detective Scaturro raised an eyebrow and cocked his head. "So are you going to tell us the story?"

"Not much to tell," Elwood said. "A while back I hit a rough patch. I spent several wasted nights at the Starlite, drinking bourbon, inhaling chocolate, and reading Philip K. Dick novels. But not before I stashed the abominable bedspread in the closet."

Detective Scaturro dispatched a unit to the Starlite. Officers were soon able to view the motel's surveillance videos. At four-thirty P.M. yesterday, a man walked into Room 112 with our Miss Doe on his arm. At six thirty-seven this morning, the man, who had registered under his own name, Ted Seeley, left the room carrying a cumbersome object swaddled in the bedspread and dropped the load into the trunk of his rental car. Seeley was a convicted sex offender only recently released from prison. He was picked up that evening at his mother's house in North Las Vegas. His mother wept at the kitchen table as the officers read Ted his rights and cuffed him. She made the sign of the cross and said, "He's sick in the head. My poor baby's sick." She scraped the uneaten lasagna from Ted's plate into the toilet in the hall and flushed. We would soon learn that the victim, Ariel Gonzalez, was a fifteen-year-old crack addict, who liked to write poetry, and who had been working as a prostitute for three years. When police finally located her family, her older sister said, "Thank god you've found her."

Elwood asked Detective Scaturro what he'd heard about the woman who fell to her death at the Luxor. Not a thing.

"I did a report on the news."

"I'll watch it."

"They took it down."

I asked Detective Scaturro, "What do you think about the casino denying it ever happened?"

"Want to avoid bad publicity."

"What about a police department denying it?"

"That would be wrong."

"But not inconceivable?"

He looked at Elwood and then back at me. "When you say police department, I take it to mean the high command." And then he turned his back and the conversation was over.

Elwood and I agreed we needed a drink. He had a well-stocked bar at home only a few minutes from here. From the backseat of his car, I said, "So what does Scaturro have, like, five kids?"

"Yeah, how did you know? All boys. One on the way. He's hoping it's a girl. He'll never stop having kids, that guy. Every new child makes him feel more alive."

Elwood mixed us a drink he called a Chekhov, made with vodka, elderflower, and gooseberry liqueur, which Rachel Maddow had taught him to make at an after party at some press gathering back East. He garnished the drink with a thin slice of green apple and a sprig of mint. Delicious. And one drink led to another. We sat out on his back porch. He pointed to a mockingbird perched in the palo verde and took out his iPhone. He played the two-note text-tone tweet, and the mockingbird answered in kind. He said to me, "Why don't you call me, so I'll have your number."

I pulled out what I thought was my iPhone but was, in fact, a Trader Joe's sardine can. So I told Elwood my number. I said, "The cat makes me crazy."


MY CONVIVIAL CABDRIVER suggested I browse through the advertising postcards and pamphlets in the seatback pocket in front of me. I told him I was familiar with the material, and I wasn't looking for any action this afternoon, hoping he could detect the ironic quotation marks in my pronunciation of *action*.

He said, "You don't like it live in the lap?"

"Not when I have to pay for it." I asked him how pathetic he thought a man's life would have to be if he had to purchase sex.

He said, "You are what is called a brood, no?"

"Prude, yes," I said.

He said that not all men were as fortunate and handsome as I was, and I did note the gentle ironic quotation marks around his adjectives. He said, "Loneliness corrodes the heart." He told me his tautonymous name was Ilarion Ilarion, that he was a Macedonian from Bulgaria, spoke five languages, and had been in the USA seven years. He pointed to a photo on his visor of his wife and two young sons. "Names Joe and Tom. Americans."

I told him I was Wylie from South Florida.

He told me that a ride to one of the advertised destinations would be free.

I said, "How does that work?"

"I get the juice from the grateful establishments."

"Kickbacks?"

"You seem incredulous, my friend. Are you sure you're not Canadian? Juice is how I feed my family. Can't make a living driving people six blocks. Twenty-five hundred cabs in this town."

"You own your cab?"

"No driver owns his cab here. The unions pimp us; the owners fuck us up the ass. Pardon my Serbian."

"Tips aren't good?"

"All the money goes to the casinos and the whores." He held up two fingers. "Two sounds a driver doesn't want to hear: change in a pocket or bullet in a chamber."

We were stopped at a red light in front of Caesars Palace when we both noticed a squabby fellow in a Lakers basketball jersey—15 WORLD PEACE—and bulky denim shorts, harassing a young girl. She walked in a circle, trying ineffectively to get away from this lout, who was screaming in her face and poking her shoulder with his stubby forefinger. Ilarion hit the horn, threw the cab in park, opened his door, stepped outside, and told the punk to stop right now or face the wrath of Ilarion. The Laker gave him the finger, but walked away just the same. That's when I recognized the victim as the girl I'd seen at the Crisis Center two days ago. And she was still crying. I wondered if she had ever stopped. I handed Ilarion a twenty, thanked him, and hopped out. He said, "Watch yourself, my friend."

Now that World Peace had fled the field of combat, the frazzled girl put her face in her hands and took a deep breath. She had slipped her arms up to the elbows into the sleeves of a thin green hooded sweatshirt, and left the rest of the sweatshirt doffed. She saw me watching her and told me to fuck off.

I said, "I know you."

"You wish you did."

"I mean I know who you are."

She had the monogram PG tattooed on her upper arm. Parental Guidance? The swelling on her face had diminished and she'd hidden the bruise with makeup.

I said, "PG?"

"Pretty Girl."

"You were at the Crisis Center. I volunteer there."

"You'll go to heaven."

"Are you okay?"

"You want a date?"

"They took you to Refuge House."

"And I left."

"Where are you staying?"

"In the tunnels. With the mole people."

"Why not Refuge House?"

"Girls don't stay at Refuge House. They're shipped out."

"Probably want to get you away from your triggers."

She shook her head. "You're clueless."

She told me she could take care of herself, had been since she was twelve. No, she had no phone, no change of clothes, no friends in Vegas, and nowhere to go except underground. I told her I wanted to get her a room for the night. She asked if I came with the room. I did not. Had she eaten? She had not. Supper and a room, I said. With a room she could soak in a hot tub, wash her clothes, watch a movie, get a good night's sleep, and go back to the Crisis Center tomorrow. I said, "I'll be there at ten."

She smiled. "I'll be sleeping."

A short, heavyset woman wearing a Reno Aces ball cap and a GIRLS! GIRLS! GIRLS! DIRECT TO YOU IN 20 MINUTES OR LESS T-shirt handed me several advertising photos of naked women. I handed them back, pointed at her T-shirt, and said, "Fewer."

"Qué?"

"Your T-shirt is grammatically abusive."

"No entiendo."

"I thought prostitution was illegal in Las Vegas."

"Prostitute? No! Girlfriend? Sí!"

A blonde woman in a blue cape sat on the sidewalk playing a small accordion and singing opera with a piercing falsetto. Her cigar box was empty. The T-shirt lady smiled, pointed her chin at my companion, and said, "Ya tiene las manos llenas."

The girl told me her name was Ruby Tuesday; she was eighteen; she grew up in Smallville. Three lies. I was the handsomest guy she'd seen all day. Four. I suggested we duck into Serendipity 3, where we ordered her a buffalo wing pizza and a chocolate milkshake to go. I showed her a photo of Layla. She looked at the photo and then away. Said she didn't recognize her. Five? Something had leaped out of that image and stung Ruby. I asked her to look again. She said she could look all day and nothing would change. I asked her if the name Blythe Davis rang a bell. It did not.

We took the walkway over Las Vegas Boulevard to Bill's Gamblin' Hall & Saloon. Ruby sucked on her milkshake, and I carried the pizza. When a woman wearing a fanny pack and flipped-up sunglasses looked at me and then at Ruby and then back at me, I realized what we must look like to passersby and to any law enforcement officers lurking about—an odious pedophile and his supple young bedmate. And Ruby, apparently, thought the same. She said, "Don't worry. They can see your halo."

The registration clerk told us we'd be able to see the Eiffel Tower from our room.

I said, "She will. I'm not staying."

Ruby said, "The what?"

I handed her the key card and the pizza and told her to enjoy herself.

"When I lay down and close my eyes, and it's quiet—that's the best time there is." She put her drink on the desk, shook my hand, and thanked me. Her sweatshirt still hung from her arms.

*Lie*, I thought, not *lay*.


BAY SAID THAT my brother-in-law Oliver had been trying to reach me all day. I explained my can of sardines. Bay said Oliver told him that his wife, my sister Venise, had suffered a heart attack, was in the hospital, and wanted to see me. Patience had booked me a flight on the red-eye tonight. She'd meet me at the airport in the morning. Bay said, "I've got your suitcase packed and in the car. We'll drop you at McCarran at nine."

I said, "Do you think that's wise?"

"Your sister is very sick."

"She can be an alarmist. What if I'm seen by the wrong people?"

"Open Mike reports that no one's really all that interested in teaching us a lesson anymore. They're all too busy scheming with their lawyers, keeping their hands clean, and putting on happy and honorable faces."

"So we can go home soon?"

"Soon enough."

We ordered Cajun martinis. Mercedes was on her way. Bay handed me his iPhone. Julie Wade had sent him a screenshot of Blythe Davis, aka Fawn Monroe, captured from an escort service ad: "This dark-eyed beauty is playful and intuitive to your needs. She loves attention and doesn't mind being in the spotlight. A bargain at any price." The ad promised discretion, safety, and veracity. Blythe's back was arched, her neck was exposed, her allegedly dark eyes shut, and her mouth open in a pose she hoped approximated ecstasy, but more accurately suggested stupor. I asked Bay to forward me the photo. He said, "Aren't your sardines packed too tightly for that?" And then he handed me my phone.

Mercedes kissed Bay on the cheek and sat. He pulled a white rose out of the air and handed it to her. She thanked him and slipped it into her water glass. She ordered a Sidecar. I asked her how her creative writing class went.

"We wrote about what keeps us up at night."

"So what did you write about?"

"Being alone. Feeling abandoned. Forgotten. The party's over and everyone has gone home, and I'm alone, and I don't even live here." She thanked the waiter and sipped her drink. "What keeps you up at night, Wylie?"

"What I haven't done. What I've done. What I have to do. What I've done wrong or sloppily or mindlessly. What might have been. What I can't forget. What I can't remember. Death. What I've lost. What I gave away. What I'll find. Layla Davis."

"Have you tried Ambien?"

I said, "What keeps you up, Bay?"

He smiled. "She does." He took Mercedes's hand.

# 5

I WAS DREAMING without sleeping. Bay hadn't packed my sleep mask, so I bought one at the airport terminal along with silicone earplugs, Dream Water, and a foam neck pillow. I swallowed the Lunesta that Bay had given me. I planned to sleep my way to Florida, but that didn't happen for more than five minutes at a time. I tossed; I turned; I may even have whimpered and moaned. I dreamed I was crammed into Seat 23D on a Virgin America flight to Everglades International Airport. My dead father told me his brain was on fire, and I could see that his head was smoking. The young man in 23E tapped my arm, said he had to visit the lav. While he was gone, I drifted back to dreamland and told Venise I was en route. Venise weighed 357 pounds in my dream and in her actual life, and she hadn't spoken to me since our father died a couple of months ago.

Patience was parked at the curb outside Terminal 3, leaning on the hood of her cayenne-red Cube and reading *An African in Greenland*. On the way to breakfast, Patience told me about the Mickey Pfeiffer auction preview at four at a Boca Raton warehouse. Mickey had been the managing shareholder, the CEO, and the chairman of the law firm Pfeiffer Kline & Lukeman in New River. He was a well-known philanthropist, an indulgent husband, a reckless philanderer, and the operator of a $1.7 billion Ponzi scheme. He owned a Boeing 727, an eighty-seven-foot Warren yacht, a fleet of luxury cars, including a silver Rolls and a Lamborghini Murciélago. He wore $20,000 Savile Row suits and $200,000 Rolex watches.

As befits a luxurist of ostentatious wealth, Mickey had his own security force, made up of ex- and off-duty Everglades County sheriff's deputies, and New River and Eden police officers, but all these king's men were ultimately unable to keep Mickey safe. He was tortured and beheaded by criminals or cohorts unknown or at least unacknowledged. It was all part of a recent and aforementioned county-wide bloodbath involving cops, lawyers, mobsters, lobbyists, businessmen, and federal, state, and local governments, which was the reason Bay and I—peripheral players at best—left for Vegas.

At six-thirty at the iConnect Café and Yoga Spa on Plumeria, we found two young waitresses asleep, their heads facedown on a table, their extravagant hair (aubergine and caramel) draped over the place mats, their arms in their laps. We cleared our throats. We coughed. Patience shook Aubergine awake. The girl wiped crust from her eyes and tapped her colleague on the elbow. Daisy and Dahlia, their name tags read. I asked for coffee with cream.

Daisy said, "How much cream?"

I said, "Make it blond."

Patience ordered a latté.

The waitresses looked at each other. Dahlia said, "How do you make a latté?"

Patience said, "Do you really work here?"

Daisy said, "Yes."

Patience said, "How do you get stoned so early in the morning?"

Dahlia said, "Busted."

"Make that two coffees," Patience said.

Another customer walked in, a man who had nicked himself shaving, whose hair was damp and slicked back, and whose tie was unknotted. I figured him for a lawyer who had to stand before a judge in two hours, to defend a predatory client whom he knew was guilty as sin, and he should not have stayed so late at his colleague's retirement party last night, but then he would not have met Saskia the intern, whom he'd recently left dead asleep at his condo, and whom he should give a wake-up call to in about fifteen minutes. He ordered a vegan scramble and a cleanse-and-detox smoothie. He opened his valise and took out his iPad.

Dahlia asked him if he'd like a boost with his wellness drink. Did she have a recommendation? She did. Bee pollen. He told her to go for it and went back to his scrolling.

Patience said, "How's Vegas?"

"Bay's enjoying it." I told her about Mercedes Benz. Patience said she went to high school with a guy named Ford Falcon. She asked about Layla. Had we learned anything new? I told her about Layla's sister, the drug addict and prostitute.

The customer pulled a Dopp kit from his valise, stood, and asked Daisy, "Dondé esta el baño?"

"Por aquí." She pointed down the hall.

Patience opened her journal and showed me a fortune cookie fortune she'd pasted on a page: THIS BOOK SHOULD BE A BALL OF LIGHT IN ONE'S HAND. "You're not worried at all?"

"About Venise."

"Not yourself?"

"I've got Open Mike on speed dial."

"Just be discreet. Don't spend a lot of time in public."

"I'm here to see you and Venise."

"Why do you suppose the urgency?"

"I'm her brother."

"Whom she doesn't talk to."

"Maybe she's had a change of heart."

"Pun intended?"

Two bikers parked their Harleys out front, walked in, took off their gloves and their wraparound sunglasses, and sat at a table by the window. Gray ponytails, full gray beards, black boots, blue jeans, black T-shirts, black vests, leather vest extenders, red bandannas, black bi-fold wallets on metal chains, and holstered cell phones. They ordered earth-balance bagels and banana muffin smoothies, hold the boosts, thank you very much. The bulkier one announced that he had a urologist appointment at eleven. "Not looking forward."

"Everything okay down there?" his friend said.

"Serviceable, but no longer maintenance-free."

"Ouch."

"Leaking some oil."

"Loose plug, maybe."

"What's on your agenda?"

"Building a gun cabinet for my grandson. Turns fourteen Friday."

When their breakfast arrived, the bikers held hands across the table, bowed their heads, shut their eyes, and prayed.

Our suppositious lawyer told whomever it was he was speaking with on his cell phone that he was stuck in nightmarish traffic on 95. Some kind of horrific accident ahead. "They're pulling bodies from the wreck as we speak."

I dropped Patience at Jaunts & Junkets Travel on Mangrove, drove to my empty house, parked down the block, and waited a bit.

My friend Red Soileau had been recently murdered in my front yard, and the people who did the killing, thinking Red was me, those who were not themselves dead or else in jail awaiting trial, might still be after their intended target. I let discretion be the better part of curiosity, decided against a tour of the house, and drove to my office, where I found the door ajar and Mecca Pressman sitting at my desk, wearing a green jumpsuit and a gray cowboy hat. Mecca was the Ephemeral Building's janitor and handyman. He lived in #102, a former dental office. Mecca looked up and said, "Don't you ever knock?" Mecca once pitched for the Bristol White Sox in the Appalachian League for three months (meatballs over the plate and a hanging curve), then struggled for years with a substance abuse problem—the family curse or hobby, depending on whom you asked—became a client of mine, joined AA, straightened out his life—clean and sober six years now. I asked him what he was reading.

"Your case files."

"That's illegal."

"And fascinating."

I pointed at the files. "Did you read your own?"

"Only the two you left on the desk." He held up a file folder. "When this Wayne here told you he cried when his dog died but not when his dad died—that was a red flag."

"Thank you, Dr. Pressman."

"Save your sarcasm for therapy, Dr. Melville."

"Did I get any mail?"

"I tossed it."

"Why?"

"Gullibility is not a desired trait in a therapist. The bills are on the windowsill."

"Listen, Mecca, I got to run, but before I do . . ." I held out my hand, and he gave me the files and some narrative advice.

He said, "Show us the eyes. The eyes are the windows into the abyss."

ON THE WAY to the hospital I stopped at Bay's to see Open Mike, who was watching Bay's canal-side home in our absence. I found him out on the dock with a Bloody Mary, the *Daily Racing Form*, a head of lettuce, a pile of currency, and a hair dryer hooked up to an extension cord. I asked him what the lettuce was for. He said, "Watch."

He picked up the lettuce, walked to the end of the dock, and dropped the lettuce into the canal. In a few moments, the water bubbled, a shadow appeared below the surface, and a manatee emerged, caught the lettuce in its mouth, rolled over, and dove.

I said, "Holy shit, that was a big manatee."

"Twelve feet, I figure."

"And the hair dryer?"

"I'm straightening all my bills. I hate a messy wallet," he said.

We went into the kitchen and Mike fixed me a Bloody Mary. I told him I wasn't hungry. Mike had crammed Bay's substantial freezer with a hundred or so stacked fast-food burgers wrapped in their paper jackets. He told me he didn't cook. This way, he explained, you just pop one or two of these puppies in the micro-wave and you're good to go. Mike inherited his baggy cognac-brown eyes from his mom and his widow's peak from his dad. The orange hair came courtesy of a mutation in the Lynch family DNA. "Every other generation," Mike told me, "the Connemara Lynches punch out another ginger." And like all the male Lynches, Mike was built like a drystone pillar.

Mike answered his phone. And passed it over to me. Bay told me that the Vegas police were looking for a man in connection with a kidnapping. A fifteen-year-old girl was on the TV news, her face in shadow, describing to a reporter her abduction last night by a man who claimed to work at the Crisis Center. I told Bay what actually happened, and then I wondered if she'd shown up with the cops at the Crisis Center at ten when my shift was set to begin, and then I realized I hadn't called in to tell them I couldn't make it. Would that make me look guilty? I wondered why she would do this to me. Bay said the artist's sketch made me look a tad shifty. They've got you on video, too. He told me to stand by. He'd find out what he could and get back to me. He told me to put Mike back on the phone.

I called Oliver from the car to get Venise's room number. "Oliver, it's me."

"How is she?"

"I haven't seen her yet. Are you in her room now?"

"You know I can't stand hospitals."

"But you do call her, right?"

"Whenever the Weather Channel does the local report."

"You keep the Weather Channel on all day?"

"There's quite a bit of tornadic activity in the upper Midwest right now."

"What's going on, Oliver?"

"I can't live without her."

"You'll have to unless she loses some weight."

"I know."

"They can't do another gastric bypass."

He told me he had a confession to make. Venise did not want to see me. He wanted Venise to see me. "I want you two to end this nonsense. I think it's the stress killing her."

"She thinks I squandered her inheritance on Dad's assisted living facility and on our trip to Alaska. She thinks I killed him."

"You need to try, Wylie."

"I will, but we both know she's not a reasonable woman."

"You two need to reconcile before anything . . . happens."

"And you have to do more—"

"You're breaking up, Wylie."

"I am not. You're just saying that."

"If you're talking, I can't hear you."

AT EVERGLADES GENERAL I found Venise in her private room, sitting up in bed in her pink waffle-net pajamas, watching Rachael Ray and eating an alarming Rabelaisian meal of mashed potatoes *and* french fries; beef *and* chicken; fried pie *and* chocolate cake. I asked her where she'd gotten the food.

"Downstairs in the lobby."

I said, "Maybe you're at the wrong hospital. You've just had a heart attack, Venise. And here you are eating mounds of saturated fats and carbs."

"It makes me happy."

"You're morbidly obese."

Venise lifted the sesame seed bun off her three-story bacon cheeseburger, applied a handful of fries to the tower, squeezed a packet of ketchup onto the unsettling agglomeration, reset the bun on top, looked me in the eye, and took a predacious bite out of the ungodly mess.

I said, "I'm not going to watch you kill yourself."

She lifted a flap of fried chicken skin from her bowl of gravied mashed potatoes, held it above her mouth, and dropped it in.

I said, "I'm going to speak with your doctor."

"You do and I'll kill you."

I gave her a kiss on the forehead. She did not pull away or stop chewing.

I TOOK A SEAT at the beachside bar at Slappy's Wonderland and ordered a dozen oysters and a beer while I waited for Donny L., he who had lost his family and his job, to arrive. Quentin, my shucker, welcomed me back and called my attention to a lovely young woman on Rollerblades, gliding past us on the boardwalk, weaving gracefully through the crowd in her stunning blue bikini with a matching hyacinth macaw perched serenely on her bronzed shoulder. When I asked Quentin what was new, he told me he had developed these polaroids that itched like hell. He said, "Tried Benadryl on them and everything."

I said, "What are you talking about?"

"Cold sores on my ass. Polaroids."

I got the joke and laughed.

He said, "No joke, Wylie. Hurts like heck."

"You're serious?"

"As a Pentecostal preacher."

Donny and I ordered fried grouper sandwiches. I told him he looked like shit and he told me why he did. He'd recently interviewed a fifteen-year-old Filipina, who had been enslaved for three years by her "employers" in their home in Grassy Haven, a tony enclave of CEOs, professional athletes, and diplomats in west Everglades County. The girl was purchased from her parents in Manila and brought to the States by a development officer with the Philippine Consulate in New River and his wife. The girl's passport was taken away. She was charged for her transportation to the U.S. and for her room and board. She was forced to cook, clean, and care for the couple's two preschool children. She was beaten regularly by the wife, a pediatrician, for perceived violations of house rules. She was not allowed to contact her family. She was told her parents would be killed if she ever tried to run away. But run away she did.

One afternoon, she walked the children to the neighborhood park, sat them in the sandbox, told them to wait right there while she went to the ladies' room, and she left. She walked to an Asian market she often shopped at with the wife and told the clerk her story. The clerk called the police. When the children did not arrive home for the dinner that had not been prepared, the parents contacted the police, who were just then interviewing the girl. The children were with Child Protective Services. When the police charged the couple with kidnapping and enslavement, the couple invoked their diplomatic immunity, collected their children, and returned to Manila.

After he heard the girl's story, Donny decided to investigate slavery in South Florida. He identified three areas of concern: domestic workers, farmworkers, and sex workers. He told me about young girls, mostly, but a few boys, being recruited into sex work in the halls of juvenile court by men and women posing as lawyers and social workers. The kids weren't told they were being recruited, of course. These were kids that no one would miss. Once the recruiter earned the child's trust, then the cycle of intimacy and violence began. Kiss, kiss! And then bang, bang!

Donny looked around, leaned forward, and whispered, "Here's a story I'm trying to confirm. A seventeen-year-old Guatemalan told me she was smuggled into the country at fourteen to work the fields in Homestead. She was forced into prostitution. She had a baby. The baby was branded with a heated belt buckle by the pimp. And then he sold the baby when the mother gave him some sass.

She and three other girls were brought to a house in Naranja and gang-raped in front of each other."

"Have you gone to the police?"

"Need to make sure that the girls are safe before I write anything. Just remember, when you see a prostitute, don't think *criminal*; think *victim*. Some of the women you see working the streets of Vegas were shipped there in box trucks from the tomato fields of Florida."

"I can't believe this."

"The Islamists kidnap three hundred girls at a time. Here we do it one by one." Donny ordered two more beers and went off on Muslim fundamentalists, eviscerating the medieval barbarians who degrade women, murder those who believe in any deity but their own, a god who's nothing more than a nightmarish invention of some delusional pigs needing an excuse to justify their lust for plunder, slaughter, and oppression. The Koran, Donny said, spends more time telling Muslim men they can keep women as slaves than it does telling them they need to pray five times a day.

When I suggested that not all Muslims agreed with the fundamentalists and had condemned the atrocities, Donny said he was sick of cultural relativism that defended the deprivation of human rights, murder, and intolerance in the name of respect for religious beliefs and cultural tradition. Religion, he said, doesn't deserve respect.


PATIENCE CALLED TO SAY she'd meet me in an hour at the Wayside. I'd been coming to the Wayside my whole adult life. First with my ex, Georgia, often with Bay, and at times with my dad, both in his vigorous and stocious days and in his sundown days of dementia.

The Wayside ignores the state's smoking ban, which makes it a favorite of the folks from the mission on Main and the backsliding folks from the AA meeting at the Episcopal church across the street.

Not very long after I'd moved out of our house, Georgia called to tell me that she had a stack of mail waiting for me and that she was dating a fellow with the rhyming name Marty Hardy, a Realtor, divorced with two kids. She said she could do without the kids, quite frankly, but Marty was a garrulous fellow, not given to fits of melancholia like someone she knew. And then she got around to talking about us. She wondered if we hadn't been too hasty in our separation. Maybe we should, you know, talk. By then I had settled into a solitary life in a studio apartment on the beach over a Mexican restaurant run by Persians. We agreed to meet Saturday afternoon at the Wayside, which was around the corner from Georgia's.

I kissed her on the cheek, sat, and asked her how she was doing. "All in all," she said, "comme ci, comme ça. Good days, bad days. Ups and downs." She handed me Marty's business card. "He wants you to have it. You can't be renting forever."

There was a picture of a stout, bearded fellow, wearing a TRUST ME, I'M A REALTOR T-shirt and the slogan WE KNOW WHERE YOU LIVE across the bottom.

Georgia looked around at the half dozen shabby tables, at the torn vinyl chairs, at the Alonzo Mourning poster, at two of the six Boswell brothers playing cribbage at a pub table, at the dented cigarette machine, and at Twyla behind the bar, smoking a cigarette, sipping a Tom Collins, and watching NASCAR on TV, and said, "A lot of memories here."

We ended up at Georgia's. We ordered lamb shawarma and Moroccan fish, and we drank even more. We looked through a photo album of our life together and grew mawkish. Nothing had changed in the house except my cluttered office. Now my books were in a storage unit on Lantana, and the office had been converted into what Georgia called a meditation room. Mats and cushions on the floor, potted plants in every corner, candles on the windowsills, Japanese prints on the walls, and a hand-of-Buddha indoor water fountain on the coffee table, burbling away. Eventually, Georgia cut Marty loose and found the man she would marry, Tripp Morris, and had two kids of her own. Georgia and I were like DeFonda and Abrel and should never have been together to begin with. She was Beatles; I was Stones.

TWO WOMEN OF MY casual acquaintance, Desirée and Baby, were sitting at a shaded table on the Wayside patio enjoying their high-balls and a blunt. Baby had her shoes off and her feet up on a chair. Desirée wore a hairnet.

Baby held up the blunt and said, "Kind bud, Wylie."

Desirée said, "Hawaiian black."

I thanked them for their thoughtfulness, walked into the bar, ordered a Bloody Mary, and asked Zeke, the bartender, what was up with the eye patch. He said it helped with his double vision. "The headaches are a bitch."

"How long has this been going on?"

"Six, seven weeks."

"This is serious."

"No shit." He stuck a celery stalk in my drink on the second try and slid the glass to my hand.

"You need to see a doctor."

"Or two." He smiled and held up his hands. "No dinero."

I told him I was calling a doctor friend to make an appointment. "Won't cost you."

While I was on hold, Baby and Desirée came in and sat at the bar. Baby handed Zeke a plastic sack full of meat ends from the Italian market where she worked, and he poured them each a Dewar's and water.

I explained to Zeke that Dr. Chao was a holistic ophthalmologist and would probably talk with him about his diet and his supplements, so he might want to keep the meat ends a secret. I told Walter to send me the bill, but he probably wouldn't—he'd be so fascinated with the mystery of Zeke's vision that he'd consider it a privilege to have a go at him.

Patience walked in and gave me a kiss. I ordered another Bloody Mary, and we went to a table. She slid her hand over mine and squeezed. We toasted our reunion. I said, "When are you coming to visit?"

"Soon, I hope."

An orbiculate fellow wearing a VIRGINITY ROCKS! T-shirt and carrying a tub of fried chicken from Chicken Lickin' (*It's So Clucking Good!*) under his arm, walked in, put the tub on the bar, pulled up a stool, and asked Zeke to turn on the bowling channel. He ordered a pitcher of beer.

Zeke said, "Don't you have high cholesterol, Warren?"

"If you call six forty-seven high."

"How the hell are you even standing?"

"In fact, I'm sitting." Warren pulled a drumstick from the tub, held it up, and admired its succulence.

And that's when my cell phone played "Abracadabra." I answered. Bay had some distressing news. My grainy face was all over the Vegas TV newscasts. My young friend Ruby, whose real name, at least for now, was Misty Roses, had gone to the police with a story of her rape by an anonymous-looking man she met on the street. That much we knew.

I said, "*Anonymous* hurts."

Bay said that surveillance videos of me and Misty on the boulevard were the lead story on every channel. The authorities had trouble getting my name at first because I'd been fortunate enough to have paid for the pizza and room in cash, but it had been only a matter of time before someone in our neighborhood or the Crisis Center recognized me and called the cops. And, in fact, as soon as he saw the story, Gene Woodling did call the police. He gave them my name and said I could not have done what the girl they were calling Misty, but whose real name was Audrey Blick, said I had done. I was a straight shooter, one of the good guys.

"This is ludicrous, Bay. They'll ask the hotel clerk, and he'll tell them I left her there."

"Unless he's been persuaded otherwise."

"They won't find my DNA on her." Then I remembered. "Well, I did shake her hand. Why would she do this?"

"Maybe someone wants to fuck with you."

"Cops?"

"No, but someone else who put them on your trail."

I told Bay that I was sure the girl had recognized Blythe from the photo.

Bay told me not to fly. As soon as my name turned up on a flight manifest, I'd be scooped up. Better to walk into the Vegas Metro Police Department with my lawyer than be caught by surprise. My lawyer's name was Meyer Cohen, Bay told me, a crackerjack attorney but a mediocre poker player who owed Bay a favor. "Open Mike's going to pick you up at six A.M. It's a thirty-eight-and-a-half-hour drive, give or take. See you Thursday."

I let Patience know the developing complications and the disappointing but necessary travel plans. Our reunion would be short-lived. She asked about Venise, and I told her about the overeating and the emotional outburst. I'd called Venise's heart specialist, Dr. Wasgatt, while I was still at the hospital, but he couldn't tell me anything: the HIPAA rules and all. He did give me the number of the Obesity Clinic at Florida International University. He said to think of it as a last chance and then he said he didn't say that. I called and got Venise a bed in their thirty-day inpatient holistic bariatric clinic. I called Oliver and left the info on his voice mail. "Don't let her tantrum her way out of this, Oliver."

I lay in bed with a copy of *Travel + Leisure* unfolded on my chest while Patience showered. I told myself not to worry. They couldn't prove I did something in one place while I was busy in another.

Whenever I have to wake up early I have trouble getting to sleep and staying asleep. I drift off to dreamland only to resurface reluctantly minutes later, and in this restless way I seldom reach the third act of my dreams. I felt someone shaking my leg, and I opened my eyes, and Patience said, "Wake up. Mike's downstairs."

"He's early."

"He brought coffee and doughnuts."

"I guess I fell asleep before you came to bed."

"And you were talking in your sleep."

"What did I say?"

"You said you put Venise on ice so she wouldn't spoil."

"Damn! I'd better call Venise."

"I'll pay her a visit after work."

# 6

"I'VE DONE SOME bad things in my life," I heard Mike tell Patience as I walked into the kitchen. "But I've learned to accept myself, warts and all. This is who I am." He spooned honey onto his strawberry-frosted doughnut and licked the spoon.

Patience said, "You've got yourself one righteous sweet tooth there, Michael Lynch."

I poured myself a coffee and sat down.

Mike said, "I've stopped holding on to my unworthiness."

I reached for a cinnamon doughnut and asked Mike if he was quoting Thich Nhat Hanh.

"Goldie Hawn," he said. "I just go with the flow, you could say."

"Like a dead fish," I said.

"Resistance only creates sorrow," he said.

"Like a fallen leaf in the current," Patience said.

Mike said, "Are you ready to do this, Coyote?"

"I am."

"Back to the belly of the beast."

"I haven't done anything wrong."

"We all have."

"I've got a lawyer. An alibi."

"And yet the cops are on your trail."

"You're not being very comforting."

He asked me for my cell phone and took a flip phone from his pocket and slid it to me. "I got you a burner. Leave your cell here. Cops can get your call activity from the cell. Every call you've ever made, your contact lists, voice mails, photos, videos, messages, apps, your passwords, your geolocation points—all without a warrant." He handed the cell phone to Patience. "Patience can bring it when she visits."

I said, "Pretty soon we'll need IT support to get lost."

Mike said, "I've got my GPS locked into your Vegas address. I've got a cooler full of Italian sandwiches from Stranieri's Market, a thermos of coffee with cream, a case of Red Bull, a six-pack of beer, a first-aid kit, and I filled the car with gas." He put down his doughnut and wiped his mouth with the napkin. "We'll want to evacuate our bowels and bladders before hitting the road. I plan on making good time."

MIKE HAD RENTED a gleaming graphite-blue Nissan Rogue. Patience said, "You really did fill your car up with gas." She opened the back door and I peeked inside. The cargo space was crammed with five-gallon plastic gas cans.

Mike said, "Eighteen cans. You're looking at ninety gallons of high-test right there."

I said, "We have gas stations in America."

"They can't beat my price." He explained that the Rogue got thirty-three miles to the gallon, had a twenty-two gallon tank, and we had 2,259 miles to go, give or take. Eighty gallons should do it. "We have more than enough."

I said, "We'll have to drive with the windows open."

Patience said, "What price is that?"

Mike said, "I've got an associate in security at the tank farm over at the port who was willing to look the other way in exchange for future services rendered."

Patience clapped her hands. "Okay, then. I've heard enough. Good luck, boys." She kissed me goodbye and waved to us as we backed out of her driveway. Mike grazed the mailbox and said, "No harm, no foul."

The overwhelming smell of the gasoline was already assaulting my sinuses. Could a throbbing headache be far behind? I leaned my head out the window and sucked in the relatively fresh air.

"Satellite radio," Mike said. "Watch this." He powered the radio on and told it to go to *The Richie Mulhearn Show*, which turned out to be a sports talk show. Richie's guest prattled on about parity in the Association. And then followed fifteen minutes of commercials for erectile dysfunction medications and personal injury attorneys. We merged with the turnpike north, and I asked Mike what the other smell was.

"My new scent." He held out his wrist for me to sniff. "Kon-Kwest. They call the fragrance *animalic*. It drives the female of the species wild."

"What species?" I sneezed. "I think I may pass out."

"You'll get used to it."

"What if we get stopped?" I said. "What happens? All this fuel can't be legal."

"We won't get stopped."

On the radio, Richie launched into an unprovoked rant about women who were ruining sports with their ridiculous emotions and their stupid opinions. Women, Richie said, had turned professional sports into a world of sissies. I looked at Mike. "Really, Mike. We have to listen to this?"

Mike told the radio to call his bookie. And then he put $500 on the Heat in tonight's game. When we got back to Richie, he was talking about restraining orders and pepper spray and cock teasing, and he said he didn't care what the pussies calling in had to say. He told them to talk to Oprah. He was right, he said. He was very right.

Mike took out a cigarette and lit it.

I said, "What the hell, Mike? You trying to kill us?"

"I'm nowhere near the gas."

"It's the fumes that burn, not the liquid."

"I did not know that." He held his cigarette outside the window and the wind blew sparks to the backseat. "I'll be careful."

We stopped on 75. I bought some oranges at the roadside fruit stand while Mike refueled the tank and tossed the spent cans into the Dumpster. He smoked a cigarette before we hit the road. I thanked him for his courtesy. He said the courtesy would last forty minutes. I asked him when the car was due back at Enterprise.

"It's a disposable."

"A what?"

"A burner. It's rented a to guy named Paul, D. for David, Reed, from Richardson, Texas, SS number 465-97-1224, who does not actually exist in our world as we know it. Mike showed me Paul's Texas driver's license with Mike's photo on it. Mike opened a second Red Bull and drank it in one swallow. "Time's a-wasting, amigo."

I WOKE IN A FOG. "What the hell is that?"

"The battleship *Alabama*."

"Are we at war?"

Mike swerved to avoid an armadillo, but the armadillo jumped up into the car's grille. Mike made the sign of the cross and asked me to grab him a sandwich from the cooler. We ate as we drove through Mobile. He asked me if I had noticed anything about all the perky weather girls on the news-at-noon shows in Miami. He told me they were all pregnant. All at once. "What do you suppose is going on?"

On the radio a pair of apoplectic dopes were screaming about a referee's missed call that cost the Mavericks a win, and they weren't surprised when irate fans started sending threatening e-mails to the ref's family.

We checked into the Ville Platte Night's Inn at eight-fifteen, and when I say *we*, I mean Paul Reed. No lifeguard on duty, no water in the pool. No soda in the vending machine. Mike had driven every mile of the way. I'd taken four naps totaling three hours of blessed sleep and relief from the nightmare of sports talk radio. Never was so much said by so many about so little. We'd passed dozens of state troopers, and I held my breath to still my heart at every pass. We'd seen the aftermath of three accidents, one of which was magnificent. A man driving a Ford F-150 pickup, towing a twenty-eight-foot travel trailer and towing a pop-up camper behind that, managed a three-vehicle pileup all on his own when one vehicle in his convoy jackknifed. The resulting triangular wreckage blocked all eastbound traffic on I-10 from Gulfport to the Louisiana state line.

Mike kicked off his loafers, collapsed onto his bed, and fell asleep fully dressed. My own body was still vibrating from the rhythm of the road. I sipped a glass of cognac to take the edge off. The image of my imminent arrest in Vegas had me jittery and semi-alert. The motel room wasn't helping my mood. The faucet on the sink was installed at a ridiculous angle; the security chain door lock was missing the button-link that attached it to the track mounted to the wall. On the toilet lid in the bathroom I found a yellowed nap sack "for disposal of sanitary napkins" with a drawing on it of a vase with a sprig of blue flowers, a visual motif repeated in the framed art—screwed into the bathroom wall as if a woebegone traveler might want to steal it—a painting of a brown vase laden with large pink blossoms. The orange paint from a recent renovation dripped down the bathroom wall and over some of the tan tile. And I thought maybe I deserved to linger in this squalor.

I turned on the TV and imagined myself on the screen doing the perp walk from the squad car to the courthouse the way this guy in Opelousas who'd allegedly murdered his wife was doing. The perky weather girl on Channel 4 was pregnant. I caught myself nodding off, but I was unable to stay under, until I seduced myself with the idea that I was already asleep and none of this hellacious odyssey was happening, and then, unburdened of the truth, I drifted off to slumberland.

I woke up in my not-so-comfy chair with a sore back. The TV was off and Mike was gone, but he'd left his clothes in a pile on the floor. I shaved, showered, dressed, packed my overnight bag, gathered Mike's clothes, and headed out to the parking lot, where I saw Mike filling the Rogue's gas tank.

"You forgot these," I said.

"I left them."

"Why?"

"The stores are full of that shit. I don't need to be schlepping soiled clothes around with me. Just not very classy, my friend."

He had used a room towel to wipe away the armadillo residue from the front bumper. He stuffed the towel, the clothes, and the empty cans into the trash receptacle. We bought leaden doughnuts and washy coffee at a drive-thru called Sinkers, but not before I had hurried into Evangeline Drugs and bought Mike an electronic cigarette. I gave it to him and said, "Humor me."

I almost had a heart attack somewhere in West Texas. I'd finally been lulled into tranquillity by the passing landscapes and the soothing music of tires on concrete. We were cruising along at eighty-five or ninety, keeping pace with the sparse traffic. Mike was drinking a beer, eating a sandwich, and listening to a baseball game when we heard a siren and felt, as much as we saw, the flashing lights from the cruiser behind us. Where the hell had that guy come from? Mike told me to relax and to let him do the talking, but if I had to say something, I was to call him Paul. Got it? Just as Mike eased the car to the shoulder, the trooper blew by and nabbed the car ahead of us. I breathed again. Mike said, "We are some lucky bastards, Coyote."

I FOUND OUT about our substantial arsenal in Moriarty, New Mexico. We'd stopped at a gas station/convenience store and parked on the side by the Dumpster. I noticed an apartment upstairs over the store. An open window, lacy curtains fluttering in the soft evening breeze.

Mike said. "Go in and get us ten lotto tickets while I top off the tank. We're on a lucky streak."

"We are?"

"On fire."

I gathered food wrappers, tissues, napkins, empty cans, and empty bottles from the car and tossed them into the Dumpster. Mike grabbed a gas can from the wayback and lit up an actual cigarette. He raised his eyebrows and gave me a look like a defiant adolescent would, like, *I can smoke if I want to.* I headed for the store. I saw a young woman sitting in the apartment window, dandling a baby on her lap, and watching me. I smiled and nodded. I wondered what she was thinking about one more stranger passing through her life, and I tried to imagine her existence upstairs and imagined it noisy, cramped, and drab.

I bought ten Powerball quick picks. The ginger-haired clerk asked me where we were headed. I told him Vegas and asked him if he lived upstairs.

He did. "Short commute."

"That your wife and baby in the window?"

"I'm just the baby's daddy. Not one to be tied down, you know."

"Where you going?"

He smiled. "Places."

Once I was back outside, I saw Mike holding a pistol at arm's length and aiming it at the Dumpster. And then I heard *pop!* He must have slipped a noise suppressor over the barrel. I looked up at the apartment window. Ginger's woman and child were gone—she to call the cops, I was certain. I said, "Let's get out of here."

"I hate rats."

"Is that rat bothering you?"

"Not anymore."

"Rats don't want trouble; they want food." I opened the passenger door.

"What animal do you hate?"

"You mean *hate* it so if I saw one, I'd kill it?"

"Right."

"None."

"Not even those fish that swim up your dick and stay there? Not them?"

"Fish?"

"Toothpick fish. Jesus, Coyote, your knowledge of the animal kingdom is pitiful."

"Can we get a move on?"

"Now I have to pee."

"So pee right here."

"Like a dog? No, thank you."

When Mike returned and drew out the pistol he'd tucked into the back of his slacks, he opened a storage space beneath the cargo deck where you might expect to find a spare tire and a jack. What we found were two rifles, a shotgun, another pistol, and an AK-47.

I said, "What if that cop had searched us?"

"All legal."

"All necessary?"

"We'll see."

WHAT SHOULD HAVE BEEN a sweet and leisurely evening for Mike and me turned sour and turbulent in an Albuquerque minute. Mike had dozed off to sleep in our room at the Rodeway Inn Midtown while I watched the local news and learned that we had won $5,000 in the lottery. I couldn't help myself. I slapped the arm of the chair and said, "Goddamn!"

Mike stirred. "What?"

I told him what. He said we should celebrate.

We drove down Central Avenue looking for a bar that sang to us. Zinc Bar, nope. Kelley's Pub. Nope. Scalo's? Too grand. Two Fools Tavern? Too close to home. Something Brew Pub. Something Else Bistro. Cantina Lobo—that's it! We found a parking space across the street and down the block. And then we found a guy slapping a woman in the face down the alley beside the cantina. Strapping fellow, wispy woman. Then the asshole grabbed her by the throat and shoved her against the brick wall. I looked at Mike and thought, We can't even go out for a drink without finding trouble. Mike grabbed the guy's shoulder, spun him around, and head-butted him. The goon's shattered nose gushed blood; he dropped to his knees and threw up. The woman cried.

I said, "Are you okay?"

Mike said, "He won't bother you again."

I said, "We should call the cops."

Mike said, "But we don't want to see the cops."

"Right," I said. I took the trembling woman's elbow. "Come with us."

The assailant tried to speak. Mike planted a foot in the guy's ribs and rolled him over onto his back. His Duke City Gym T-shirt was soaked in blood and dribbled with vomit. The guy said, "You'll be sorry."

Mike cupped his hand behind his ear. "I don't hear so well in the dark."

I said, "We really need to go," and we hurried to the car. I hopped in back with the remaining gas cans.

Mike opened the passenger door for the woman and said, "Pardon our appearance while we're remodeling."

Her left cheek was swollen and bruised. She did not want to go to the ER, and she was afraid to go home, and she didn't want to get friends involved. She asked us to drop her off at the Best Western in Old Town.

I said, "I'm Wylie, and this is—"

"Paul," Mike said.

"Tracy," she said.

Mike said, "Here comes the cavalry." Tracy's assailant and three other bald, tattooed, pinheaded prednisone freaks with bitch-tits were waddling toward us, one of them wielding a baseball bat.

There would be no reasoning with these four cock diesels in the throes of 'roid rage. Mike started the engine. The four jamokes surrounded the car. The batsman swung at the passenger window, sending Tracy into hysterics. The window shattered but did not break.

When Mike backed up, we heard a nightmarish scream. The dashboard monitor showed that we had pinned one bonehead against the car behind us, and that sent Barry Bonds into a frenzy of window-clubbing. Another lummox climbed up the hood and onto the roof and began stomping. Mike excused himself to Tracy, reached across her to the glove box, took out a pistol, and fired a bullet through the roof. The stomping ceased. Tracy's bloodied mugger stood in front of the car, pointing his finger at her, and slamming his mighty fists onto the hood. Mike ran him over, and we headed down Central away from the lights of the city center. I looked behind us and saw our flattened beast struggle to his feet. We made a right at the first dark street we saw, and the rooftop passenger slid off the car, onto the pavement, and rolled to the gutter.

At the Best Western, Tracy thanked us for saving her life. We told her she should give the cops a call. She said she would. We watched her walk to the lobby. I said, "Her name's not Tracy."

"What I was thinking."

"And Sluggo was her boyfriend."

"She'll probably bring him soup at the hospital."

Mike dropped me at the Rodeway, said we needed a new car, and I'd only be in the way. He'd see me in the morning. I thought I'd never sleep, given the violence we'd just endured—all very disturbing, of course, but I was relieved, if not elated, that we had survived. After a glass of cognac, I was out.

When I got out of the shower in the morning, Mike was sitting

at the desk reading the complimentary newspaper. He told me that
Paul Reed's virtual cousin, Walter Becker, had rented a new car,
and Mike led me out to the parking lot to see the sparkling silver
Rogue, complete with fuel cans, arsenal, and beverages. I didn't
ask. I did beg for coffee. We stopped at a drive-thru place in a
dingy neighborhood near I-40 for breakfast burritos and coffee.
Mike called my attention to a burned-out shell of a car that was
still smoldering on the swale of a dead-end street. He shook his
head. "Someone's having a worse day than we are."

WE CRESTED A BARREN hill at dusk, rounded a curve, and as we
descended into Las Vegas Valley, there below us lay a sea of glister-
ing light in the blank and pitiless expanse, and I agreed with Mike
that the view was both exhilarating and miraculous, especially
after driving so many hundreds of etherizing miles through empty
and inhospitable desert.

Bay called me on Mercedes's cell and told me that Mike
and I had reservations at the Aria. I was to go to our suite and
stay put. My lawyer, Meyer Cohen, would be by at seven in the
morning to escort me to police headquarters. Bay would meet
us there. We'd enter through a side door, thereby avoiding any
newspeople who might be lurking out front. We were actually
doing the cops a favor. They were a little embarrassed, what
with the revelations they accidently uncovered in their rush to
judgment. The interview should be brief, and I'd be released.
The hotel video showed me leaving the building and did not
show me returning. The clerk verified the video. The video at
Emeril's showed me dining with Bay and Mercedes at the time
of the alleged assault.

"Your accuser admitted her mistake to the authorities, who

then took her to Refuge House. Someone who wants you out of the way got to that girl."

"We need to go home, Bay. This town is preposterous."

"We have Layla's case to solve. And maybe that's what's pissing someone off. Maybe you got hold of a loose thread, and someone's afraid that if you keep tugging at it, you'll unravel the whole valuable fabric of whatever it is they're trying to keep secret."

I told Mike he was doing a hundred, and wouldn't this be a silly time to get busted.

He apologized and slowed. "I get excited."

Bay said, "I don't know what that fabric might be, but we do know, as you said, there are a lot of people conspiring to keep her death a secret. A confederacy of the culpable."

"Why?"

"Because all the felonious libertines know who killed her. And they also know that crime is the engine driving the local economy. Even the cops depend on it. And the criminals need the cops to keep the other criminals in line so no one gets the upper hand. Otherwise—chaos, and that will get the entertainment czars to fold their silken tents and slouch off to Macau, and this place becomes a waste of desert sand once again." And then he said, "I'm going to be a brother."

Bay's dad, Little Bob, it seemed, had indeed gotten his forty-three-year-old inamorata, Lorena Linkletter, pregnant. "If it's a boy, they're naming him Pierre."

"Pierre Lettique," I said. "Sounds like an expensive men's fragrance."

"I'm thinking about suing the Viagra people for child support."

"Is he sure it's his?"

"Yes."

"How does he feel?"

"He's all swollen up like a bullfrog about to croak. The Flaubert Stud."

"And how's the expectant mom?"

"Lorena looked radiant in the photo they sent. Hair's cantaloupe-colored, but that could be the light." And then he told me to take the SIM card out of my phone, destroy it, and toss the phone when we hung up. Then he said he thought he and I should send flowers to the happy couple. And I agreed. And maybe money for a crib. Or maybe the crib instead of the money.

# 7

I SAID, "We need more data."

Bay said, "About?"

"About Layla's death. It's a mistake to theorize before you have sufficient data. You begin to twist the facts to fit your theory, instead of the theory to suit the facts."

Bay cited my source. "Sherlock Holmes, 'A Scandal in Bohemia.'"

I said, "On the other hand, Einstein said that if your facts don't fit the theory, change the facts."

Bay held out his hands, palms up, as if weighing the merits of our experts. "Sherlock?" He raised his left hand. "Albert?" His right. "And do we even have a theory? And what is a fact?"

We were standing—actually, I was pacing—in the hallway of the police station while Meyer Cohen had a preliminary conference with Detective Sergeant Spooner and the Vegas Metro PD spokeswoman, Celia Rojas, who was both pregnant and perky, and evidently in the wrong line of work.

Bay said, "A photograph is real. You can hold it in your hand. A photograph is a fact. But the image that the photograph depicts is not necessarily a fact." He opened his wallet and slipped out a photograph of Little Bob in the seat of a John Deere tractor and little Bay on his lap, both of them smiling beneath their tractor hats and squinting into the camera.

"You look blissful," I said.

"Not a fact," he said. And then he fanned his fingers, and the photograph vanished.

We were out of the police station by eight. I did not receive an official apology nor an explanation for the harassment, unless "These things happen" is one or the other. When I changed the subject and asked Spooner about the investigation into Layla's baffling death, Meyer squeezed my elbow and shook his head. Rojas looked at Spooner; Spooner looked at his watch.

The three of us went out for breakfast at Your Eggsellance. Eggs Benediction came with wafers of unleavened bread. I got the Benedict Arnold. Bay and Meyer built their own Sin City Omelets. Bay told us that he'd heard from Julie Wade. Blythe, aka Fawn, had shown up in Memphis ready to move into her deceased sister's condo and to claim her inheritance. She arrived on the arm of a Vegas attorney named Lester Daum. Meyer smiled. He knew Daum. Crooked as a sack of snakes. And just as cold-blooded. A man fond of letting people know that the courtroom injunction to tell the truth, the whole truth, and nothing but the truth does not apply to the lawyers in the case. He practiced with his brother Leslie, in a firm known to other lawyers as Daum and Daumer or Less and Less. "Lester once defended a white man who had murdered three of his Mexican neighbors over in Pahrump by invoking the Bush Doctrine of preemptive strikes, saying his client only murdered the neighbors before they could murder him, a simple act of anticipated self-defense."

When Daum heard that Layla had left all of her assets to St.

Jude's Hospital and not to Blythe, he booked the next flight out. Julie knew the lawyer handling Layla's estate. Julie found Blythe, fed her, got her into detox, and was hoping to find out what else Blythe might know about Layla's passing once she was coherent. Julie told Bay her assistant Anita had resigned to have a baby, and if he knew anyone looking to get into detective work, to let her know.

Bay said that Ruby Tuesday/Misty Roses/Audrey Blick had not resurfaced as far as he knew. And with that verb I remembered that Ruby had told me about the tunnels and the mole people. After Bodhi, our waiter, refreshed our coffees, I asked Meyer what he knew about the tunnels. Three hundred miles of them under the city, conduits for rainwater, he said. And, yes, folks live down there, some of them for years. Safer than the streets. Black as pitch, for the most part. Some people have furnished their camps with the mattresses and furniture the hotels discard. Bay asked me if I was going to eat those last couple of Marmite soldiers.

DJANGO HAD LEARNED a new trick in my absence: the Prisoner. He enters a room, gets behind the door and up on his back legs. Then he walks the door to the jamb and pushes until it clicks shut, and now he's stuck inside. He was clever, all right, but he still couldn't turn a slippery doorknob, so he ended up scratching like crazy to be sprung. We'll have to start shutting all the doors when we leave the house, Bay said.

I found Django locked in my bedroom. When he saw me open the door, he blasted by me and into the living room, ran over the sofa, the chair, the TV, and up the curtains. I sat in the chair and he leaped to my lap. And then he who will not be cradled climbed my chest and licked my face.

Bay made Irish coffees, told me Mike was asleep in the guest room and Mercedes was on her way. I called Elwood and asked him if he'd like to explore the tunnels with me this afternoon. He most definitely would. He'd be by soon. He told me he was working on a story about Lake Mead, the city's shrinking reservoir. It seems all the male fish in the lake were becoming hermaphrodites. Probably a good idea to drink bottled water, he said.

Mercedes arrived with a bouquet of red tulips and blue irises in honor of my vindication. Bay set out a tray of cubed pepper jack cheese and garlic-stuffed olives. We toasted the delusive judicial system.

I asked Mercedes about her creative writing class. She told us that there were two warring factions in the class, the realists— of which she was one—and the fantasists, the people who don't believe in climate change or evolution but do believe in elves, angels, and werewolves. Django hopped on her lap and gazed at me over the tabletop like I could so easily be replaced. Then he closed his golden eyes when Mercedes scratched the sweet spot on the top of his little noggin.

Mike padded into the kitchen in his Venetian Casino robe. He said to no one in particular, "I'm not a *has*-been; I'm a *will*-be." Mercedes said she was working on a story about identical twin brothers who'd been separated at birth. Django licked Mercedes's fingers and stared at me. Mercedes said, "The one named Nyler was raised by their biological mother, the one named Teyton by their biological father. They never had contact, never knew that they were half of a matching pair until Nyler's mom, on her deathbed, told him so, and Nyler went looking for his brother. And found him."

I said, "And then what?"

"That's as far as I've gotten. One's happy, the other isn't."

•    •    •

WE PARKED ELWOOD'S tiny car at Caesars Palace. Elwood had come prepared with two Maglite incandescent flashlights, two headlamps, two pairs of size-ten green Wellingtons, and a five-inch butterfly knife—just in case. He'd been down in what he called the Drain before, with social service workers who were trying to convince the tunnel dwellers to move to more conventional, if temporary, housing above ground. We walked behind the casino and entered the Drain below Caesars' parking lot. Elwood estimated that there were thirteen thousand homeless people living in Clark County, two thousand kids living on the streets, and two or three hundred people who called the Drain their home.

The graffitied walls gave way to unpainted cockroach-dappled walls about a hundred yards in. It smelled sour, dank, and mildewy, but not as funky as I had feared. We sloshed through an inch or two of standing water, slick with algae, beneath colonies of spiders dining on their feasts of ensnared mosquitoes, past solitary scorpions, and past bright red, six-inch-long crawfish that Elwood told me had migrated from Lake Mead.

"Hermaphrodites?" I said.

"Shall we check?"

We stopped and listened: rattling crickets, trickling water, a dog's bark, and a radio set to a cool jazz station, it sounded like. Elwood said, "I think we've found Mario." We trudged ahead. Elwood announced our approach. "Mario, it's Elwood, Elwood Wingo, Channel Fourteen news. I got you a carton of smokes. My friend Wylie and I want to talk with you a minute."

We found Mario sitting on his cardboard floor in his blue medical scrubs and flip-flops. He turned down the flame on his camp stove burner and told us to have a seat. A woman in red scrubs was asleep and snoring on a makeshift bed—a mattress atop forklift pallets atop plastic milk crates. An orange tabby nestled into the woman's neck and purred like a raccoon. Mario said, "Zoë keeps the rats away and gives Carolyn someone besides me to talk to."

I pointed my chin at the pot of now-simmering water on the stove. "Making lunch?"

"Crawfish."

"Taste like chicken?"

"Taste like shit. But if I had me the right spices—cayenne, garlic, cloves, paprika, allspice—I could make a boil that would make those mudbugs sing."

Elwood told me that Mario had been a sous chef at Charlie Palmer's place on the Strip.

Mario said, "Lots of drugs in restaurant kitchens. Pretty soon I liked the taste of crack better than the taste of bone-in rib eye."

Mario had been living in the Drain for four years and had hooked up with Carolyn eight months ago. Carolyn had been an ER nurse at Mountainview Hospital with a key to the drug locker. I noticed a shit-stained bucket and two piss cups beside the bed. Before Drainville Mario had been happily married, with two kids, and lived in a snug two-bedroom house in Henderson, but the guy he was renting from, it turned out, did not own said house. He'd just changed the locks on a foreclosure, had the utilities turned on, asked for first, last, and deposit, and signed a one-year lease with Mario. "One night the cops came and tossed all our belongings out onto the street." The phony landlord never went to trial, Mario said. "If I ever see that dago motherfucker again, I'll kill him."

Mario crushed his cigarette out on the sole of his flip-flop and dropped the butt in an inch of revolting liquid in a plastic cup. On the CD player, not a radio, Dexter Gordon played "Ghost of a Chance." Mario said, "I found out Daria and the kids moved back to Texas when they got tired of waiting for me to come home. Home was the Gospel Rescue Mission shelter."

I said, "Have you gotten used to life down here, then?"

He said, "You don't get used to wretchedness." He looked over his shoulder at the snoozing Carolyn and told us he and Carolyn managed to stay afloat, as it were, with temp work for Labor Ready. He did janitorial jobs, mostly, some waste removal, and landscaping. When I asked him why not cooking, he said how could he get a legitimate job with no address? Can't rely on a cell phone, either—no service in the caves. Carolyn, he figured, turned some tricks, but they didn't talk about that.

He said, "I don't want to die down here." He turned up the flame under the pot of water. "It just kills me, tears me up inside. But there's nothing I can do about it."

"Sure there is," I said.

"I mean, it's okay sometimes. It's cool here in the summer, warm in winter. It's quiet, private. Used to be more private. Now we get guys like you nosing around. And filmmakers. Social workers. Mormon missionaries. No one stays long. Mostly, it's peaceful. It's like having the superpower of invisibility."

About once a month, Mario said, he and Carolyn and the cat checked into a modest motel and got cleaned up—scrub-a-dub-dub—washed their clothes, watched TV, ate a hearty breakfast. "It's all good," he said.

I said, "What about the floods when it rains?"

Elwood said, "The water rushes through here at thirty miles an hour."

Mario said, "I'm of two minds about the floods. I've gone through a few. Sure, you lose all your possessions, but a big flood is like flushing the toilet—all the crap gets washed away, too." He reached for a cardboard box beside the bed. He said, "I was pulling your chain before. What's your name again?"

"Wylie."

"Wylie, I wasn't making lunch when you two arrived. I was about to cook up some meth." He took out a glass coffeepot and set it beside the heating water. "Got everything I need right here," he said, and named the ingredients as he pulled them from the box: "Ephedrine, codeine crystals, red phosphorus, filter, lye."

I said, "How do you take it?"

He pulled a hypodermic needle from the box. "Cook it and slam it!"

I noticed a distinctive wallet in the box where the coffeepot had been—light brown leather with a red baseball stitch design. I said, "Where did you get the wallet?"

He'd found it right where Bay had tossed it, in the tunnel about a half mile east. Just out for a walk and there it was. "There's never any money in them, but the credit cards come in handy if you can use them quickly. This guy had his PIN number written on his ATM card. Pretty foolish for him, lucky for us."

Elwood said, "Before we go, could you take a look at a couple of photos for us?"

I held up photos of Blythe and Ruby. Mario didn't recognize either. He said that not many young folks lived down here. Mostly it was single guys and the occasional couple.

Elwood said, "What was that?"

Mario turned the radio down. Zoë sat up and hissed. Carolyn stirred.

"Dogs," Elwood said. "Howling dogs."

"Or coyotes," Mario said.

"Howling like hammers," I said.

"We've been hearing a lot more of that lately."

•    •    •

I TOOK A VERY LONG, very steamy, very soapy, and very thorough shower while Django curled himself into the bathroom sink with his little cloth soccer ball. I scrubbed myself with a bar of lemon-scented goat's milk soap and washed my hair with violet and jasmine shampoo. Bay stuck his head in the door to tell me he was leaving, his backup cell phone was on the kitchen table for my use, and the photos had been downloaded to it. He was dropping Mercedes off at school, and then he and Mike would meet me at Main Street Station, a locals' casino downtown. We hoped we might meet someone who recognized Blythe or Ruby. And Bay was also hoping that the poker tables attracted more fish than sharks.

I was famished but couldn't eat. Everything in the fridge smelled stenchy. I mixed a vodka martini in a go-cup and called a cab. I closed all the doors in the house and settled Django on the couch. I asked my cabby, Umar, to look at the photos of Blythe and Ruby on the phone. He shook his head and handed me back the cell. "All these bone-white hookers," he said, "they all look alike."

I showed the photos to a security guard at the casino door. He refused to look at them. I said, "Please."

He said, "Sir."

I said, "A young woman has died, and I'm trying to find out why."

He said, "People die left and right. Life goes on."

"Not for everyone," I said. "Why won't you just look?"

"You want to know why? I'll tell you why. Because." And then he warned me about harassing the patrons inside. "We'll be watching you."

I found Bay entertaining a baby in a stroller while the baby's mother played blackjack nearby. Bay showed the baby how he could pull his index finger apart. Magic 101. The little guy seemed disinterested.

Bay said, "That usually kills." So then he levitated the baby's pacifier, dangled it right in front of the baby's chubby little face, but the baby was remarkably unimpressed.

I said, "Maybe you should have explained Newton's law of universal gravitation to him first."

The baby's mom went bust and joined us. She thanked Bay, looked at her little one, and said, "No new shoes for Pookie today. Let's go find your daddy."

Pookie said, "Ah bah," and they strolled away.

I said, "Isn't that illegal? A baby in a casino."

Bay said, "The essence of law is enforcement." And then he slipped on a pair of surgical gloves that he pulled out of the air and told me to wish him luck. Poker chips are a significant source of the bacterium *Staphylococcus aureus*, and Bay wasn't taking any chances.

I said, "Where's Mike?"

"The sports book. We may have seen the last of him tonight."

I took a seat at the end of the Boar's Head Bar. I thought about the subjacent Drain dwellers hunkered down beneath my feet right then. The thought was a picture of a man smoking a cigarette while his wife stirs some soup in an aluminum saucepan. Beyond her I could see a child's tricycle. Jesus, don't tell me there are kids down there. I put the phone on the marble bar. I ordered a Ketel One martini from Chad, my metrosexual bartender. He sniffed the air and said, "Lush, right?"

I said, "I drink a bit, but—"

"No, I mean Lush, the store—you used Lush bar soap today."

"I did."

When Chad brought my drink, I showed him the photos of

Blythe and Ruby. He didn't know them, but he leaned forward and told me quietly that he could hook me up with much sweeter twat than that. I explained the grim situation.

He apologized. "My bad, dude."

"It's okay, Chad."

"You're a dick?"

"Pardon me?"

"You're a PI?"

"I'm not."

"Cop?"

"Interested party."

"Are they with the Asians?"

"What do you mean?"

"They work for someone. There's no freelancing in Vegas. It's not a right-to-work town, if you know what I mean. Someone owns them."

"You're kidding."

"Sometimes they're branded with a tattoo. Did you see one? On the arm, the wrist, the eyelid."

PG, I remembered. Pretty Girl.

"Like if it said SWAG then Swag owns her. Whoever Swag is. Or are."

"Are?"

You know like *Southwest Asian Gang*. SWAG. Like that."

"Is there such a gang?"

"No." Chad slapped the bar, said, "Let me know if there's anything you need, my friend," and left to wait on a couple wearing matching lilac polo shirts and leather fanny packs. PG, I thought. Posse Galore? I turned my seat around to face the casino, rested my elbow on the brass rail, and sipped my drink. I thought I saw my Crisis Center colleague Gene Woodling's oval head bob up behind an aisle of slot machines. I heard a familiar voice. A man two seats down ordered a Wum Wunner. I looked past the empty seat between us and saw a squat fellow wearing a blue and silver I'M A BELIEBER ball cap and texting someone on his phone. He caught me looking. I smiled. He nodded and smiled back. Chad brought him his drink.

"Nice T-shirt," I said.

He turned and pulled at the hem of the shirt so I could get a better look. The profile of a police dog and I ♥ MY GERMAN SHEPHERD.

I held out my hand. "Wylie," I said. "And you look like a *Tom*."

He looked perplexed. "How'd you know?"

"Dog lover?" I said.

"Yes, I am."

"Man's best friend," I said.

"Unconditional wove."

I showed him the photos.

"Fwiends of yours?" he said.

"No."

He nodded and smiled. "I seen you on TV. You waped that whore, the one on your phone."

"I did not."

"That's what they're wooking for, bwoads like that." He finished his drink, stood, and winked. He gave me a thumbs-up and left.

So it *was* Gene Woodling I'd seen earlier, and here he came bounding toward me and holding hands with a girl who looked far too young to be out so late on a school night. I waved to Gene. He squinted in my direction but kept walking. I called his name. He couldn't ignore that, and he and the girl came over. I shook his hand. He said he'd heard my legal troubles were over. I thanked him for the call to the cops on my behalf. No biggie, he said. The

girl excused herself, said she needed to visit the ladies' but would
be right back.

"Kind of young?" I said, and I didn't know why. Was Gene's
private life any of my business?

"She's twenty-two, Coyote."

I tried to make up for my rudeness. "What are you guys
drinking?"

"We can't stay." Gene adjusted his crooked glasses to no avail.
Was one ear lower than the other?

"Have you seen Ruby around?"

"Who?"

"Misty Roses. My accuser."

"Audrey Blick. I have not."

"She laughed at me when I asked why she left Refuge House.
Said I was clueless. Do you know why she would?"

"No idea."

"How are things at the Crisis Center?"

"Busy busy."

"I'll stop by."

"You should call Helen first."

The cell phone chimed. A text from Bay. Bad news. *Blythe dead.
Details at the top of the hour.* Shit.

Gene said, "You okay?"

"What's your game, Gene?"

"I'm not playing games."

"I mean in the casino. Keno? Slots?"

"Video poker, mostly." Gene jiggled the keys in his pocket and
shifted his weight from one leg to the other.

The girl returned from her visit and held on to Gene's arm
with her two hands. I held out my hand. "I'm Wylie. Pleased to
meet you . . ."

"Chyna with a *y*. Likewise."

I showed Chyna the photos of Blythe Davis and Audrey Blick. She said, "I know Fawn. She is totally messed up, that girl."

"Not anymore."

"Well, good for her."

"She's dead."

Gene said, "We should get going."

"Were you friends?"

"Acquaintances."

Gene made a show of checking his watch—black face, white arms, green canvas strap. "Chyna, we got to get a move on."

Chyna told me they were going to see Criss Angel at the Lux.

I said, "You like magic?"

"Love it!"

"And not just stage magic, I bet."

"Real magic, you mean?"

Real magic isn't real and stage magic is, but I nodded. "The supernatural."

"When I was twelve I was in a horrific traffic accident. My aunt Jodi and me were hit head-on by a semi. They used the Jaws of Life to get me out of the mangled car. They found no pulse. I was dead."

Gene said, "Chyna!"

She said, "I left my body and looked down at the paramedics trying to save me. I saw a light so bright it should have blinded me. I heard choirs of angels singing. I smelled the odor of sanctity. I saw a faceless man in a white robe who told me I had a choice. I could stay in heaven or I could return to my body."

I said, "But don't we define death as permanent?"

Chyna shook her head. Gene rolled his eyes and bit his upper lip. She said, "Death is not a moment, Wylie. It's a process, and like anything worth doing, you can't rush it. Death takes time."

"I'm glad you came back to us."

"He has plans for me."

"Gene?"

She pointed to the ceiling. "The Lord."

Gene said, "We've got to go," and then he took Chyna's elbow.

She said, "Now that I know what death is, I'm not afraid of it. Are you?"

"Pretty much," I said.

Gene nodded goodbye. "We're out of here."

I asked him to let me know if he heard anything of or from Audrey Blick. I held my fist out for an affable bump. He left it hanging. I watched this inconsolable man and the seasoned but unjaded Chyna leave the casino and wondered if Gene realized how eloquently his kinetic asymmetry, his tricky eyes, and his clumsy gait expressed a pain he was unwilling or unable to confront. In this way, Gene was not unlike the folks who pay good money for therapy, sit down in my office, and do all they can to avoid talking about their wounds and heartache. They talk, instead, about obstacles, misunderstandings, and disrespect. To succeed, I tell them, to grow, to heal, you must first admit you have a problem, admit you want change, which I know, I tell them, is scary. And they stare at their hands or the floor or the ceiling without blinking, and I wait, and they re-gather their resolve and poise and resume their evasion. Gene held the door for Chyna and looked around to see if anyone was following them.

I turned back to the bar and signaled Chad for another. Then I Googled *Audrey Blick* on the cell and found an Ancestry.com entry from the 1940 U.S. census. An Audrey Blick, then twenty-five, lived on Williams Avenue in Houma, Louisiana. Her husband, Norman, also twenty-five, would likely have been drafted into the military in the next few years, leaving Audrey to raise their baby,

Norman Junior, by herself. Was our Audrey Blick the grandchild of baby Norman? Chad set the martini in front of me. Not for the first time in my life, I thought maybe I shouldn't drink so much.

The gentleman standing at the end of the bar facing me looked familiar, but was for the moment unplaceable. My recollection may have been muddied but my visceral response was unnervingly clear. I didn't like this man I didn't know. I didn't trust him. I turned my head to cough and snuck another glance. He was either scrutinizing an e-mail or taking a photo of his Rob Roy or of me. His nose was blunt, his mouth wide and thin, and his cheekbones prominent. He wore his thinning gray hair in a scruffy crew cut. His tiny dark eyes looked like watermelon seeds pressed into bread dough. When he bit the cherry off his toothpick, I thought I had it and closed my eyes. Almost, but not quite.

I opened my eyes and he was gone, and Bay was sitting beside me with a martini in one hand and his cell phone in the other. He read me the text from Julie Wade. Blythe Davis left the La Paloma Treatment Center two days ago, but not before posting an e-mail to Julie explaining some of what had happened to her big sister. According to Blythe, Layla had tried to kidnap her, against her will, but she, Blythe, caused such a commotion at the airport that she was not allowed to board the plane. When the two of them checked back into the Luxor and Layla would not stop with the reprimands and the harassment, when she would not let Blythe leave the room unescorted, then Blythe called her handlers, K-Dirt and Bleak. She just wanted them to put the fear of god into Layla. They beat her, drugged her, and made Blythe watch as they threw Layla over the thirtieth floor railing.

The Memphis police found Blythe's body in Hickory Hill, in a Dumpster behind the mall, dead of a heroin overdose, a needle jabbed between her toes. The Shelby County medical examiner ruled the death accidental.

"Murder, she wrote."

Bay said, "If she wrote it."

"Do you trust this Julie Wade? I'm starting to doubt everything."

"I do. But she can't know for certain that Blythe wrote the e-mail. And if she did, how do we know she was telling the truth?"

"Still, it's worth investigating."

"The coroner ruled Layla's death an accidental suicide."

"Pretty fast work, don't you think? What about the drugs in her system?"

"Recreational, according to the coroner's report."

"You don't believe that."

"What I believe doesn't matter," Bay said. "The cops had their evidence; they came to their conclusion. Why bother to look if everything you need to prove your convenient hypothesis is right there in one place?"

"But now we have new evidence."

"Like you say: maybe we do."

Chad leaned over the bar and said, "Get a load of those powder monkeys."

We turned to see seven or eight handsome young Asian men in flashy rockabilly suits, aviator shades, Colonel Sanders ties, and cowboy boots. They all sported imposing ornamental pompadours, and they seemed to be swaggering across the room in slow motion. I asked Chad who they were. "Are they a band?"

He said, "No offense, amigo, but did you just fall off the turnip wagon? Call themselves Saigon Boyz."

Bay asked Chad if he knew a guy named K-Dirt.

"Heard the name."

"Bleak?"

Chad pointed his chin at the flock of Asians. "They'll know."

The Asians took seats at an empty poker table that seemed to have been reserved for them. I recognized one of the gentlemen as the failed pickpocket who'd unleashed his bee on my finger. When I pointed him out to Bay, the guy in the heliotrope suit and the lemon-yellow shirt, Bay told me to let it go. The beekeeper met my gaze, but did not seem to place me.

I settled our tab. I called Elwood and left a voice-mail message with the names of Layla's alleged killers. Bay said I shouldn't bother the cops with this right now, but I called Spooner anyway, expecting to ask him to return my call when he got the time, but he answered. He let me tell Blythe's story. He said, "You're taking the word of a drug-addicted hooker?"

"An eyewitness."

"And a dead one at that?"

I asked Spooner what he knew about Refuge House.

He said, "The homeless shelter?"

"Yes. On Bridger."

"That's all I know."

"Ever had any complaints about it?"

He had not.

We stopped at the men's room, and as we stood at the urinals, I read Bay the crude latrinalia, and he explained that it was not licentiousness, but puritanism that made Las Vegas, with all its farcical extravagance and vulgarity, possible, maybe even necessary. If all these naughty tourists weren't god-fearing religious zealots, they'd have seen to it that debauchery was legalized back in Centerville, and they wouldn't need a plane ticket to Oz. They'd be kicking it with the neighbors back at the homestead.

I was blow-drying my hands when our charming beekeeper

burst into the loo, waving a pistol and demanding his money, his wallet, and an apology, the latter of which I thought was a nice touch coming from a douchebag. I was slightly terrified as I always am when I see a gun, but I knew not to look like I was frightened or amused. When you grow up with a drug-addicted twin brother and spend too much of your time dragging him out of crack houses, you get unwisely inured to the casual display of handguns and to the blundering jerkoffs who use them.

Bay told him to put the gun away if he wanted to be taken seriously. "You're not going to shoot anyone in a casino, Junior."

He smiled, slipped the gun into the back of his belt, drew an automatic knife from his jacket pocket, and fired the four-inch blade out the front of the grip.

Bay said, "Now, that makes more sense."

He said, "You owe me four hundred dollars."

Bay said, "Three-sixty, but I don't know what you're talking about."

"Why the bee?" I said.

"You were being warned."

"I see," I said. "A pun."

He said, "What the fuck are you talking about?"

Bay said, "The essence of a warning is the identification of the offending conduct."

Mr. Heliotrope brought the knife blade to Bay's throat and did not hear Open Mike enter. The beekeeper held out his hand. Bay held up a wallet, and Mr. H. lowered the knife. Our assailant's very own leather bifold replacement wallet. Mike crept up behind Junior, reached his hand between Junior's legs, grabbed Junior's pecans, and crushed them until our gasping, trembling, wailing erstwhile mugger dropped the knife and dropped himself to the tile floor. Mike told him to shut the fuck up, and when he wouldn't or couldn't, Mike stepped on Junior's throat and lifted himself up on his tiptoes. Bay used a pick to open a locked custodian's storage closet, and Mike dragged Junior inside by the nuts. We shut and locked the door. When he finally caught his breath, Junior, now a man of diminished voice, managed to yell, rather hoarsely, that we were dead men.

Bay counted the money in "Danny Choi's" wallet and dropped the wallet and the black diamond watch and the iPhone and the sterling silver money clip and the pocket tin of condoms into the trash. "Medianoches at the Florida Café?"

# 8

"WAS I SLEEPING, while the others suffered?" Didi asked Gogo, while they waited for Godot, suspecting, perhaps, that his own untimely slumber was, in fact, treasonous. To be ignorant of the suffering of others is to be complicit in that suffering, isn't it, whether the ignorance is willful and convenient or oblivious and genuine?

I spoke with Patience before bed. She told me she was up at three because she was worried about Charlotte, who had not been returning phone calls or answering her text messages or e-mails. Patience said that Charlotte lost her job at the fish camp when she raised a stink about serving tomatoes and lectured her boss, Fatty Goodenough, about the immorality of buying produce from the local growers who forced their fieldworkers to labor under dangerous conditions. There's blood on these tomatoes, she told Fatty, and he told her to put mayonnaise on them and get back to her station.

Then Charlotte got involved with the farmworkers' union, picketing Publix supermarkets and Hattie's Burgers restaurants in southwest Florida. She spoke to the press about the horrific living conditions of the workers. She spoke with authorities. The only people listening to her, however, were the growers and their boot-licking subcontractors, and those folks weren't happy at all. Patience worried that something dreadful might have happened to Charlotte, and she was driving over to Immokalee in the morning to knock on Charlotte's door.

I ended the call and lay on the bed with Django asleep and dreaming on the other pillow, his tiny black paws twitching. I closed my book on parasomnia and tried to imagine Layla's final hours, thinking now, if I could trust Blythe's putative confession, that Layla had not taken her own life. She got word from Julie about Blythe's whereabouts and planned a rescue mission over a weekend. She took a cab from the airport to the Luxor, checked in, and without unpacking her luggage—filled with clothes for Blythe—hurried to the Strip, where Blythe presumably conducted her business.

Blythe would not have been happy to feel the familiar hand on her chafed elbow and to hear her unduly protective sister say, It's time to go home, sweetie. Layla would have been distressed by her baby sister's thinning, lusterless hair, her gray, almost translucent teeth and receding gums, by the cold sores on her lips and the tracks on her arms, and would have had to fortify herself against tears and commence her persuasion. Layla would have said, You have the chance, sweetie, maybe your last chance, to save yourself, to start over, to take control of your own life, to fall in love, to start a family. And Blythe, being high, might even have believed this fantasy of a luminous future because everything is possible and imaginable when you're feeling euphoric. And so they hurried to the hotel, dressed for their flight, checked out, got a taxi to McCarran. Layla would have noticed Blythe growing quiet, unresponsive, and dangerously reflective on the short drive. When

Blythe brightened a moment and pointed out that she had no identification, Layla would have produced Blythe's duplicate Tennessee
driver's license from her purse.

And then the meltdown and the hysteria on the Jetway, the scold-
ing of the flight attendants, the arrival of security, the humiliating
escort back to the terminal, and the consultation with TSA agents.
Official conclusion: panic attack due to pteromerhanophobia.

Layla would have held her trembling sister on the cab ride
back to the Luxor as she devised an alternate plan for getting the
petulant one back to Memphis. She'd drive Blythe back, even if it
meant tying her down in the trunk of the rental car. She would
not fail to save her little sister from this vile and merciless life of
perdition. She would fulfill her promise to Saint Jude, the patron
saint of lost causes.

They checked back into the Luxor and settled into their new
room on the top floor. Layla called the rental car company, reserved
a mid-sized sedan, and arranged for a pickup in an hour. Blythe
went to the bathroom, turned on the shower and the vent, called
her associates, K-Dirt and Bleak, explained that she was being
kidnapped, and told them to hurry and to bring along something
for the pain.

When Blythe answered the knock on the door and introduced
her friends to Layla, Layla asked them to leave. They laughed. She
asked them again, a bit more forcefully. Blythe smoked heroin on
the sofa. When Layla picked up the phone to call security, K-Dirt
took the phone from her and stomped it with his foot. One thing
led to another, and I didn't want to think about it anymore. Blythe
might have said something like, Don't hurt her too bad, before she
nodded out.

In the morning I made coffee, filled Django's stainless steel
bowl with coconut milk, and called my journalist pal Donny L. in

Melancholy to see what he could tell me about the farmworkers in Immokalee. He told me he was sitting on the beach among tanned and stout French Canadians, reading Upton Sinclair, and drinking Moscow Mules out of a thermos.

"Are you okay?"

"I'm okay."

"You want to talk about it?"

"Why?"

I had been trained to think that if you could only articulate your thoughts and feelings, you could discover *the* truth or *a* truth about yourself, and the truth, as gospellary wisdom has it, would set you free. But I was being persuaded to believe that some of us can't face the truth. The truth we've buried would crush us. We need the lie so that we can go on, and the point of therapy is to go on, isn't it?

So my developing theory was that sometimes therapy works because it allows us to be less truthful with ourselves, and we would like our circumvention to be "blessed" by the therapist. And in this way we become someone we can live with, someone flawed but not, thank god, repellent.

Donny told me there were three hundred thousand farmworkers in Florida and every one of them lived in poverty. The average annual salary of a farmworker was $7,500. "We subsidize farmers and growers to the tune of twenty-five billion dollars. That's double what we spend on welfare for the needy, for the farmworkers. Socialism for the rich and capitalism for the poor."

To take home $50 a day, Donny said, a worker in Immokalee has to pick four thousand pounds of tomatoes, 125 buckets, each weighing over thirty pounds, has to haul that bucket hundreds of yards across a field at times. The workers live in barracks housing, most of them, owned by the growers, and their rent is deducted from their paychecks. They live in perpetual debt. They work bent over in the hot sun, exposed to toxic pesticides for ten to twelve hours a day, and they get no benefits, no holidays, and no health insurance. All of that so that we can eat flavorless tomatoes that are gassed with ethylene so they turn red, and are then given cute names like UglyRipe or Tasti-Lee.

MIKE CAME HOME with his right hand wrapped in a bloody Brunswick bowling towel. He told me he'd cut his knuckles when he punched an annoying little Ted Nugent–impersonating cocksucker who was trying to sell him a paintball gun and wouldn't take *Get the fuck out of my face, needledick,* for an answer.

"I've still got a piece of his tooth in my knuckle."

Mike rinsed his hand at the sink, and I filled a plastic bag of ice from the freezer. Django swatted a fallen cube across the floor and sped off after it. I gave Mike the bag. "So you punched him, and then what?"

"I picked him up and punched him again. And he cried." Mike said good night, headed to his room, slipped on the ice that Django had abandoned, and said, "That cat's going to kill someone."

Elwood stopped by the house on his way to the TV station. He told me he had found out the identities, but not the whereabouts, of K-Dirt and Bleak. He'd brought along two bowls of jook, a kind of rice porridge, that he'd picked up at Seoul Brothers. I sniffed and decided that maybe jook was an acquired taste and saved my bowl for Bay.

Elwood said, "Kaiden Castle and Ben Alexavier. A pair of Jack Mormons from Twin Falls, Idaho. They were on their mission here in Vegas and were preaching the good word to a clutch of hookers in what they suddenly realized was a brothel and not the home of a large and very blessed Catholic family. The girls did some laying on of hands and speaking in tongues, as it were, and there ensued the weeping, the moaning, and the gnashing of teeth, and then the boys dropped to their callused knees and praised God and the Angel Moroni for delivering them to their terrestrial kingdom."

"What do they do?"

"Whatever they're told, apparently. Except go to temple anymore."

"But you can't find them?"

"I'm expecting a call."

Elwood sprinkled sugar on his jook. He said he was posting a story on his blog later today about Layla's horrific death and about the seemingly incompetent, perfunctory, and perhaps compromised investigation into her case. "The authorities won't be able to ignore this."

He asked me what we had to drink.

"Milk? Juice?"

"I was thinking breakfast spirits."

"I've got this bacon-infused vodka in the freezer."

"Drop a raw egg in it."

He would report what we had learned from Blythe through Julie Wade and what he had learned from an anonymous source at the coroner's office. Zohydro had been found in Layla's system. Didn't sound recreational to me.

I said, "Did you speak with the police?"

He told the police what we knew about the killers. No corroboration, no comment. He asked them if they knew that Layla's sister was a prostitute and drug addict. No comment. He asked if anyone in the police department understood the nature of their job. No comment. "When I got back to my car, I had seventeen citations on the windshield, a broken sideview mirror, and a note that threatened me with arrest should I persist in interfering with an ongoing police investigation."

"But they closed the case, I thought."

"Keeping it open just enough so no one gets in."


I GOT A TEXT from Patience. Charlotte would be arriving at noon in Vegas on a flight from New River. Could I fetch her? Evidently, Patience never made it to Immokalee, but Charlotte made it out. Bay joined me for coffee and jook. He decided the jook needed a little salt. And a little sriracha. I told him about Charlotte.

He said, "I love a full house."

"Should we all meet for lunch?"

Django hopped up on the table and sniffed at the jook. Bay said Django needed a time-out. Django sneezed and backed away from the bowl. Bay said, "Where should we meet?"

"Mladinic's. One-ish."


THE EAGER PASSENGERS arriving on Virgin flight #321 were so hell-bent on gambling that they stopped to play the slots in the terminal. A slender Filipina in a zebra-striped jersey and black pedal-pushers hit the jackpot on Firehouse Hounds and got so excited, she had to suck on her asthma inhaler.

I saw Charlotte walking toward me up the ramp, holding a canvas shoulder bag with both hands. She looked a bit weary and a lot relieved. She wore a blue cotton short-sleeved shirt dress, red running shoes, and a red Fort Myers Miracle baseball cap. We hugged.

"So good to see a friendly face," she said.

I said, "You're staying with us, of course, but first lunch."

"Great. I'm starving."

I saw no pet carrier. "Where's Henry?"

MLADINIC'S TAVERNA IS ONE of the city's most venerable eating and drinking establishments. It's nestled in the surprisingly verdant John S. Park neighborhood, far enough away from the Strip and from downtown to escape the hyperstimulated hordes of tourists held in thrall by the scintillant neon. When Pete Mladinic, a Croatian immigrant, opened his bar in 1935, he could see as far as Red Rock Canyon to the west and all the way east to Frenchman Mountain. The vista has changed; the tavern has not. There's a shaded patio out back where Charlotte and I would be meeting Bay and Mike, and a cozy little bar inside—six stools and two tables— where I sat on my first visit here when I fell in love with the place.

That day I sat at the only vacant barstool, a stool, I would soon learn, that was normally reserved for one Ren Steinke, but Ren was, on that day, over at Green Valley Gastroenterology Associates enduring a colonoscopy. I ordered a Croatian beer. The wiry cowboy to my right, the one who told me about his pal Ren, introduced himself as Ellis Derringer and tipped his Stetson. He said that for the past fourteen, fifteen years, he and Ren met here every weekday at noon to watch *The Young and the Restless* on the TV over the bar. He asked me if his cigarette was bothering me. I said it wasn't. I'd been a smoker once myself. Then you know the hunger, he said. He told me he wished his life was like the lives of the characters on *Y&R*.

He held up two fingers to the bartender, Tatjana. He said he would put up with all manner of betrayal, infidelity, and deceit if only his life could mean something. "Not one person on this show is happy. Me, I'm happy as a dung beetle in a shit storm, but I'm just sitting here on my bony ass going nowhere fast." He pointed to the TV screen, where a gray-haired gent with several chins and ropy forearms was telling a skittish blonde that his wife knew about everything.

"Take Adam and Chelsea," Ellis said. "They're doomed. But theirs is a magnificent train wreck of ruin. Something you could write home about."

Tatjana brought our beers. Ellis lit a Lucky Strike and said, "My old lady stole away in the middle of the night. Gone like she never happened." He sipped his beer and said maybe he deserved the desertion: he was no day at the beach.

He said, "Sometimes I think I'm happy because I have unfulfilled desires and that gives me hope. It's not all belly-up for old Ellis, you know?"

The credits rolled on the show, and Ellis said, "Sometimes I imagine I have amnesia. I'm not Ellis Derringer at all. I'm Clu McClure. I'm from Genoa Falls, and I'm related to the Abbotts and the Newmans, only I, sitting here talking to you, don't know it."

"You do know the show's made up, right?"

"And what I imagine is I get bonked on the head again, and I wake up in a hospital, and I know who I am, and I ask the nurse for a telephone." Ellis put down his beer, left his money on the bar, shook my hand, and said he was off to fetch a polyp-free Ren and drive him home.

I noticed that the stocky woman with a gray chignon to my left was solving quadratic equations on her iPad. I smiled and told her I'd flunked algebra twice in high school.

"And yet look at you now!" she said.

She told me her name was Colette and that she'd been a nun— Sisters of St. Joseph—for twelve years, during which time she taught high school math.

I bought us both pints of Wittgen Amber.

She said, "And then I left the convent. I married Mr. Buzzy Schott in Chillicothe, Ohio, and we had two daughters, a house in the 'burbs, and a border collie, and then I realized I was a lesbian, and I moved out on Mr. Schott. The older girl, Clois, is a doctor and a mom. Her younger sister is an idiot just like her father." Colette sipped the ale. "Now I live two blocks from here with my partner, Mary, who's an accountant at the MGM Grand."

I held out my hand. "Wylie."

"As in *cagey*?"

"I prefer *artful*."

Colette put down her stylus and picked up the iPad. She said that when she looked at a math equation, she saw a world so exquisite it was beyond words. "And every time I look at the equation again, I see something I hadn't seen before." She borrowed a pen from Tatjana and drew an equation on a napkin:

$$e^{i\pi} + 1 = 0$$

She smoothed the napkin and asked me to tell her what I saw.

I said, "Whatever it is on the left, it all adds up to zero."

She squeezed my arm and said, "Poor baby." But she wasn't giving up. "This elegant equation is known as Euler's identity. Gorgeous, no? Such purity and simplicity."

I told her that I'd suffered a lifelong aversion to numbers.

She said, "Any in particular?"

"I'm arithmophobic."

"I see, a concrete thinker. Well, then, let's think of the equation as a story and the figures as characters."

"Go on."

"*1* is a constant and it's where we begin when we count. *0* is our youngest number. It indicates absence, and yet without it, there could be no math. You've probably met $\pi$ before."

"Pi are square."

"$e$ is Euler's constant, and, like $\pi$, is irrational and transcendent. $i$ is an imaginary number." She cocked her head and searched my face for a glimmer of understanding. "Your face is as empty as a null set."

I said of the equation, "It's all Greek to me."

She said, "Euler's identity is as sublime and beautiful as Van Gogh's *Starry Night* or Mozart's *Requiem*. And here's the kicker," Colette said. "We can't understand it; we don't know what it means, but we've proven it, and so it's true."

We raised our Wittgen steins in a toast. Colette said, "Here's looking at Euclid!"

I said, "And here's to Euler's pi that was infinitely delicious."

I asked her if she thought there was randomness in the universe, that it had no purpose, no method, no order, and no coherence. She said not random, but unpredictable sometimes. Until we find a theory that explains it all. She asked me what I thought.

"There is no aim or purpose. There's just what happens."

"The universe does seem to be on a drive to maximal disorder," she said.

I said, "The evidence is all around us."

"Numbers are infinite," she said. "If you love numbers, there will be no end to your happiness."


WHEN CHARLOTTE AND I arrived at Mladinic's, Bay was dazzling Mike with some basic but deft sleight of hand. He did the French drop with a silver dollar, making it vanish and then reappear beneath Mike's hat. The straw trilby, by the way, was part of what I could only describe as Mike's unanticipated but snazzy golf ensemble: blue polo shirt, red slacks, white belt, and saddle shoes.

We ordered a pitcher of Karlovačko beer. Mike said, no, he didn't golf, but that didn't mean he couldn't look sharp. Bay ordered for the table: sardines in lemon juice to start, squid ink risotto, ground grilled meat, and pork kabobs. When the beer arrived, Charlotte gathered herself and began.

She told us that she had seen migrant labor camps surrounded by cyclone fences, razor wire, and armed guards. In Florida. In the twenty-first century. She'd seen twelve-year-old children working in the fields—child labor laws don't apply to agricultural work. The Obama White House scrapped the proposed rule changes that would have kept children away from hazardous work.

She'd seen men locked overnight in unventilated box trucks so they couldn't escape. She'd seen contractors confiscate workers' passports for "safekeeping." She'd seen twelve men living in a dilapidated single-wide with faulty plumbing, rotted floors, leaky ceiling, and without AC, for which they were charged $2,000 a month rent. Pregnant women worked in tomato fields that were soaked in terotogenic toxins. "I'm not a troublemaker," Charlotte said. "I've never had much nerve. I've never been one to stand up and scream. But I couldn't stand by."

She'd seen heartbreaking photographs of children born without limbs, with fused limbs, with extra digits, one baby with a parasitic head attached at the neck, another with a single eye in the middle of her forehead. The congenital abnormalities were not a coincidence. Those fields were sprayed with methyl bromide, a Category 1 autotoxin that kills everything it touches. And all the while, Charlotte said, the growers themselves, the corporate farmers with their ag and business degrees from the University of

Florida and their bespoke suits and their vigorous children, enjoy their afternoons at the country club, their weekends in Vail, and their philanthropic fund-raising galas, and feign horror when they learn of the injustices inflicted on the workers by their trusted subcontractors and note that they, too, are victims, betrayed by heartless supervisors.

Bay said, "So what happened when you rattled their cages?"

"Someone trashed my motel room. My tires were slashed. My windshield shattered. And then someone killed Henry. Hacked him open with a machete and left his body at my motel room door."

Bay said, "I'm so sorry, Charlotte."

"I'm very, very pissed off right now," Mike said.

ELWOOD HAD LEARNED from a reliable-ish source that Messrs. K-Dirt and Bleak were lounging poolside at the Grand Dragon Hotel. Elwood suggested we pay them a visit. He picked me up at the Barnes & Noble in Summerlin, where I'd bought a book on traveling the back roads of Nevada. I learned that there were floral sculptures in Hawthorne made out of old bomb casings. I hopped into the back of the Fiat mobile office, moved sacks of stale pastry off the seat, and settled in. We went nowhere fast.

"The convention's got everything tied up," Elwood said. "The NRA's in town."

I told him that Walker Lake used to have an annual Loon Festival, was home to schools of cutthroat trout, but now nothing can live in the saline water. And did he know that the old Tonopah Cemetery was across the street from the Clown Motel? That there were over thirteen thousand abandoned mines in the state?

•　　•　　•

WE TOOK A SHADED poolside table at the Jade Mountain Bar and ordered two Maogaritas. (Just what you'd think, but with lychee liqueur added.) Elwood told me that the station wouldn't let him post the story about Layla's murder mentioning the names of the alleged killers. He couldn't run it, not on the air and not on the blog.

I said, "The station's worried about lawsuits."

"The cops won't talk; maybe the killers will."

"*Alleged* killers, and I doubt it."

"Won't know till we ask."

I asked Elwood how he'd recognize our dangerous friends. He said he'd seen their high school yearbook photos. Kaiden was treasurer of the Camera Club. "And there they are," he said, nodding to a pair of fair-haired gents lounging by the pool on foam mats.

I thought they'd be burly, neckless skinheads with droopy mustaches and lugubrious tattoos, like a couple of Motörhead fans on the way to WrestleMania. These two inconspicuous fellows seemed harmless, angelic even, every-mother's-son material, and looked like they might be on the way to a hootenanny. Their slim bodies were tanned and hairless. They were as sleek as harbor seals. They wore identical Oakley sunglasses and black sports watches on their left wrists. One of them rubbed oil onto the other's back and shoulders.

I said, "Does that move seem a little peculiar to you, Elwood?"

He said, "The sun's a bitch."

"Would you let me rub tanning oil on your back?"

Our waitress, Elizabella, returned with our drinks and overheard me say that being a Jack Mormon must be like being a lapsed Catholic. She said, "Jack or lapsed?"

I said, "Lapsed."

She looked at Elwood. He said, "My people don't get that choice."

She said, "All Mormon men are premature ejaculators."

I said, "Really?"

She said, "Trust me. I've done extensive field research." She smiled, folded the drink tray under her arm. "It's from having to hold it in all those years."

Elwood said, "Those two are not armed unless those are Glocks in their Speedos, so now might be a good time to ask them some questions. In public and all."

"I'll wait here."

Elwood stood. "Wish me luck."

I watched him flip down the tinted lenses on his glasses and approach K-Dirt and Bleak. I took out my cell phone and prepared to dial 911. Elwood handed one of the pair his business card and then spoke, asking, I imagined, the sixty-four-dollar question: Why did you murder Layla Davis? Elwood was not one to back and fill. Both men shook their heads. Elwood then may have reminded them who Layla Davis was. One of the men stood and got into Elwood's face.

Elizabella returned with our check and said, "I see your pal has met Chip and Dale."

"He has, and I'm worried."

"Preemies," she said.

"You know them?"

She nodded. "And quite nearly in a biblical sense."

"They have unsavory reputations."

"So I've been told."

I noticed that Elizabella was no longer red and silky. "Did you change your kimono?"

"I didn't want you to get bored."

"Well, that was thoughtful."

"Easy on, easy off." She flashed her dimples and widened her Egyptian-blue eyes.

Waitresses are my weakness. I wanted to know the story behind the tiny scar above her left eyebrow. I said, "Is Elizabella your real name?"

She said, "Look at you, getting all ontological on me."

I looked up to see Elwood being frog-marched away from the pool by two uniformed guards. I looked up, and Elizabella was gone. I looked at the Mormon twins and realized that I *had* seen them before—with Blythe leaving the elevator after Layla's death. As I ran to rescue Elwood, I switched on my image-generating future receptor, took the pepper spray from my pocket, turned, and fired several bursts into the pursuing preemies' eyes. I met Elwood outside, where he was taking a selfie with the two mollified guards and checking the spelling of their names.

I said, "Did they deny everything?"

"They said they did it because they wanted to and they could. But they might have been lying."

"And you can't prove it anyway."

"I've got it in a file." He held up his phone. "Every mumbled word."

"Did you show them Layla's photo?"

"I did. They started talking Mormon."

"There's no such thing."

"That's what I said. They told me it was actually reformed Egyptian."

And then I told Elwood what I had just discovered. They were both at the scene of the crime.

Elwood said, "They may have pulled the proverbial trigger, but Eli did the killing. I'd bet on it."

I said, "Eli?"

We drove to Elwood's. He carried two folding chairs into the kitchen from the porch and set them at the table. He explained, "I eat standing up at the sink." He cleared the table of the piles of unopened mail and newspaper clippings. I sat. Elwood opened the freezer, where he kept iced martini glasses, a cocktail shaker, vermouth, vodka, and twists of lemon. He mixed and poured the drinks while standing there. He set the drinks on the table, shut the freezer, opened the fridge, pulled out a large manila envelope from the vegetable drawer, opened it, and unfolded an organizational chart on the table.

I said, "What is this?"

"This is the chain of command of the anonymous monopoly that operates the very lucrative illegal prostitution business in Nevada. The Invisible Empire, I call it." Elwood explained that while legal brothels operated in eight rural counties in the state, most of the prostitution happened where it was illegal—in Vegas and Reno. Sixty-six percent more money was spent on *illegal* prostitution. "We're talking hundreds of millions of dollars."

"How do you know about this Empire?"

"I've been investigating prostitution in Nevada for four years, and for six months of that time I had a willing informant within this organization. Called himself Babe Parilli, but I have no idea what his real name was."

"Why would he talk to you and presumably risk his own life?"

"Vanity, I think. He didn't like the anonymity. He wanted to feel important and wanted people's esteem; after all, he rubbed shoulders with very bad men and with movers and shakers. He felt appreciated when he spoke with me. Babe drew this org. chart right here at the table."

Below the directors' box and the CEO's box were four department boxes: Recruitment & Distribution, Operations, Enforcement, and Public Relations.

I said, "PR?"

"They throw hush money around to media outlets."

"You can keep the media out of it, but how do you keep the cops out of it?"

"Cops are public servants who do what they are told. You don't have to influence the cops, just the high command."

Elwood said, "Babe worked in enforcement for a man he called Eli, the head of local and regional enforcement for the company. All the independent brothels in the state, legal and ill-, are a part of this centralized network. Eli's responsible for policing the network. Anyone who stepped out of line got a visit from Eli and friends. A stand-up guy, according to Babe. MBA from Wharton. Worked his way up the corporate ladder. A team player."

"And who are these directors?"

"Babe said they were your corporate types, solid citizens, weekend golfers, entrepreneurs, investors, guys with Gucci briefcases and pocket squares, the same sort of trash who run Goldman Sachs and Chase."

"Slave traders."

"That's not how they see it. Prostitution is a victimless crime, they say."

"You don't see the bruises when you're counting the money."

"Babe never told me their names, and I doubt he knew them."

"And Babe is . . . ?"

"No longer with us. Vanished. One night he's at my house getting editing help with his nephew's college application, and the next day he's gone."

"Did Eli have a last name?"

"Belinki. Babe let it slip one gin-drenched afternoon."

"You have a photo of this Eli Belinki?"

Elwood opened his laptop. "As you might imagine, Eli is camera-shy. He's the Thomas Pynchon of hit men. But I found him tagged in a Facebook photo at a frat party at Penn." Elwood turned the screen for me to see. "That's him with the ukulele."

"Looks like Abraham Lincoln."

# 9

WHEN BAY AND I saw the enormous dog chase down, catch, and then drown the lemur, we were out for a stroll in the neighborhood alongside Lake Jacqueline, talking about Charlotte's dilemma. Then he said, "The next car that comes down Regatta will be a red Audi R8." And it was. He'd been doing this all evening, and he hadn't missed a car yet. Clearly he wasn't guessing, but I couldn't figure out how he was doing it, which brought us to speculate on the origins of magic. Bay quoted Clarke's Third Law: Any sufficiently advanced technology is indistinguishable from magic. "Imagine," Bay said, "the first *Homo erectus* who discovered fire and how to conjure it with flint. He must have seemed like a god to those nearby clans still cursing the darkness. They would have fallen at his feet."

That's when we heard the piercing screams of the loping monkey, which was what we thought the terrified creature was at first, and saw him or her coming toward us down Regatta Drive, followed by a bounding bullmastiff, closing the distance between them. The pair of them veered left, crossed the street, the swale, and the sidewalk, and splashed into the lake, where the dog grabbed his sodden prey and dove under the water.

When the beast emerged from the lake with the limp body of his dispatched prey in his jaws, he shook himself dry, spied the two of us, raised his hackles, and snarled. Bay said, "Silver Ford Focus," and that's when I noticed the deceased's ringed tail in the glow of the approaching car's headlights. The dog trotted off up Regatta Drive with his trophy; the Focus stopped; the driver rolled down her window and called to us. Kit told us she'd just delivered a half dozen Maui Wowee pizzas to the House of Mirth, she called it, a brothel four doors up Regatta on the left.

"Really?" I said. "A house of ill repute in our proper little subdivision."

Kit said, "The girls need fuel, and the johns tip well." She smiled. "Beach Pizza—doing our part to make the world go 'round." She pointed to a pair of extra-large pizzas on her front seat. "Got to run. Two Vege-terraneans for Charo."

Bay said, "Fourth house on the left?"

"The one with the taxis idling out front."

We walked to the House of Mirth. Bay said he didn't know the neighborhood was zoned for business. "I wonder who's running the show." He entered the address into a real estate app on his phone. A cabdriver asked if we were looking for anything special. We weren't. Anything at all, he said. You name it. A suited gentlemen stood on the porch, legs spread, hands folded over his crotch. I thought of how proud his mother would be to see what Sonny's made of himself. All that worrying for nothing. Sonny nodded. Bay told him we'd lost our dog. Had he, by any chance, seen a huge dog lumbering by?

He nodded.

"You did?"

He nodded again and pointed up Regatta Drive.

Bay thanked him and yelled, "Here, Rambo!" He held up the screen of his phone with the real estate details. The house was owned by Clive Chesser, the treasurer of the Desert Shores Home-owners' Association.

I WAS EARLY for my late lunch rendezvous with Elwood at Mla-dinic's. I sat alone at the bar with a pint of Kaj beer, watching the local news on TV. I'd been trying to reach Helen Lozoraitis at the Crisis Center, but she was not returning my calls or texts. On TV, men and boys, some of them very young, all wearing camo outfits with rifles or shotguns slung over their shoulders, walked out into the desert. The NRA had sponsored an early morning Wild Dog Roundup as a public service and a thank-you to its host city. And by "roundup" they meant slaughter, if the mass grave we were shown was any indication. A spokesman for the NRA told Fox 5's Lyle Candeleria that the roundup was a rous-ing success: forty-five dangerous and possibly rabid and diseased dogs were neutralized and no longer posed a threat to the citizens of Clark County. And only two hunters and one oblivious hiker were injured.

A man with a hooded gray sweatshirt obscuring his profile sat down beside me in what I had come to think of as Ren Steinke's barstool, ordered a Campari and soda, and stared straight ahead. On TV, a local vet in a blaze-orange vest said that there was now convincing evidence that the feral dogs were mating with the indigenous coyotes, a word he pronounced in two syllables. "What we never want to see is a pack of Rhodesian ridgeback coyotes prowling our streets." Lyle then crouched down to interview a seven- or eight-year-old boy who knelt, proudly, beside his kill, a Tuxedo Boston terrier. "Back to you in the studio, Ted."

The cowled gentleman beside me, who must, I thought, suffer from very poor circulation, said, "Everyone who matters knows what happened. And you don't matter." On the news, a judge ordered a nearly catatonic woman, who had been stalking a professional golfer, back to jail for violation of her restraining order. The man beside me continued staring straight ahead. He hadn't touched his drink. He folded his hands and cleared his phlegmy throat. He said, "Do you read me?" His raspy voice evidenced years of whiskey and smoke. I cast a discreet glance at him. He did not seem to be speaking on a mobile device. His flawless and preternaturally white complexion suggested youth, confidence, vitality, and plastic surgery. I said, "Are you talking to me?"

He said, "Everyone who matters has moved on. And so should you. We all have so much left to accomplish."

"What the hell are you talking about?"

"She's dead. That's life. It is what it is."

"I hate that phrase."

"Whatever."

"And that word."

"And that's *my* problem?"

"Are you talking about Layla Davis?"

"Am I?"

"Who are you?"

"A friend."

"No, you're not."

"A friend is a man who tries to keep you from getting hurt. I qualify."

"Is this a threat?"

He looked at me. "A warning."

Tatjana returned from the kitchen with a rack of cleaned cock-tail glasses.

I said, "You're wearing a mask."

"I'm wearing a face."

"But it's not your face."

With that, this man with a prosthetic face stood. He said, "Thank you for the drink, Mr. Melville," without moving his latex lips, and he left.

I asked Tatjana if she knew him.

She said, "He looks like Frank Sinatra."

"Only younger."

"Ronan Farrow."

"Who?"

"Guy on the news. Little Blue Eyes."

Elwood texted that he was five, maybe ten, minutes away. I settled up with Tatjana and asked her to say hello to Ren and Ellis when she saw them. I told her that Ren was looking fine the last time I saw him with Ellis.

She said, "Ellis is in hospice."

"Is in what?"

"The cancer. When they found it, it was everywhere. Like God. Morphine drip. Not much longer to go."

I carried my drink to a table out on the patio and found myself angry with Ellis and his fucking cigarettes. The happy little dung beetle had come to a long, steep hill. Not wanting to continue on this freighted train of thought only to find myself at Terminal Station, contemplating my own mortality without my therapist Thalassa Xenakis sitting across the patio table from me, I Googled an image of Ronan Farrow, and he did, indeed, resemble my dis-sembling messenger. And then I called Helen Lozoraitis, and this time she answered.

She said she would prefer, and then she changed *prefer* to *insist*, I not come back to the Crisis Center. The center did not need the distraction of adverse and avoidable attention, nor the damaging negative publicity my presence would provoke. I asked her if she was kidding. She said the perception of impropriety was as toxic as the impropriety itself.

I said, "In what world?"

She said, "People won't remember that you were innocent. All they'll remember is the grainy video of you and that child on the Strip, she looking like a little girl at her first state fair and you looking, for all the world, like a skeezy pedophile."

So I hung up on her. And then I called right back, got her voice mail, and apologized for my rude, impetuous, and immature reaction, said I'd like to talk, hoped she would pick up, said I completely understood her wanting to protect the Crisis Center and all, but just the same, I said, I'm good at what I do, and there are lots of folks out there in distress, and our not doing everything we can to address their critical needs was simply irresponsible, and what, by the way, was going on over at Refuge House that a client can just walk away? Do you think you ought to be referring runaways to a place so lacking in basic supervision, and then I came to a realization as I spoke. I said, "You think I'm guilty, don't you?" And then I told her to fuck herself and hung up.

Elwood said, "You seem angry. Would you like to talk about it?" He smiled and sat. We ordered light. Octopus salad and cuttlefish risotto appetizers. Two beers. He told me he'd been fired, and he felt liberated.

"Why?"

"I posted the story about Layla's murder on the station's site."

"No, you didn't!"

"They took it down before anyone could read it."

"I'm sorry."

"I'm better off. TV news is pretty people reading press releases."

"Maybe you can write for the *Sun*."

"No future in print journalism." Elwood flipped up the shaded lenses on his glasses. "News is *now*. The dailies are all about *then*. They're in the wire service reprint business. And the city weeklies are all about pain clinic, massage parlor, and escort service ads."

"So what will you do?"

"I'll blog and I'll freelance. I'll write articles for *Parade* magazine for cash. 'The Miracle of My Mother's Pudding'; 'Can Bugs Be Cute?' Write them in my sleep. 'Four Uses for Honey That Will Blow Your Mind.'"

Our waiter, Tobias, arrived with our beers, said the food would be out in a jiffy, and introduced us to his shadow, Dunstan, waiter-in-training. Dunstan bowed slightly from the waist.

"I'll have the blog site up by tomorrow morning latest. I'm calling it the *Wingo Star*."

"Ouch."

"And I'm going live with the Layla story and naming names."

"Do you have a lawyer?"

"Uncle Shelly."

Our lunch arrived. We took a look at the gorgeous food, found its quantity wanting, and ordered two bowls of chicken broth with Dalmatian grits dumplings. How could we not? "And those fries," I said, "with the sriracha sour cream."

"Excellent choice," Tobias said.

Elwood's phone chimed an alert. He checked the message. "Holy shit!"

"What?"

"Wayne LaPierre's been shot dead."

"At the convention?"

"In the middle of his welcoming speech."

I said, "'The only thing that stops a bad guy with a gun is a good guy with a gun.' Not judging, just quoting the terrorist-enabling deceased CEO."

"I should get down there."

"And leave me here with all this food?"

"It does smell good."

"He'll still be dead in the morning when you launch your blog."

"I wonder who did it."

"Did he think the avenging angels of irony were never going to swoop down and carry him away?"

"He's Catholic, and so lived without the burden of irony."

Another chimed alert. Elwood read me the news. "They caught the guy."

"Alive?"

"Whisked him away."

We ate. We waited for more news. Elwood called a few of his sources and colleagues, but no one knew anything more than we did. We wondered how K-Dirt and Bleak would react when Elwood's story went public. We ordered crumb cake with walnuts for dessert. I suggested to Elwood that he move, at least temporarily. He thought he was in no danger, that the Doublemint twins might even savor the publicity, since no one was about to arrest anyone anyhow.

Another chime. Elwood said that eyewitnesses described the shooter as a burly balding guy in his thirties wearing a T-shirt that read HB1840. "That was a Washington State bill requiring domestic abusers to turn in their firearms. The NRA did not vigorously oppose the bill this time around."

"So then Wayne loaded the rifle that fired the shot that did him in."

Elwood raised his glass, said, "Let us, as a nation, never forget that the Second Amendment is the bedrock of our liberties and our freedom."

WE ALL SAT at the kitchen table. Bay was dressed for his poker game later at the Bellagio—black synthetic slide sandals, brown socks, creased jeans, and a green T-shirt that read I'M BLUFFING. He was drinking a club soda. Mike and I were enjoying our preprandial martinis and snacking on pickled bologna rings and chipotle beef jerky slabs. Health food. I held Django in my arms while we watched Bay demonstrate the five different grips he used to throw playing cards, in ascending order of potential damage: the Flick, the Butterfly Swirl, the Sea Urchin Spin, the Dolphin Dart, and the masterful Four-Finger Fist, where he tossed all four aces at once, and when he was finished there were eight playing cards solidly embedded in the watermelon on the kitchen counter. I released the excitable Django, and he leaped to the counter and warily sniffed the cards. When the doorbell rang, he jumped straight up in the air and then bolted for the bathroom and shut himself inside. Bay invited the two cops into the house, and I let Django out of his prison. We all stood in the living room with Officers T. Virgin and M. Hettich. Mike said, "What can we do you for, Officers?"

Virgin said, "We're looking for Charlotte Edge, and we understand she might be here."

"No Charlotte here," Mike said.

"Or we would have invited her to our party," Bay said.

Hettich said, "Are you Melville?"

"Nat Hawthorne."

"And you can prove it?"

"Of course."

Virgin said, "Hawthorne and Melville?"

I said, "You an English major?"

Hettich looked at Mike. "Melville?"

"Becker."

I said, "The last time I heard from Charlotte, she was in Florida."

Virgin and Hettich looked at each other. Virgin puffed his cheeks and exhaled. Hettich raised his eyebrows and pursed his lips, and I knew I was busted, but I also could see from the neck-rubbing and the feet-shifting, they didn't want to be here. So whose errand were they running?

Django did a figure-eight dance around and between Hettich's legs.

Hettich winced. "I'm more of a dog person."

"I'm guessing a big old dog who sleeps in your bed. Likes a bear hug before you leave for work."

"Dan."

"Retriever?"

"How did you know?"

"The smell on your uniform. You might want to check to see if Dan's anal sac is impacted."

Mike said, "You guys should have your names on the backs of your uniforms like the ball players do. Then we wouldn't have to squint to read your name tags."

Hettich said, "That's ridiculous."

Mike said, "That's a million-dollar idea right there."

Bay said, "What's this all about, if you don't mind my asking?"

Virgin pulled a business card from his pocket and handed it to Bay. "If you do hear from Miss Edge, ask her to give me a call."

"I sure will."


BAY AND MIKE left for the Bellagio once they learned that the Strip was unaffected by the shooting and commotion at the Convention Center. I reached Charlotte on her cell. "Where are you?"

"Well, I took the 210 Lake Mead bus, but now I'm at Summerlin and Rampart."

"You've gone too far."

"So I've been told."

I told her to wait right where she was, at a Walgreens, and I'd be by to fetch her. And then I told her about the cops and asked if she might have any idea why they wanted to speak with her.

"I may have roused a sleeping dog."

"Who's that?"

"Some of the union work I did in Immokalee made the national news. Good for the union, bad for me. You remember Mr. Kurlansky, of course."

"The man who fell from grace with the cliff."

"Yes, well, his family learned of my whereabouts on CNN and dispatched Mr. Kurlansky's younger brother to find me."

"The death was ruled accidental."

"No evidence, no trial. The case may be cold, but it's not on ice, not as far as the Kurkanskys are concerned. They've been telling everyone who'll listen that I murdered their son."

"And somehow the brother got the local cops involved."

"Dieter's a cop in Fort Bragg. A nasty cop."

"So the visit to the house was a professional courtesy."

"Dieter showed up in Immokalee snooping around and asking

questions, and the Ochoas, the thugs who supervise the workers, were only too happy to show him where I lived. I saw him before he saw me. He'll kill me if he gets the chance."

"Do you want to go to the cops?"

"Hell, no."

"That's the spirit. But here's the thing. You can't stay here. They'll be back. I'll pack your suitcase and meet you right where you are in twenty. You'll stay with Mercedes till we figure out our next move."

Patience called to say she'd be arriving tomorrow afternoon. Not a minute too soon, I said. I told her about Charlotte's fix. By the time I'd packed Charlotte's overnight bag per her instructions and then drove the few miles to Walgreens, she had made some calls to friends in Immokalee. I drove south on Fort Apache to West Flamingo, and Charlotte filled me in. "It's bad," she said. "But not Leroy Brown bad."

This she learned from the union's lawyer: Her stalker, Dieter Kurlansky, got himself into some trouble, mouthing off at the Club Lumina, got jumped, pulled out his pistol, fired a shot through the ceiling, and took a shot in the jaw from an unknown assailant. The place cleared out pretty quickly. Dieter survived the gunshot but not without the loss of several teeth, some gum, an inch or so of jawbone, and copious blood. Un hombre con suerte, the ER doctor called him. Mucha, mucha suerte. He would be taking his nourishment through a straw for quite some time, and he would require reconstructive surgery. The lawyer told Charlotte that, of course, no one saw a thing because, quite frankly, Dieter couldn't pick four thousand pounds of tomatoes in a day, but whoever fired the shot surely could.

"This is quite the mess," I said.

"He found out I was here."

"By tracing you to us, no doubt."

"Time to vanish again. Alone this time."

MERCEDES SET CHARLOTTE UP in her den with a fold-out bed. Charlotte excused herself, saying she was going to take a long, contemplative bath. I sat at the kitchen counter. Mercedes set out a plate of Manchego cheese and Sardinian parchment crackers. She told me her roommate Mindy was at her boyfriend's friend's condo. The boyfriend's married. Mindy gave him an ultimatum. Tonight's the night. He has a wife and two kids. Mindy's been seeing the asshole for two years. Found out about the wife at Christmas.

I said, "He's not likely to leave the wife."

"I know that and you know that."

"Of course, he might tell her that he is."

"So what are we drinking, Wylie?"

"I'm driving."

Mercedes wasn't buying the charade. "We all drink and drive in Vegas."

"But that doesn't make it right."

"But it hurts a lot less when you crash if you're flushed."

"We're being irresponsible."

She held her thumb and finger an inch apart. "A little one."

"What's your specialty?"

"A Paralyzer."

"Well, that sounds harmless."

"Kahlúa, vodka, and Coke."

"A little one."

"The caffeine'll keep you alert."

I got a text from Gene asking me to meet him tomorrow: *Name the time and the place. A quiet place. And wear your therapist hat. I need to talk.*

I replied, *Aloha Shores Park at eleven.*

I asked Mercedes how her twins story was going.

"I started a new one."

"What about?"

"A dying man wins the lottery."

"I wanted to know what happened to the twins."

"So did I, but they stopped cooperating."

"Lock them into a room until they come clean."

"What are we going to do with Charlotte?"

"Get her out of town."

# 10

'M HONEST ENOUGH to know I have to lie from time to time. I lied
to Gene because I thought he needed me to. I told him I didn't
think there was anything inappropriate about his dating Chyna,
and I was sorry if I had left that impression. "Sometimes I speak
without thinking."

"Sometimes the spontaneous utterance is the unvarnished
truth," he said.

"I thought you were trying to ignore me."

"I was. I know these girls are safe with me. I do what I can to
help them leave this place."

Gene and I were sitting at a shaded picnic table near the roller
hockey rink in Aloha Shores Park. For the next hour and a half,
Gene talked candidly about his life, and I listened. All his previous
reticence had vanished. He lived, he told me, a celibate life. By
choice, he said, or, more correctly, by compulsion. He understood
that he was being irrational, but he believed that all sexual inter-
course was an act of violence.

I said, "We can work on that."

He said, "I don't want to work on that."

I said, "Where did this notion come from?"

Gene's father, Delmer, president of the Farmers and Merchants Bank in Star City, was both a pillar of the community and a monster in the home, a man who enjoyed cruel and brutal sex with Gene's mom and with his assorted mistresses. Gene had twice witnessed his naked father choking and punching his helpless mother after he'd run down the hall to see why his mother was screaming. After that, his parents mercifully locked the door, and he stayed in his bed with the pillow and blankets over his head, trying to block out the sobs from down the hall and the slap of his father's leather belt on his mother's raw skin. "Accident-prone," they told their friends, to explain the bruising and welts and burns. "All thumbs." "Clumsy as a June bug."

"Eventually she killed him. Left me with his millions. Drove herself and his sorry ass off the 165 bridge and into the Arkansas River down in Pendleton."

Long story short, he said, his unwillingness to copulate had alarmed Kiernan, who made it quite clear that she was not about to live in a sexless and childless marriage, and then she hopped a bus to Las Vegas. Gene followed her and began the six-month search that culminated when she was found murdered in her condo. No one was ever arrested for the crime. Gene bought a small house and began his volunteer work, hoping to do some good.

I said, "How are you feeling?"

"Good." He lied to me because he thought I needed to hear a cheery answer.

I said, "If you want to work on the sexual issue—"

He said, "It's not that big a deal. Think of me as a priest."

"You told me to wear my therapist hat."

"I've never talked about my father before. It helps."

On the walk back to our cars, Gene told me that he suspected, and had for some time, that girls at Refuge House were being sold into slavery. "That's what it amounts to," he said. "The girls were being shipped out of Vegas to the small towns around the state, maybe around the West, where there was a demand. "Sorry I lied when you asked about it that time."

He'd gone to the police and the FBI with his suspicions and his anecdotal evidence—straight from the girls' mouths—and the FBI and the cops did nothing. Unless they were doing something undercover. We could hope. He told Helen Lozoraitis what he had learned, and at first she laughed at the implausibility of the story, but then became furious. At him, not at Refuge House. He didn't think Helen knew anything about the trafficking, that she, in fact, worked very hard at not knowing the truth. The truth would upset her world too much. She had to think of herself as doing nothing but good in order to live with herself. "I suspect she has some serious demons locked in her attic."

He'd heard rumors that the Danites, a Samoan Mormon gang, were behind the enterprise, and rumors that it was the Polynesian Saints or the Vascos, a gang of Basque cowboys out of Elko, but he didn't buy any of it. Yes, they were all useless and dangerous people, but the gangs had enough on their plates already. It was much simpler than that. What we had here was a gaggle of unaffiliated entrepreneurial businessmen taking advantage of an auspicious investment opportunity. Sex sells and greed motivates. Lust and lucre; supply and command. But it wasn't exactly free enterprise and the American way. It was a feudal system, and the lords lived here in Vegas.

When Gene spoke with Mr. Jory Teague, director of Refuge House, Inc., and told him what he suspected was going on, thinking that Mr. Jory Teague had no idea what certain of his perfidious employees were up to behind his back, Mr. Jory Teague put down his egg salad sandwich, picked up his brass desk lamp, and smashed it against the side of Gene's head. Gene was then threatened with further bodily harm by a bruiser with a black truncheon but no neck, and threatened with a lawsuit by a cadaverous attorney with half-glasses and loose dentures, if he were to go public with these obscene lies and unfounded allegations.

I asked Gene how shit like this could happen in a civilized country, or any country, for that matter. Gene responded with a history of the world in thirty-seven seconds. Fade in: A hulking troglodyte with a boulder crushes the skull of a terrified little herbivore who's had his beady eyes on one of the feracious females in the cave. Might makes right. He who wields the biggest club runs the meeting, gets the girl, eats at the head of the trough. When the more discerning of the diminutive others grow tired of being pummeled or worse, they invent gods and worship and priests. Vengeful and capricious gods. Solemn and uplifting worship. Arrogant and pietistic priests, they who must be obeyed, who then preach to the shock-heads on the necessity of turning their clubs into plowshares or risk the same dire oblivion that befell their cousins the Neanderthals. And then come villages and cultivation and testosterone-soothing domesticity, and with settlement come laws and courts, and crime and punishment, and private property and money, and wealth becomes muscle. He who wields the largest stock portfolio runs the meeting, gets the Kardashian, eats at Per Se. And we're right back to where we started.

So, Gene said, we give everyone enough money to live with dignity and not a penny more. When everyone lives with dignity, he said, religion will rise on its slow haunches and slouch off to oblivion.

Gene said, "Here we are." He put both his hands on the driver's window of his red pickup, pushed the window down, reached inside, and opened the door. "Refuge House is one of several distribution centers run by an affiliation of investors that I haven't yet been able to identify. But I will."

I gave Gene Elwood's contact info and told him to give Elwood a call.

AND THEN I GOT a call from Elwood on my way to the airport to pick up Patience. Told me his car had been stolen. I said was he sure it wasn't impounded. Good point! He called back to ask if I could drive him to the bank for cash and to the police impoundment lot.

"Will an ATM work?"

"Need more than the limit."

Patience looked more beguiling than ever. She wore a white linen shirt with a paisley necktie, a black sport coat, jeans, and blue sneakers. She asked about Charlotte, and I filled her in. I told her our first trip would be with Elwood and our second with Charlotte. Said she couldn't wait. "Great to see you, Wylie."

Elwood was waiting outside his house. He had sad news, he said, after he shook hands with Patience. His pal Detective Lou Scaturro had suffered a stroke. He was at Desert Springs intensive care, and his wife was due any day now. When Elwood learned that Patience was a travel agent—another moribund profession—he told her he had always wanted to go to Tristan da Cunha, the most remote island in the world.

Patience knew Tristan. "There are two hundred and sixty people, all farmers, and eight surnames. There's one pub, one volcano, one crayfish-packing plant, and one cop who's made zero arrests ever. The jail cell door is made of plywood. No one's rich. No one's poor. No one's alone. And there's no place to hide. There is no private property."

I said, "It would be a great place to set a murder mystery."

Patience said, "You can't fly there. You can take a ship from Cape Town, but that takes six days, and you might have to wait awhile for the next ship."

Elwood said, "Let me think about it."

BAY TOLD CHARLOTTE she had a reservation at the Silverland Inn and Suites in Virginia City under the name Alice O'Malley. She said she'd always wanted to be Irish. Bay said he wouldn't hold that against her. She asked why he would say that, and he said, "The eight hundred babies buried in a septic tank by nuns in County Galway."

"I see."

He said, "We'll have all the necessary paperwork in Alice's name in two days. In the meantime, you'll stay with Mercedes."

Four of us were sitting out on the patio at Mladinic's nibbling on platters of fish carpaccio and grilled spicy sausage. Bay, Charlotte, and I were drinking beer. Patience thought she'd try the Croatian national cocktail, which was made with cherry liqueur, sour cherry juice, candied orange peel, and garnished with wild cherries. She loved it.

Bay and Charlotte had already gone shopping for prepaid phones, prepaid phone cards, prepaid credit cards, an iPad mini, and a cute little ten-million-volt pink stun gun. They'd taken ample cash out of Charlotte's Wells Fargo account and set up a Nevada corporation online for a few hundred dollars. This way, in the future, in an emergency, she'd be able to use the corporate credit card without her name being attached to the purchase.

Patience might have been enjoying her Crocktails a little too much. She was smiling brightly at a black bird under our table that was wrestling a scrap of fish into submission. I asked her if she was okay. She said, "I'm lovin' that buzzard."

"It's a grackle."

"Just lovin' it to death."

Charlotte owed no back taxes and had no outstanding debts, which was good, Bay said, because people you owe money to are better at tracking you down than the cops are. You can't vanish forever under an assumed identity, but maybe you could confuse the authorities and any skip-tracers the Kurlanskys might have hired long enough for the skies to clear. As we spoke Mike was driving his Hummer through northern Arizona and southern California with Charlotte's debit card, leaving a trail of ATM transactions and gasoline and sundry purchases that would keep any investigators busy for a while.

WE DROVE THE MIRAGE up the mountain to Virginia City and arrived in midafternoon. It felt like it might snow. This was not a town you passed through on your way to anywhere. This was a destination, though not necessarily, we hoped, a final one. Virginia City seemed remote enough to be overlooked by sleuths, public or private, small enough to simplify Charlotte's obligatory vigilance, but not so small she couldn't blend immediately into the community of eager tourists, grizzled eccentrics, shopkeepers, artists, and artisans. We checked Charlotte into her room and walked out for a farewell meal. We found a place that served crispy pork bellies and medieval duck and had a fully stocked bar, and we knew Charlotte would be okay for a while. She told us that she had memorized her new Social Security number and had made up her family, the O'Malleys, in case anyone should ask.

Alice O'Malley grew up in Revere Beach, Mass. Her brothers

Tommy and Stephen were Massachusetts state troopers. Little brother John Jo was a Maryknoll priest, and was preaching the good word in the South Sudan. Her big sister Maureen had passed. Little sister Meg, the feisty one, was a flight attendant for United. Alice's dad's family hailed from County Mayo. Mom's family, the Mad Lomasneys, were from Cork. "I'm working on cousins now. The family's like a fisherman's sweater—large and tightly knit."

We followed our farewell meal with farewell drinks at the Bucket of Blood Saloon. We toasted our friendship, long may it wave. We said our goodbyes.

Sometimes when I drink too . . . make that *whenever* I drink too much . . . no . . . whenever I drink sufficiently, but not uncontrollably, I become relatively euphoric and somehow tranquil at the same time, if that's even possible. When that happens, I imprudently disarm the filters of caution and good sense, which I normally rely upon as impediments to complete honesty. Whatever cheerful thoughts float across my buoyant mind, I express. And so as we descended the mountains toward Reno, a city 220 miles from the sea and somehow west of Los Angeles at the same time, and as I admired the delightful and sexy Patience asleep beside me in the passenger seat, I thought about wedding chapels and quickie marriages and the ensuing bliss forever after, and I shook Patience's arm, and when she opened her eyes and smiled, I said, "Do you want to get married?"

And she said, "To you?" Which I thought was a peculiar and disheartening answer. And when I didn't respond, she said, "We can talk about this when we're sober."

And I thought, No, we won't. And I hit the accelerator a little harder. And the little engine skipped a beat.

# 11

I HAVE A better chance of understanding the origin of the universe, the laws of quantum physics, and the motivation of the sly pheromonal agents responsible for the carnal misalliance of James Carville and Mary Matalin than I have of understanding my own bewildering and miscreant self. This is not something a therapist should be proud to admit. And, trust me, I'm not. Why do I sometimes behave reprehensibly and against my own best interests? Every answer I come up with—stubborn, depressed, confused, distracted, hurt, blah, blah, and blah—seems brazenly false and insolently banal. I watch myself act boorishly, nastily, obnoxiously, and I tell myself to stop, but then go right ahead and do it anyway.

So there I was in Valmy, Nevada, in my cramped little Mirage, in the parking lot of the Golden Motel, on an unseasonably cold morning in early June, waiting for my sweetheart Patience, who had seemed to be ready to leave ten minutes ago, but was now delayed for whatever reason, and I sat in the idling car, fuming for no acceptable reason. We were five days into our desert odyssey, and I was finding myself increasingly anxious and irritated. It had been my bright idea to roam the Silver State without an itinerary, to trust in serendipity—the journey *is* the destination and all that. So we followed our whim at every fork in the road, put our faith in chance to lead us on, and I arrived at the realization that where I really wanted to be was at home. In Melancholy, Florida. In my own house with my cat and my stuff and my work, helping my anguished clients to shape coherent stories from the chaos of their bewildering lives, doing so because, I believe, a simple narrative, and the awareness that is its consequence, are the only control we may have over our lives, and sometimes, for a while at least, that is enough to get us by. And in helping to give shape to their lives, I give meaning to my own. But out here, wandering in the desert, I felt expendable, false, and useless, like some malingering vagabond.

UNION BIOLOGICAL TRANSPORT was the company name stenciled to the driver's door of the box truck that forced me off the two-lane mountain road. I woke from this—last night's final dream—before I sailed off into the uncompassed void. And now I realized the truck's cargo had been human—undocumented women from the tomato fields of Florida—a reminder to my unconscious self that Blythe and Layla were dead, Charlotte was in hiding, and Audrey/Ruby Tuesday was indentured, most likely, to the Affiliation, as Gene called it. If I'd been a better dreamer, I would have rolled down the tinted window of the cab and seen who was driving the rig.

When Patience finally backed out of Room 12, she tapped her pockets, cut the lights, and shut the door. When she turned, lowered her head, and held the collar of her jacket closed at the neck, I didn't recognize who she was or understand what I was doing with her, and for that moment I was a stranger to myself. I recall the scene now in high-contrast, badly focused black-and-white, like a jumpy, eight-millimeter home movie, and I'm watching myself watching Patience walk toward the car, and when I cut to her, she lifts her brow, smiles into the camera, casts her eyes up and to the right like a child who's been caught being naughty.

Patience settled into the front seat and leaned over to kiss me, and when our lips touched in the cold, dry air, we were zapped with the sting and click of static electricity. Patience made a joke about my high-voltage smooch, and I pulled my head away. I drove toward Battle Mountain. Patience apologized for the lumpy bed and asked me if my back still ached. She had chosen the motel for the sign out front: THE GOLDEN MOTEL/BEAUTYREST. For years, she told me, she'd been letting signs guide her life. If you need something, open your eyes, and you will find it. Sometimes the signs were the written kind, like the one we'd seen at the New Wine Church of Jesus Christ in Tonopah, announcing Sunday's sermon: SURELY, I COME QUICKLY. REV. 22:20. This Bible verse had become our bawdy mantra on the trip. Other signs might be zodiacal. I was an Aquarius, a wonderful match for her Libra, she assured me. Air meets air. It was all or nothing for the two of us.

I looked out at the lightening sky and the scrubby landscape, so vacant it could blunt the senses. I felt the car jerk and hesitate, or thought I did, like it had been doing for the last five days. Patience said she didn't notice it. Maybe it had something to do with the altitude or the cold engine. I tried to relax.

She said, "What's the matter?"

"Nothing's the matter."

But she was right, of course. I felt distressed, uncomfortable, tense, annoyed. I was still preoccupied by Layla's murder, exasperated by the infuriating and inexplicable cover-up, and shaken by my own absurd but slightly terrifying brush with the law. I saw a restaurant in Battle Mountain, pulled to the curb, and parked in front of the green pleated-aluminum façade of the Coffee Shop.

Patience took my arm and walked us to the door. "When you're agitated, you set your jaw and flare your nostrils."

We took a booth beside the depleted breakfast bar. A hand-printed sign taped to the sneeze guard reminded the customers that it's "all you can eat," not "all you can heap on your plate." We ordered coffee. The man sitting alone at the adjacent table wore wide red suspenders crisscrossed over his chest. He seemed to be reasoning with his pliable waffle and losing the argument.

Everything about the Coffee Shop was bothering me, the brown Formica table with its cigarette burns, the plastic cruets of powdered nondairy creamer, the red and yellow squirt bottles of catsup and mustard, the bamboo basket of saltine twin-packs, the sugar and sweetener packets stacked on their plastic caddy, the peel-back cups of ersatz jam jumbled in a cracked wooden salad bowl. The coffee arrived in a coppery plastic thermal decanter. Patience poured coffee in my cup. When she poured her own, she moved her eyes from the cup to the menu, and for some reason her hand followed her eyes, and she poured the coffee on the table. She quick got a rag from our waitress and sopped up the mess. I tasted the coffee and said, No harm done. Weak and stale.

Tennille, our waitress, took forever to get back to us. When she did, Patience said she'd stick with the coffee. We passed on the uninviting breakfast buffet. I ordered bacon and eggs sunny-side up. I said, "Do you have any butter?"

"Yes, sir."

"Real butter?"

Tennille didn't understand the question. She dipped into her apron pocket and took out a small sealed tub of what turned out to be something called Country Morning Blend. I said, "No toast, thanks."

Patience took her journal out of her backpack, flipped it open, and read me her last entry, something she'd overheard in the Shop n Go in Lovelock: *Bottle caps don't break down, why should you?* The man in the red suspenders at the next table barked and rubbed his hands together. He had spread typewritten pages across his table. He touched his eye with a finger, touched his forehead, his chin, each of the pages in turn. He barked again.

Tennille arrived with my breakfast. I didn't remind her I didn't want the toast. Patience asked the waitress about the barking man.

"That's Eric. He's not all there, if you know what I mean. But he's sweet as honey, just the same."

Patience took a slice of bacon. My ex, Georgia, used to pilfer my food all the time. Drove me crazy. I said, "Should I order you bacon?"

"It smells so good."

Eric was suddenly standing by our table contorting his face, flicking his fingers until he got our attention. He looked at me and forced a crooked smile. "We're all impressed with your strength of character and sense of self-worth." And with that assessment, he saluted, turned, and marched back to his table.

The front door squealed open, and I saw a man walk in whom I didn't know, but who looked vaguely familiar. Plaid shirt, dusty jeans, work boots, sunglasses over eyeglasses, and green ball cap. He looked like he was trying to grow himself a chin with his scraggly beard. I sensed that he was annoying, whoever he was. And then I remembered that he was the guy pumping gas while I was filling the car last night at the Shell station in Valmy. I noticed him then because while he was fueling his pickup, he was talking on his cell phone and smoking, two risky behaviors that the sign on the gas pumps warned against. The S on the enormous neon gas station sign above our heads had burned out, announcing to any poor soul approaching this benighted town out of the pitch-black desert that they had arrived in HELL.

I asked Patience where she'd like to drive to today, hoping we'd head in the general direction of Vegas. She unfolded her state map on the table. We decided to drive 305 to Austin, eighty-eight miles of unpeopled open range. I figured the car's little jerkiness wouldn't be a problem. Gas up and buy water before we leave town. Tennille brought our check. Patience paid her. Eric brought another check and laid it facedown on the table. Patience read what he had printed: *This happens rather than that. And that's the way things like this come about—you and me in the same place. A miracle.*

I SET THE CRUISE CONTROL to eighty, adjusted my seat, stretched my legs, and watched Patience glue Eric's message into her journal. She said, "In ten years, all I'll need to do is look at this check, and I'll remember everything—the red suspenders, the threads of white saliva at the corners of Eric's lips, Tennille's brown mascara, these salt flats. It'll all come rushing back to me."

I felt the car flinch and balk, and so did Patience. I said, "We're forty miles from anywhere." And then the car ran well for ten or so miles before it jerked a few more times, knocking the car out of cruise control. Patience suggested stopping to let the car rest, but I was afraid if I turned it off, it wouldn't restart. I figured we were now twenty-eight miles from Austin. It took all of my concentration to keep the car running. All I could think of was this damn sputtering car and the salesman who had sold it to Bay and me at Rick Ferguson Auto Sales in Vegas, Danny Mascola, "Dan the Can-Do Man," white shoes, white belt, carbon black toupee, and yellow aviator shades, Danny Mascola, whom I wanted to throttle right then. She sound like a creampuff to you now, Danny? Patience told me to breathe.

Carl, at the Last Chance Chevron in Austin, told me the problem was vapor lock. I stared at the engine and wondered if I was being fucked with. Vapor's a gas. How can it lock? And if it did, how would you know? Carl said, "What that means is your engine's running so damn hot that the gasoline begins to boil, and that creates vapors that your fuel pump can't handle. When the car cools down, the vapors condense to liquid, and the car runs fine—for a while." Carl said what he would do with this little Asian car was he would install a new thermostat to keep her running cool. "Suit yourself, of course." Carl wiped his hands with an orange shop rag, tucked the rag in his back pocket. He pointed to the Mirage. "Myself, I could never buy a Jap car like this. You don't know how cruel those people were. You heard of the Bataan Death March?"

"That was a long time ago."

"It was yesterday."

"We're allies now."

"You think so?"

Carl figured two and a half hours to fix her up, given as to how he was backed up and all—his mechanic Grady Hall didn't show up for work this morning. Had his girlfriend-du-jour call to say Grady's gone fossil hunting with the Ramos brothers down to the Toiyabe Range, if you can believe that.

Patience and I walked to the Lucky Boy Saloon, sat in the dark and empty room, and ordered drinks. The bartender said he was sorry, but he didn't know what a Vulcan Mind Bender was. When Patience explained it to him, he said sorry, but they didn't carry ouzo at the Boy.

Someone—the Chamber of Commerce, maybe—had built a large letter *A* out of whitewashed boulders on the hill across the street. *A* for *arid*. *A* for *abject*. The bartender brought our vodka and tonics and a bowl of Wheat Chex and pretzels.

Patience asked him if he was a Virgo.

He blushed. "Hell, no!"

"Not that," she said. "Your birth sign, I mean. What's your birthday?"

"First of September."

"This should be a good day for you, then. Welcome the intrusion of a healthier perspective."

"I sure will, ma'am. Will that be all for you all?"


PATIENCE LATER HEADED for the Main Street shops to look at jewelry. I said I'd be right here obsessing about vapor lock. I caught Virgo's attention and ordered another cocktail. He closed his book, using a drink stirrer as a bookmark, and hopped to it. A couple walked in. The elegant silver-haired gentleman took off his sunglasses, slipped them into his jacket pocket, and ushered his young companion to a table across the narrow room from mine. His smile was bright, his forehead sloping, his eyes avocado-green, like my mother's refrigerator. He wore a tailored black suit, a starched white shirt, and a pink-and-blue-striped silk tie. His nails were manicured and polished. The young woman wore a red strapless dress and silver wedge sandals. Her eyes were dark and her hair shoulder-length and brown with blonde highlights.

Virgo brought my drink. I asked him what he was reading. He said, "*Self-Esteem Affirmations, Volume II*." And then he recited an affirmation. "I am in the right place at the right time, doing the right thing."

When my table neighbors got their glasses of red wine, I held up my vodka and tonic, and we drank to Virgo's worthy self-regard. Virgo smiled and said, "I am making the right choices every time."

I said, "I'm Wylie Melville."

The gentleman's name was Clifton Luciano and hers was Bella. "I just go by the one name," she said. "Like Lady Gaga."

I said the obvious. "That's two words."

Bella smiled. "Two words but one name. 'Lady' is her title."

Clifton told me no, Bella was not his daughter. She was his wife and business associate.

"What's your line?"

"Sales." Clifton glanced at Bella and smiled. "You are looking at the last of a dying breed, Mr. Melville: the door-to-door salesman."

"Really?"

"I've been a commercial traveler since I was thirteen. I've sold Fuller brushes, the Cadillac of cleaning products. I've sold vacuum cleaners, Japanese knives, cookware, yo-yos, *Encyclopedia Britannica*, miracle cleaner, illustrated Catholic Bibles, and indestructible dinnerware. I could sell a TV to a blind man and knee socks to an amputee. I favor a life on the road. I'm a people person—love that face-to-face contact."

"What are you selling these days?"

"A product that sells itself."

"And what's that?"

"You're looking at it."

And with that, Bella smiled my way, drew her tongue along her lips, raised an eyebrow, and cocked her head.

I said, "This is a joke?"

Clifton said, "What can I do, sir, to get you into this woman today?"

"You're pimping your wife?"

"Managing her career."

She said, "I'm a big girl. I know what I'm doing, and I like what I'm doing."

Virgo appeared. "Care for another?"

Clifton said, "And our handsome young waiter finds himself once again in the right place at just the right time."

PATIENCE AND I drove south out of Austin and into the desert listening to Marcella Riordan perform Molly Bloom's soliloquy on the CD player. "Isn't this exquisite?" I said.

"She does go on about bottoms, doesn't she?"

We were thirty miles outside of Austin when the car coughed and sputtered. Molly said *yes*; I said *NO!* I turned off the CD and clenched my jaw. Patience rubbed my neck and told me to breathe from my diaphragm. Five miles later the car bucked, lurched, and rattled. I slammed my fist on the steering wheel. Patience said that wasn't going to solve anything. I said, "Don't start, okay?" I cursed that son of a bitch Carl, the goddamn thief. And then the car ran smoothly again. I willed it to run, but after a mile or so, the car trembled, gasped, and died just beyond the Shoshone County line near the alkali flats.

I said, "I cannot fucking believe this."

Patience told me to try my cell and call Carl to come tow us back. But there was no service. I got out of the car, walked ten steps, tried the phone again, walked ten more steps, tried the phone. And ten more. And then I tossed the phone across the highway and started walking south. Patience got out of the car and asked me what I thought I was doing. I suppose she thought I was going to explode, but she didn't want to be the detonator. She told me I needed to recombobulate. I told her I was going for help. She let me go and retrieved my phone, which was scratched but intact and workable.

She tried starting the car. When it hesitated, she revved the engine, and it caught. She pulled out onto the highway. After a hundred yards or so, the car shimmied, skipped, but settled itself. I heard her approaching, turned, and walked back toward the car. She slowed, stopped in neutral. Pumped the gas. I hopped in. We had to pull over every three or four miles to let the stalled car recuperate, and in that way we made it to within six miles of Pesadilla. Where we were stopped, someone had fit a mannequin's head atop a rusted barbed-wire fence post. They'd put a white plastic fedora and yellow sunglasses on the tanned head and tied a paisley necktie to the post at the mannequin's throat.

And that was when three cowboys in a pickup saw us stranded, made a U-turn, and stopped. I told the men about our predicament and about Carl's diagnosis and glaring incompetence. The men laughed. Grady Hall introduced himself.

I said, "Carl's absent assistant! He mentioned you."

Grady introduced Nacho and Chili. The men nodded. One of them tossed a beer can into the sagebrush.

Grady said, "Easiest thing to do is we'll tow you into town."

"We really appreciate your doing this. You don't know."

The cowboys towed us in to the Smoky Valley Garage. Grady introduced us to Tinker Beaty. Patience found the ladies' room key in the office, attached to a cowbell. Tinker took a shop rag from his pocket and slid under the car. I said, "Can I buy you boys a drink before you head back?" Grady said, "Sure can," said they'd meet me across the street at the Full Moon Saloon. Tinker slid out from under the Mirage and held up the fuel filter. "Here's your vapor lock, pardner. So clogged with dirt and shit won't nothing get through. Let me see do I have a replacement."

Patience put the key back on its hook beneath the old metal advertising thermometer. On the thermometer cans of Dubl-Duty motor oil were lined up at an angle, one behind the other, so all you could see was DUTY DUTY DUTY. And then Patience noticed a small black dog curled beneath the metal desk, obscured by piles of grease-smudged *Chilton* manuals. Patience crouched down and said hello. The dog lifted its head, sniffed the air, and slapped its tail on the floor. Patience said, "What's your name, baby?"

Tinker told me, "I don't have a filter for this particular car, but I can jury-rig one to fit. Get you folks on the road again. First chance you get, you have a proper one fit on, hear?"

Patience said, "What's the dog's name?"

Tinker said, "Doesn't have one." And then, "This'll take a while."

We walked outside. I told Patience it would be rude not to show our appreciation. Patience had a bad feeling about the cowboys.

"We'll buy them a drink, thank them, then say our goodbyes."

"They're bored. And that makes them dangerous."

I kissed her nose, took her arm, and we crossed the road.

The Full Moon was dark and quiet. I bought a round of drinks for the table, beers for the cowboys, water for Patience, whiskey for me. We were the only folks in the bar except for the bartender, who spent her time pulling slots by the bar, smoking cigarettes, and drinking something green. She had an unfortunate do-it-yourself tattoo on her right shoulder: NO REGERTS.

I told the boys this was our first trip out West. We were from Everglades County, Florida.

Grady said, "You're a long way from Flaw-duh."

"Couple of thousand miles," I said.

"Why?"

"Seeing the country."

Grady looked at Nacho and Chili. They smiled, leaned back in their chairs. Chili said, "Ain't got no job?"

"Taking some time off."

Grady said, "So you're like a couple of drifters out for what you can get." He smiled.

Nacho said, "You in some kind of trouble?"

"No."

Grady said, "Lacy, sweetheart, another round for the table on my good friends here." And then Grady touched the top of Patience's hand. "I never did catch your name, darling."

"No, you didn't." Patience wore a black sleeveless blouse and her right arm was tattooed wrist to shoulder in an intricate Islamic geometric pattern of stars and diamonds that seemed to fascinate our three amigos.

I said, "Hands to yourself, Grady."

Grady suggested a friendly game of Texas hold 'em. Chili took a deck of cards out of his pocket. Patience looked out the window to the garage, where the black dog was pissing against the gasoline pump.

I said, "I don't gamble."

Grady said, "Small stakes. Friendly game. Five-ten. Two-fifty buy-in. How's that?"

"You two ain't going nowhere till your car's fixed," Nacho said.

Me and the cowboys bought our chips from Lacy and moved to a corner table. I bought fifty bucks' worth, figured I'd let them win that and consider it payment for services rendered—a small price to pay for rescue, if you think about it. Lacy dealt for the house. Grady put on his sunglasses. Chili lit a cigarette. Nacho spit tobacco in his dip cup.

Patience joined us and said, "Kind of looks like we got three against one."

Grady said, "Shuffle up and deal, Lacy."

Lacy shuffled, boxed, released. "Put up your blinds, gentlemen."

I lost twenty bucks on the first two hands. Patience whispered in my ear, "You're giving money away."

Nacho hadn't taken his eyes off me except to glance at Grady when he was under the gun.

Patience said, "Wylie, you don't have to play every hand. Make them earn their money."

Grady smiled. "You can't win if you ain't in."

Lacy said, "Blinds." She dealt. Patience told me I should fold my pair of nines. I told her Grady was bluffing.

She said, "How do you know?"

Grady said, "Listen to your girlfriend."

I raised him all of my chips and asked myself why I was doing this.

Nacho and Chili folded. Lacy dealt Grady a six on the river. He smiled. I looked at Patience. I called him.

Patience said, "Really?"

"He's dancing his chips, checking his cards. He's sending me a telegram."

I took the pot and felt stupid. All this was going to do was lengthen the game. I apologized for my testosterone and tried to give the men back their money, call it even.

Grady said, "We don't want your fucking money."

Chili said, "But we would like a taste of her."

Patience picked up her purse. "We should go."

Grady said, "Are you a Jew?"

I said, "What?"

"You heard me."

"No, I'm not."

Chili said, "A Jew would never admit it."

I said, "What is this about?"

Chili said, "You look like a Jew to me."

I realized that there might not be any law here in Pesadilla. There certainly was no security in the bar.

Nacho stood up so quickly his chair fell over. He put a finger in my face. "You and me, we're going to have it out. Let's go."

Grady held Nacho's arm. "Not now."

I noticed that Lacy was gone, her cigarette still lit in the ashtray.

Grady seemed to be reading my mind. "A man could go missing in Shoshone County, and they wouldn't find a trace."

Tinker poked his head in the door and told us the car was ready. "Gentlemen," I said, "it's been real." I left the chips on the table, took Patience by the elbow, and led her out of the Full Moon, to my great relief. What an unholy mess there might have been. I told Patience, "Don't look back." Lacy leaned against the hood of a battered Willys jeep, adjusting the strap of her blouse and smoking a cigarette. When she saw me, she dropped the cigarette, crushed it out on the gravel, and walked back to the Full Moon. I asked Tinker if there was a police station nearby.

"County seat's sixty miles that-a-way."

"No deputies in Pesadilla?"

"There's only fifty-four of us here. We take care of our own."

The ring finger on his right hand was missing.

He said, "Crimes of passion, mostly."

"You know those boys inside?"

"A bit."

"Assholes," Patience said.

He told us he was from Denver when I asked.

"So how did you end up here at the end of the road in the middle of nowhere?"

"I got lost." He handed me a receipt. "Found myself at the Luck Be a Lady Motel down the road."

"Lost?"

"Long story short: My wife. My brother. My bed." He told us Pesadilla wasn't always so dead. He pointed toward the mountains and told us about a played-out marble quarry ten miles away. "When that was operating, this was one lively East Jesus."

ON THE WAY out of town, we passed the vaguely familiar man from the Coffee Shop and the Shell station, sitting in his idling truck at the crossroads, scratching his beard. Patience noticed him first and said she'd seen him in Winnemucca at the bar where we stopped to have a drink. She took out her notebook. I said, "What are you writing?"

"His license plate number. Make and model. Bronze Dodge Ram."

We headed south. We hadn't gone five miles when the car coughed, rattled, and lurched. I shook my head and stifled a scream. Patience, who'd been writing more in her journal, said, "It's okay."

I said, "It's not okay. Don't say it's okay when it's not. Okay?" I briefly considered turning around and having Tinker fix his shoddy jury-rigged repair job, but I kept imagining Grady and friends gleefully awaiting our inevitable return. I held my breath, and the car ran smoothly, but what would happen when I exhaled? Patience pointed out a bullet-riddled yellow warning sign by the side of the road with a stooped stick figure dragging a shouldered cross toward the highway. Jesus crossing.

She said, "That's a good sign."

I said, "How on earth is that a good sign?"

She said, "It's providential."

And then I saw, in the rearview mirror, the cowboys' red pickup barreling toward us, headlights flashing and horn blaring. Grady waved us over to the side of the road, and when I ignored his request, he pulled alongside. Chili rolled down his window, made a gun with his thumb and forefinger, extended his arm, shot me, and laughed. And then they sideswiped our car. Patience cried. She tried our two networkless phones. Now we were driving ten miles an hour, our front bumper on their rear bumper. The bronze Dodge Ram passed us both, the driver staring straight ahead. Chili climbed out of the cab and into the bed of the moving truck and then leaped onto the hood of our car. He hooked his fingers into the depression between the hood and the windshield and held on. Grady braked us both to a stop. Chili took a wrench out of his pocket and pummeled the windshield. I put the car in reverse and floored the accelerator. Grady gave chase in reverse. Chili lost his one-handed grip and slid off our hood and under the wheels of the pickup. I saw my chance to escape when Grady and Nacho got out to pull Chili from under the truck. He seemed to be lodged in the wheel well. I turned the car around to head for Pesadilla and what I hoped would be sanctuary. I hadn't counted on Grady's rifle. Grady shot out the right front tire. I kept going, struggling to keep the car on the road. I crested a hill, looked back at an empty highway, and felt relieved for no reason. Maybe I thought we were invisible.

When they caught up with us moments later, Grady had me drive off the highway and head for the mountains. We hadn't gotten a quarter mile when the car died. Grady pulled in front. Chili was folded up in the bed of the truck. His right arm was slung unnaturally over the back of his head. Nacho pulled Patience from the car. I decided I'd take control of the situation, ask them what they wanted, get them talking, reason with them. I heard my door open. I turned and got hit in the face with what must have been the butt of Grady's rifle. And all my troubles and all my sentience vanished beneath a shroud of thundering darkness.

I woke with a crushing pain on the side of my head. I didn't know where I was or who I was or why I was in such distress. I pulled myself up. It was dusk or it was dawn, and I was in a small car off the road in the desert somewhere. Nevada. I was in Nevada. There! One small step. I'd been in an accident. My left eye was swollen nearly shut, but my arms and legs worked. I opened a bottle of water and drank. I could feel my parched neurons firing again. I stepped out of the car and saw the four blown-out tires and the bullet holes in the side panel. I remembered the mechanic telling me about the marble quarry. I remembered the letter *A* on the side of a hill. A card game. And then it all came back, and I thought, What have they done with Patience? They didn't kill me, so they wouldn't kill her. Or did they think I was dead? I walked in a widening circle and called her name. I walked to the highway. By then it was dark. I waited for a passing car, but none appeared. I saw a dim light in the distance. I walked back to the inoperable Mirage, grabbed all the water I could carry, took my phone, and made for the light, which might have been a mile or ten miles away.

I hoped I was stumbling toward a house, not a campfire or a will-o'-the-wisp, a house where I could call or radio the authorities, put some ice on my face, and beg for a lift into Pesadilla, and I hoped that whoever lived at my destination did not turn in early. With the light doused, I'd never find my way. I looked up and tried to locate the Big Dipper and Polaris in the random scatter of stars. I hoped whoever lived at the house was not alarmingly shy of strangers and did not own a shotgun. An unexpected knock at the door, I realized, might panic a man who had chosen to live an isolated existence, a man with something to hide, perhaps, or someone to hide from. I heard the howl of coyotes in the distance.

I knew I'd eventually have to describe our assailants to the cops. I'd start by naming them: Chili, Nacho, and Grady. And Chili should be easy to find. He's got a shattered elbow, a hyper-extended right arm. He'll probably be blubbering in pain when you find him. Nacho has a porn-star mustache and three tattooed teardrops beside his left eye. Grady has brown hair, a chipped front tooth, and he blinks his tiny eyes more rapidly and vigorously than is necessary or normal.

After forty-five minutes or so I reached the house, a sixty-foot single-wide up on cinder blocks. Looked to be aqua and white, but hard to tell in the darkness. I climbed the three steps to the porch, set down my water bottles, and knocked seven beats, *shave-and-a-haircut-two-bits*, the jauntiest, most nonthreatening knock I could think of. I whistled and waited. The light went out in the window to my left. I knocked again, this time, *one-two-three*.

# 12

WHEN I SAW the pistol pointed at my hammering heart, I
expected to become a homicide statistic in the next moment.
I raised my arms, shut my eyes, and stepped back, knocking a
galvanized bucket off the canted porch. I managed to say, "I'm in
trouble, sir. I need your help." He lowered the gun to my belt. "I've
been kidnapped."

The seedy old coot holding the gun zipped his fly with his free
hand and looked past me into the night. He said, "I don't see no
bad guys holding you hostage."

"My girlfriend was taken."

"Happens to the best of us."

I said, "We need to find the abductors." As soon as I said the
word *abductors*, I knew it didn't sound right. Made me think of
muscle and flesh.

"Who took your sweetie?"

"Three guys named Grady, Nacho, and Chili. You know
them?"

"I might."

"Can I use your phone?"

"Got no phone."

"Really?" I held my face. "Got any ice?"

"Nope."

"Well, can you give me a lift into Pesadilla?"

"Can't."

"I can see your pickup from here."

"Can't drive at night. Got the macular degeneration. Be blind as a Texas salamander soon."

"I'll drive."

"No can do."

"I'll pay you."

"In the morning."

"I can't wait till morning. My girlfriend's in danger. I need a cop."

"Chili's a cop."

"He's a criminal."

"These are not mutually exclusive occupations. Real name's Angel Ramos Gonzalez. Shoshone County Sheriff's Department."

"I should go."

"You should stay. You'll get lost out there. It's not safe. Coyotes, rattlers." He opened the door wider and motioned me inside. I shook my head and stepped off the porch. He fired a shot that hit the bucket. I covered my ears. You forget just how loud gunfire is until a shot goes off by your head. The shot got some sheep bleating out there in the dark.

I said, "Are you insane?"

"Yes." He switched on the interior light. He wore a soiled white T-shirt and had a goiter the size of a mango on his neck. His eyes were Barbicide-blue.

"You'd shoot me?"

"In the blink of an eye."

I stepped past him into the living room. He was shoeless. I said, "I don't know why you're doing this."

"I'm just standing my ground here, protecting my castle from invaders."

While my ill-mannered host locked the door and fastened the dead bolt, I looked around at the dismal living room, at the ragged Naugahyde reclining chair and the black mold on the baseboard. I asked him his name. When a person hears his name, parts of his frontal cortex light up, as do parts of the temporal cortex and the cuneus, and I planned to say his name and fire up his brain a lot, get him thinking about who he was and maybe jump-start some inhibitory behavioral controls. And then when he said my name, he'd have to feel just a little closer to me, right? At work I dealt with pain, suffering, and despair on a daily basis. My job was to know how the brain works, how it talks to us, how it is a slave to our emotions.

"Creed. Creed Wackell," he said.

"My name's Wylie, Creed."

"Perhaps we should keep this on a no-name basis."

"You're living in squalor here, Creed. You know that."

The thin blue curtains were frayed at the hem. The dung-colored carpet was stained with what could have been motor oil. On the otherwise bare paneled wall hung a decoupaged plaque of da Vinci's *Last Supper* on a tree slice, evidence, I thought, of previous residents, a benighted family of Catholics, maybe even Creed's own family, long since fled to some safer haven. A shabby little artificial Christmas tree slouched in a dark corner of the room. Creed put his hand on my back and pushed me toward the kitchen.

The kitchen was under repair. Creed was in the process of removing the linoleum from the plywood floor. He took his toolbox off a kitchen chair, placed it on the floor, told me to sit at the table, and then got me a plastic cup of lukewarm milk from the fridge for some reason. It smelled like onions, and I couldn't drink it. He drank bourbon from a pint bottle.

I said, "I like bourbon, Creed."

He said, "How did you get yourself in such a mess?"

I said, "Iodine will fix that."

"What?"

"The goiter, Creed. More salt on your food."

"You a doctor?"

"Not quite."

He placed the pistol on the table and took a cell phone out of his pocket.

I said, "Liar." How the hell did he have service?

He hit speed dial and held the phone to his ear. He said, "He's right here. You want him?" I guessed the call was to Grady. "Okay. No problem. He wants to know how his honeybunch is." Creed looked at me out of the side of his eyes, raised his eyebrows, and smiled. He ended the call, set the phone on the table, and stared at me. I could hear him ticking. He was packed with explosives, the timer was set, but I didn't know when he'd go off.

I said, "The macular, Creed, is it wet or dry?"

"One of each."

"There's treatment for the wet these days."

"If He has smeared over my eyes so I cannot see, who am I to challenge God's wisdom?"

Creed the fatalist. I said, "So what happens now?"

He touched his index finger to the middle of his forehead. "You get a bullet right about here."

I almost said, You'll never get away with this, but I knew that he would. I said, "What have they done with her?"

I don't spend my alone time thinking. I spend it watching the people in my daydreams, and this immersion in fantasyland has left me vulnerable to abrupt intrusions from the here and now. All my life I've been easily startled by an innocent voice breaking the silence or a gentle hand on my shoulder. My body leaps, my heart races, my breathing stops. So how is it, then, that I'm so composed in the face of actual danger? Like just then. Here was this homicidal shithead with a loaded pistol and an empty heart threatening my life, and I was as calm as a Trappist monk. I have no control over this baffling serenity that envelops me when the pressure rises.

He drummed his fingers on his phone and smiled. "And then I haul your carcass up to the mountains and drop you off. Leave the gun, so it looks like a suicide. Not that anyone's ever likely to find what's left of you anyway." He stopped his drumming and curled his lips like an alert and aggressive dog. I knocked the cup of milk from the table. Creed said, "No use crying."

I reached down for the cup and grabbed the claw hammer from the top of the toolbox, stood, and smashed the hammer down on Creed's hand with all the speed and force I could muster, crushing it into the concrete tabletop. He screamed. I grabbed for the gun, but he had it in his unbroken hand, fumbled with it, and tried to squeeze the trigger. This time I hit him in the face with the hammer and detached the lower jaw from his skull. Creed dropped the gun, and I grabbed it. Was it loaded? I fired a shot at the stuffed sage grouse on the counter. The bird came to life and flew to the floor. I turned back to Creed and said, "Where are they?"

He slammed his head into the table. When he sat up, he spit a fountain of blood, teeth, and bone my way through his slack mouth. He wailed. He said what sounded like "Fub jew."

I realized I might not understand a word he said now, and

he couldn't write down an answer with his mangled hand. I told him if he didn't get that hand looked at soon, it would never heal properly. Not to mention the jaw. I told him to relax. I wasn't going to kill him. But now I couldn't get my own self to relax. My hands trembled. I was panting, not breathing. I kept my eye on him while I searched the kitchen.

I said, "I've got every right to kill you. You understand that. I know you do. But, dead, you'd just be out of your considerable misery, and I think you ought to wallow in it for a while." I opened the fridge to find half a can of pork and beans, three pitted, bruised, and wrinkled tomatoes, a dead silverfish, and four cans of light beer. The freezer was empty. Creed hadn't lied about the ice. I held up the empty ice cube tray and said, "Can't do anything for your pain because you live like a pig." I found what I was looking for in the junk drawer—a box of fifty .9mm hollow-point bullets and the keys to the pickup.

I took Creed's phone from the table and hit *redial* and *speaker*. Grady answered and said, "What's it this time, Creed?"

Creed said, "Mubba fuh fuh hatta hun."

Grady told him to call back when he was sober. I ended the call and called Bay on Creed's phone because mine still had no service. I told him the abbreviated story. He said he was on his way. "Keep both phones with you."

I said, "I'm going to find Patience." But I had no idea where to begin. I told Creed he should have had the phone password-protected. I knew I would not have been able to beat the password out of him. Creed valued loyalty above all other character traits, apparently, which is commendable, but leaves you open to betrayal, and, in this case, to a bleak and attenuated future. I stuffed both phones in my pocket and gave Creed one more chance to tell me where his friends had gone and what they'd done with Patience.

A listener will often lift an eyelid when something clicks. I said, "They in Austin? Pesadilla? Malachite?" He shut his eyes.

I said, "What is this, the bad guys' code of honor? You're all shithouse rats, and you know it. You tell me where they are, and I'll have an ambulance sent out here. Wherever the hell here is. And tonight you could be dreaming morphine dreams between freshly laundered sheets."

I told him to stand. When he wouldn't, I fired a shot between his legs and into the metal chair. He stood then. I shoved him to the door, unlocked it, and pushed him across the yard to the side of the single-wide. There were a dozen jittery sheep enclosed in a foul-smelling pen. I had Creed sit on the ground by the gate. I started the pickup: full tank of gas and a staticky radio. I turned off the radio, turned on the headlights, and saw Creed lumbering through the sagebrush toward the mountains. I told him to stop. He kept going. I fired a warning shot in the air. He screamed in agony and fell. How bad a shot was I? I followed the sound of his howling and found him writhing on his back in agony. He'd stepped on a spring-loaded steel leg-hold trap, and its formidable jaws had clamped down on his bare foot from ankle to instep. He screamed for me to set him loose.

There are twenty-six bones, thirty-three joints, one hundred and seven ligaments, and nineteen muscles and tendons in the human foot, and I'd bet that most all of them in Creed's foot were broken, splintered, pulled, or torn. He pounded his fist in the dirt. One more time I offered him a bargain. He said what sounded like "Joyce Kilmer," which I translated as "Just kill me." I said, "Tell me where they are, and I will." One more time he said nothing. "No water for you," I said. "No knife to cut your leg off." I told him if he were lucky he'd pass out soon from the pain. I left him crying, took a case of bottled water from the back porch, got in the truck, and made my way along a dirt road to the highway, jackrabbits bounding in front of the truck all the way.

I drove to Pesadilla, hoping to find Patience alive and alone, or the red pickup, or even the bronze pickup. I drove by every one of the seventeen darkened houses in town and by the five businesses: the saloon, Tinker's garage, a shuttered general store, a rock shop, and Ray's Antiques and Treasures. I looked through the window of the Full Moon, saw Lacy at a slot machine and a man passed out at a table. The kidnappers had an uncooperative Patience with them and a man in need of hospitalization. Either they'd driven to one of their houses somewhere between here and Austin, I guessed, or they were on their way to the nearest hospital, which I figured would be in Fallon.

Creed's phone chimed. Text message from Grady: *he at rest?* I answered: *dead u mean.* Grady: *wtf.* Me: *u want dead* ☺. I got no response. Now Grady knew something was out of whack at Creed Wackell's. He or Nacho or both would be coming to check on me or on what was left of me and to read Creed the riot act. I drove to the gravel road to Creed's, pulled off the two-lane blacktop opposite, drove fifty or so yards into the desert, turned the pickup to face the highway, shut off the lights, and waited. I didn't want to think about Patience. I turned on the radio and heard a talk-show host call for an open-minded exploration of the supernatural and then launch into a rant about the not-so-secret alien military outpost in Area 51 and the imminent launch of ghost bombs on the West Coast and the eventual subjugation of humanity under the leadership of Emperor Obama, who would reveal himself to be Ahkenaten, the once and future pharaoh of the Eighteenth Egyptian Dynasty. I turned the radio off.

Bay texted that he and the galvanic Open Mike were on their way. A five-hour drive. Give or take. I texted back that I was only semi-vigilant and having a hard time staying awake. He promised to send a text every fifteen minutes just to rouse me. The cab of the pickup smelled like an infected sebaceous cyst. I opened both windows. No approaching lights on the highway. No sound except the trill of my own tinnitus. I opened the glove compartment: a pair of binoculars with badly scratched lenses, book matches from the Moonlight Motel, a nearly spent can of WD-40, assorted screws and fuses; no title, no registration, no proof of insurance.

The throbbing pain in my cheekbone was now radiating across my face like an electrical charge. I knew Patience would not have gone gently and that her scrap and resistance might not work in her favor. I thought maybe there was a clue to where they'd gone on Creed's phone. I checked his contacts. *Grady* was there and so was *Sheriff's Dept.* Someone named *Dill, feedstore, Tinker B., Dr T, AceHdwre,* and *Angels,* plural, although Creed struck me as one of those inattentive writers who make their plurals with apostrophes and their possessives without. So this entry was, I figured, Angel Ramos Gonzalez: the incapacitated Chili. There were phone numbers, but no addresses. If Chili really was a deputy, then calling the sheriff might only make matters worse. I called anyway. The bored baritone who answered said, "What's up, Creed?"

I said, "All good."

"Chili's off today."

"There's been an accident."

"Who is this?"

I hung up and then dialed 911 and ignored the call back from the sheriff. A woman answered. "Creed?"

"Yes."

"You dialed emergency. You got one?"

"Little one."

And then she asked me to hold, which I knew was not 911 protocol, so I hung up before they could trace my location. If they dispatched a chopper, I was toast. I had to hope that, sometime before dawn, Grady would arrive to find out what had gone so wrong with Creed. I couldn't hide on a desolate salt flat in broad daylight. I cleaned the lenses of the binoculars with my breath and the hem of my shirt. I fixed my eye on the trailer and could see the lights of the kitchen and the porch. If Grady showed, he'd have three choices: A. Shoot Creed and put him out of his misery; B. Release Creed from the leg trap; C. Do nothing and leave. When he pulled back onto the road and headed north or south, I'd follow him.

Why did I suddenly think I was an action hero? I was a therapist. Until fairly recently the worst trouble in my life had been dealing with insurance payments from Blue Cross and Red Tape of Florida, Inc. But I did have a gun, and I did have the cavalry on its way: Bay, the trickster, and Open Mike, the berserker, the bedlamite of chaos. Bay once saw Mike conduct an enhanced interrogation of a police union thug by hanging the fellow, an Everglades County deputy, out the window of a speeding Lexus on 95 until the guy's shoes were gone, as were the legs of his uniform slacks and most of the skin on his legs below the knees. The petrified man talked a blue streak when Mike hauled him back inside. Having Mike around would neutralize Grady and company, I figured. I wouldn't do anything till they arrived, except to follow. At a safe distance.

# 13

I WAS RIPPED out of dreamland by the jolting chime of Bay's rousing text message on Creed's phone. When my heart finally stilled, and I could once again feel the throbbing and radiating pain from my swollen eye and the crushing ache in my head, I realized that the only way I would overcome the fear and anxiety was to act. The sitting, the waiting, the not doing anything, was making me crazy. It was time to bait the hook.

I had to find Grady in order to find Patience before I lost the cover of darkness. It was going on three; Bay and Mike were still a good two and a half hours away. I drove back to Creed's and parked the car facing the empty highway. I checked on Creed and found him to be mercifully unconscious. Or else he was dead, but I preferred to think not. I took a photo of the acerebral thug in all his indignity on his phone. I let the sheep out of their pen and shooed them off into the desert. They seemed reluctant to leave. I went inside the trailer and found what I was looking for in the medicine cabinet—Advil—to reduce, I hoped, the swelling in my eye. Creed had a rusting can of Colgate tooth powder in the cabinet, but no toothbrush. I'll spare you the repugnant details of the commode. I gathered all the clothing and threadbare linens I could find in the house and carried them outside to the fire pit. I did the same with the newspapers and magazines (*Nevada Rancher* and *Outdoor Life*). I grabbed a cold can of beer and held it to my eye. I found the circuit breaker panel and turned off the electricity. I turned on the gas stove but did not light the pilot.

In the metal shed out back I found three two-gallon cans of Coleman's fuel, a half-full can of brushing lacquer, a quart of paint thinner, a jug of kerosene, and a plastic bottle of turpentine. I piled the cloth and paper kindling beside the half cord of wood against the trailer and poured the accelerants on the pile. I lit the fire with Creed's motel matches and watched the flames leap to life. I wondered with whom, if anyone, Creed had spent his night at the Moonlight Motel in Jackpot, Nevada, and why any woman or man would spread his or her legs around Creed's mephitic loins. I found myself briefly hypnotized by the flames. I texted Creed's photo to Grady, got in the truck, and drove back to my hiding place.

I could open my left eye very gently with my thumb and fore-finger, and I hoped if I kept doing it, I could teach the eye to open by itself. I saw the beams of light approach on the highway, and the two pickup trucks slow and take the right onto Creed's gravel road. Hard to tell in the dark, with one good eye, and with fuzzy binoculars, but one truck looked like Grady's red Chevy; the other may have been blue. I saw two men park about twenty yards from the trailer. They left their headlights on and stepped out of their trucks holding rifles. One of the pair, the one I thought was Grady, walked to the back in the stream of light, to check on Creed or on the fire, which I could now see as an orange glow over the trailer's roof. The second man, Nacho, I guessed, kicked in the trailer's front door. He got a whiff of the leaked gas, covered his face with an arm, and walked inside. And that's when the whole enchilada exploded. I saw what looked like a brilliant flash of sheet lightning before I heard the blast. The trailer flew apart like a sledgehammered melon. And then I felt the concussion of the explosion in the truck, and the hula girl air freshener hanging from the rearview mirror swayed.

And then it was very quiet. And I waited. I listened for the approaching sirens of the county fire department or the sheriff's department or whatever emergency services they had here in the world of the damned. I watched for any movement at Creed's. I did see one of the liberated sheep trotting toward the highway. The fire was out, there being nothing left to burn. The trucks were there, but their windows had been shattered, it looked like. And that's when I thought for the first time that Patience might have been in one of the trucks and what an idiot I had been. I had acted but not planned, and now I would have to deal with the consequences. What if Grady and Nacho were dead? How would I find Patience? But then I saw the one I was calling Grady limp back to his truck without his rifle. He turned the truck around and headed for the highway without headlights. When he made the left turn, I waited till he was almost out of sight and followed his single taillight. And now I was thinking, Great plan, Wylie. It worked! Grady's pickup swerved and he stopped. And so did I, my lights still off. I hadn't yet reached pavement. Grady got out of the car with a handgun and shot what I would see in a minute was the sheep he had collided with. He dragged the animal to the shoulder.

I took the same left that Grady had taken at Quarry Road, a single lane of gravel alongside what might once have been tram tracks, heading west into the mountains, and drove about a half mile with the lights off. I pulled over, parked, and walked. I could still see the taillight of Grady's truck rising up a slight incline to a dead end a hundred yards ahead. An enormous owl flew by at eye level and vanished into the desert night. I never heard a sound. I had Creed's pistol in one hand and his binoculars in the other. I'd turned off the volume on his phone. I could now see a cloudy bit out of the left eye. I walked past stone foundations of what must have been houses or businesses and past old septic tank pits. I saw the window lights of a building ahead.

I crept to within fifty feet of what might have been an old hotel or rooming house and lay in the dirt. It was two stories, wooden, hipped roof with side gables, an exterior chimney, and a covered front porch. Grady got out of the pickup and walked to the front door of the building. The upstairs windows were dark, but the first-floor windows were bright, and I could now see Grady speaking with someone, and when that someone stood, I saw it was Tinker Beaty, our incompetent mechanic. Was this a dream, then, where all of the people from the recent past came together to contrive some improbable narrative? And I felt a momentary flush of relief when I thought that must be the case, but then the front door to the building opened and a potbellied fellow stepped out, and I was back into the nightmare.

The man slipped his arms into his suit jacket and shrugged it on. He took a bottle of sanitizer from his pocket and washed his hands. He walked to his car, leaning forward like he might stumble with each step. He spritzed his mouth with breath freshener. He drove past me, and when he did, I could read the magnetized sign on the car's door: KALE CHIPS—VEGAN, DEHYDRATED, ORGANIC $5 SM $10 LG. What distant planet had this guy arrived from? Kale chips in Pesadilla?

I crept closer and could see that Grady, not surprisingly, was quite agitated, Tinker, amused. I snuck around the building hoping to spy Patience in one of the windows. I heard a shuffling in the brush, a jackrabbit I figured, and then I heard a terrifying gunshot go off by my ear, saw a mound of dirt erupt by my leg, felt my heart expand to fill my chest and expel the air, and I froze. A man's voice said, "You can thank me later." He sounded like he was underwater and far away.

I turned to see the shooter kick a dead rattlesnake. "Sidewinder," he said. The man wore a Starbucks ball cap, a sleeveless gray sweatshirt, black cargo shorts, and white sneakers. "Wouldn't have killed you, but it would have hurt like a bastard." The gunshot had summoned Grady and Tinker outside and unfamiliar faces to the upstairs windows. Tinker said, "We meet again."

The furniture in the downstairs reception area was Victorian in style, cherrywood and crushed red velvet. A braid of artificial holly wound its way around the handrail and balusters and up the marble staircase. The faded red-and-white-flocked wallpaper screamed *bordello*. A large framed photograph on the wall over the sofa depicted the marble quarry in full operation. The levered blocks of stone were ghost-white. The foreman wore a pith helmet and jodhpurs. Next to the photograph hung a framed front page from the *Reese River Reveille* announcing the closing of the Adelaide Marble Quarry.

The shooter told me his name was Babatunji. I asked him why he was hanging around with these clowns and criminals. He said that's where the money was.

Tinker told me to take a seat, filthy and stinking as I was, and explained that prostitution was legal here in Shoshone County, and Misty's Wild West Ranch was a member in good standing of the county's Chamber of Commerce and was listed with and recommended by the Better Business Bureau.

I asked Grady how his two amigos were doing, and he stared at me. Tinker said, "Grady has suffered a recent hearing loss—perforated eardrums, I suspect. Nacho went to pieces and Chili will be collecting workers' comp for the duration. His fossil-hunting days are over."

"Why did you release these animals on us?"

Tinker said, "Boys were just having fun and would have let you go eventually."

"I don't believe that."

"You're right. Grady would have killed you dead."

I could see all the cards at this table, could see them in Tinker and Grady's cold eyes, knew I had a foul hand, and I also knew they weren't going to let me fold and walk away. And just then Carl the incompetent Austin mechanic came downstairs and asked how my car was running.

I said, "Can't get sex at home, Carl?"

He said, "Not since the horse died. But I do love those little fillies upstairs." He made a circle with his thumb and finger, inserted his tongue, and wagged it around. Then he said to Grady about me, "I thought you killed this knucklehead."

Tinker looked at Grady, who looked at the floor. Tinker said, "Not yet." He turned to Babatunji. "Take this jerkoff up to the quarry and dump him with the others."

Babatunji raised an arm and invited me to the door.

I said, "After you."

He grabbed my arm, lifted me from the chair, and shoved me toward the door. I realized I had three choices. I could run for it as soon as the door opened, but I could never outrun a speeding bullet. I could overpower one of these four, grab his gun, and get the drop on the others. Except that Babatunji would crush me like a stinkbug. I could try my luck and persuasive skills with Babatunji. I asked Tinker if I could just see Patience for a moment. He said I wouldn't like what I saw.

Babatunji and I stepped off the front porch and walked through the parking lot. I said, "You don't have to hold the gun on me. I'm not stupid enough to run or try to overpower you."

Babatunji told me to walk a few feet ahead of him and just follow the road. We walked.

I said, "Will you tell me where Patience is?"

"Upstairs."

"And how she is."

"She's been better. I won't lie."

"What did they do to her?"

"Right now she's under sedation."

I may have briefly thought I was speaking with a decent and reasonable man, but I was reminded by our grim circumstance that apparently he killed people for a living. Still, I had to try. I said, "Can't you just say you shot and dropped me, and let me go? Who's going to know?"

"No can do."

I turned. "Who's it going to hurt?" I saw the headlights of a convoy of vehicles turn onto Quarry Road. "We've got visitors." But, alas, not Bay and Mike.

Babatunji pointed his pistol to the brothel, shoved me toward the door, and said. "Let's go." We hurried inside.

Babatunji lifted a corner of the velvet curtain panel and peeked outside. "About a half dozen of them, it looks like."

From outside, we heard, "We're here to talk. No rough stuff."

From behind us, we heard, "Don't nobody move. Drop the guns, gents," an order that Tinker and Babatunji obeyed. "Now kick them over here."

The front door opened, and a man stepped inside. He was wearing a familiar latex Ronan Farrow mask, and so were the three guys who followed him, two of whom were dressed alike in Miami-green twill polo shirts, houndstooth check slacks, and white Keds.

I told them their shoes were untied and that was asking for trouble. When they didn't respond, I said, You two killed Layla Davis. Isn't that right, K-Dirt? He corrected me: Ronan. I said, And you, Bleak? He mumbled an indecipherable response through the mask that may have been in reformed Egyptian. I said, Why? When they didn't respond, their boss said that Blythe had belonged to his organization, real property, bought and paid for. Letting her walk away would have set a bad precedent. A simple business decision.

"So you killed her sister?"

"Collateral damage. My associates here got a little carried away. But I always take care of my staff. If people minded their own p's and q's, they wouldn't get hurt."

"You do understand that you can't own people."

Tinker said, "Babatunji's great-great-great-great-whatever grandfather was owned by President Thomas Jefferson." Then he said, "Let's be reasonable, Eli."

Eli the boss, I presumed, must be the Eli Belinki, head of enforcement for the Invisible Empire that Elwood talked about. He said, "That was a grand gesture—thirty stories down. You have to admit."

I said, "But nobody knows about it."

"The people who need to know about it, know."

"How did you make it go away?"

"Not by magic."

Eli told Babatunji that Tinker was no longer his boss. "You're working for me now, for the company." Babatunji crossed the room. Eli told him to stand out front and let any late-arriving customers know that the place was closed for renovations. And then he said to me, "I didn't expect to see you here. Or anywhere."

"Mladinic's," I said. Eli had been my wicked messenger.

Grady rapped at the side of his head with the heel of his

hand, opened his mouth in an extravagant yawn, and mumbled something unintelligible. The Ronan Farrow with the Hard Rock T-shirt sneezed. Eli said, "Nobody has to get hurt here."

What I learned in the next few minutes corroborated what Elwood had told me that afternoon at his kitchen table and then some. Eli's Invisible Empire was quite jealous of its virtual monopoly of the Nevada sex trade and vigorous in its pursuit of renegades and upstarts. You can have your brothel, your franchise, as it were, but you'd best buy your product from, and pay your tribute to, headquarters, or you would be shut down. Just like in the burger business. But then Tinker and his Merry Men decided to go rogue, bypass the organization's recruitment and distribution department, and hope that Eli wouldn't find out. But those impulsive hopes were dashed when news of the single-wide explosion and the deaths of Creed and Nacho reached Vegas—a call, perhaps from one of the other Shoshone County sheriff's deputies on Eli's payroll—and summoned Eli and his Ronans to Pesadilla. They must have flown to Austin and driven down.

Tinker said, "What about the Asians? They do what they want and get away with it."

Eli said, "They smuggle in the product and keep themselves busy with home invasions, identity theft, counterfeiting, that sort of thing. Some meth trafficking. Yes, and some prostitution. They have a niche clientele, the guys with acute cases of yellow fever, and we're okay with that."

Carl said none of this was his affair, what Grady did on his own time was Grady's own business, and Eli told him to stifle it, and Carl said he was leaving, and he took out a pistol, waved it at Eli, and backed himself to the door. Eli said, "Look at my eyes, Carl, and listen to my words: Stop right there." When Carl reached for the doorknob, Eli shot him and walked to Carl, bent over the writhing body, and said, "That there was a round-point, full-metal-jacket slug you took, and it's going to hurt like hell for quite some time, and that should keep your mind off trying to stand."

Eli straightened up. "Gets hot in here," he said. He lifted his mask, wiped his sweaty face, and said, "So how are we going to play this, Tinker? Intelligently or expeditiously?"

And there it was, Bay's *reveal* staring me in the face. I recognized Eli as the excruciating asshat poker player at the Mandalay Bay casino and as the unsettling gentleman drinking a Rob Roy at the Boar's Head Bar. I said, "How long have you been watching us?"

"Since that afternoon."

"I can't be a threat."

"You're a nuisance, and I thank you for coming to your going-away party." He nodded at Tinker and said, "We're paying Tinkerbelle a visit because he forgot he worked for me and was not an independent contractor. We're here to jog his memory."

A man walked downstairs, stopped at the landing, took in the scene, said, "Whatever you got going on here, it doesn't concern me. I'll just be going." He put on his cowboy hat.

"Not another one," Eli said. "You're not going anywhere."

"Do you know who I am?"

"I don't care who you are."

"Marv Pearl, treasurer of Shoshone County."

"And you just had sex with, what, a twelve-year-old girl?"

Marv said, "Out of my way," and stepped toward the door.

The Ronan with the blue oxford shirt slammed his pistol into the side of Marv's face. Marv dropped like a rattlebag.

Eli said, "Why does everything have to be so fucking difficult?" He told three of the Ronans to go upstairs and fetch the girls and their gentlemen.

I said, "One of those ladies is my girlfriend."

Eli said, "If you had listened to me then, none of this would be happening now. You understand that, don't you?"

The sneezy Ronan sneezed again. I told him he was probably allergic to the mask.

"Think so?"

"Latex is a common allergen."

He pointed to his mask and said what sounded like, "It's a mess in here. I'm slimed."

Eli told him to find the loo and clean up.

I said, "Why do you wear the masks?"

"At first because of the surveillance cameras and the facial recognition software the Feds have, but it's become a branding thing."

Three girls, not looking older than fifteen, in vanilla robes and strawberry high heels, a blonde, a brunette, and an electric-blue-haired beauty, came down the stairs, followed by two Ronans, followed by three bewildered men, one wearing only black socks, one a red thong, and one a dog collar and leash, followed by the third Ronan carrying an unconscious Patience in her street clothes over his shoulder. He laid Patience on the couch. I said, "I'll take care of her."

Eli told me to be still, and then he told Tinker he was taking the girls as a down payment. Tinker said how was he supposed to pay up without the brothel, and how could he run a brothel without girls. The blue-haired girl walked over to the knocked-out cowboy Marv, bent down, and spit in his face. Then she took off a shoe and pummeled his face with the stiletto heel. She beat him back into consciousness until the returning Sneezy took her by the shoulders, mumbled something in her ear, and embraced her as she wept in his arms, and I couldn't help but imagine the start of an improbable but tender love story right there, right now, wherein Sneezy and Blue get permission from the irascible but sentimental Boss, the corporation's CEO, to leave the business and start a life of their own back in Blue's hometown in Idaho, and they wait for her to graduate from high school, and have a kid and get married, in that order, because that's how it's done these days, and, of course, being out of my mind with fear, I was using the Hollywood love story to distract myself from my probable imminent death, from the loss of Patience, and from my wretched helplessness.

Eli told his men to take the three girls out to the cars. Creed's phone buzzed in my pocket. I slipped it out. A message from Bay: *We're outside.* The girls objected to being moved. The brunette told Bleak, "Get your fucking hands off me, shithead." The blonde said she was sick. Eli asked me what the text was about. I put the phone in my pocket. I said, "Mom. She worries."

He held out his hand, wiggled his fingers. "Give!"

I handed him *my* phone, not Creed's.

"Nothing here."

"That's how I know it's Mom."

When Grady bolted for the door, Eli fired a warning shot into the floor. Eli told one of his Ronans to lock the three johns in the closet, where they could have a circle jerk. Then he noticed that the bullet shot to the floor had passed through Marv's neck. "Motherfucker. Why won't people listen to me?"

Tinker said, "You killed my best customer."

Eli said, "And you're next." Then he directed his men to throw the ex-cowboy into the closet with the others.

I guessed that Eli wasn't used to this level of chaos in his operations, and I also figured the living closeted trio was probably happy being out of the line of fire, except for the leashed one, who claimed to be claustrophobic and whimpered audibly until Eli fired a shot through the closet door, and then everything went quiet for a five-count, and then Babatunji exploded through the shattered glass of the large front window and landed at my feet. His wrists were bound behind his back with plastic handcuffs. Eli and company leveled their pistols while the women screamed, and we all dropped to the floor. Tinker stood and took a bullet from somewhere in the shoulder.

Grady pointed at the west window and we all turned and saw Bay there with his gun. The oxford Ronan fired at Bay and blew out the window, then fell when a second shot hit him in the back. We heard a voice I recognized as Mike's say, "Lay down your weapons and come outside. You're surrounded." And then Bay was in the east window and the west window at the same time. Was he working with mirrors out there? And then we heard what I knew was Bay's voice coming from somewhere over our heads, and he was gone from the windows. He said, "We're going to start tossing in tear gas."

Eli said, "And we'll start tossing out bodies."

Touché. One for the bad guys. I saw that Sneezy still had his arm around Blue's trembling shoulders. Babatunji opened his glazed eyes without moving his thick head and then closed them again. Patience stirred. I squeezed her hand. She groaned and blinked her eyes.

Bay said, "Send the women out, and we'll take them and leave."

"They're hostages. And we're walking out with them."

Two.

"And if you try anything, anything at all, we'll kill them one at a time. Or all at once."

Mike said, "You okay in there, Coyote?"

"I've been better."

"Patience?"

"She's with me."

Eli and company walked out with the girls, got into their three cars, and drove off toward the highway. I looked out the front window and saw no sign of Bay or Mike. I yelled that we were not alone, as they surely knew, and said there were no weapons in evidence. And suddenly Bay and Mike were standing there in the room, Mike wielding a desert-tan tactical sniper's rifle.

Mike looked at the senseless Babatunji and said, "I know this guy, but who are these other clowns?" He walked to the chair where a very blanched Tinker was slumped and bleeding. "That's got to hurt."

Bay said, "We should be going. We have hostages to rescue."

Mike said, "Is this your establishment?"

Tinker nodded.

"It's fucked up what you're doing here. You know that." Mike fired a burst at the ceiling and the glass chandelier crashed to the floor.

Mike asked Grady his name. I said he was deaf. Patience said his name was Grady and he had raped her. Mike put his mouth to Grady's ear and yelled, "Can you hear me now?"

Grady nodded. Mike pointed to Patience and then poked Grady in the chest. "It's unfortunate you did that, pig." Mike pulled some handcuffs from behind his back and cuffed Grady to Tinker. He held his finger and thumb an inch apart, leaned in to Grady's ear, and said, "I'm about this close to shoving a grenade so far up your ass, if you burp, you'll explode."

I crossed the room to Grady. I took Grady's head in one hand, Tinker's in the other, and slammed their skulls together. Grady's eyes rolled up into his head. Tinker winced but recovered and smiled. I grabbed the two heads again but made the mistake of visualizing what a second battering would do to Grady's skull, and I stopped.

Mike grabbed my arm, shook his head, and said, "He can't feel anything now."

And then we heard yelling from the closet and pounding on the door. "Customers," I said.

Mike pulled a Hummer sport-utility truck around front, and we hopped in. It was a paramilitary pickup with a cargo bed in back. We drove a hundred yards down the road, and Mike stopped, let the engine idle, got out, and walked to the back. Patience said we couldn't let the assholes get away with the girls. Bay said the three getaway cars were now equipped with GPS devices, and he showed Patience the three beeping vehicles on his iPhone's map. He figured they had ten miles on us. Fifteen, tops. Meanwhile, Mike pulled a rocket launcher and a rocket out of the cargo bed. He knelt about ten yards from the car.

Bay said, "Really, Mike?"

"The coup de grace," Mike said. He fired a rocket at the bordello and scored a direct hit on the second floor, lit it up like a Roman candle. He put the weapon back in the truck bed and got back in the driver's seat. He fastened his belt.

I said, "Where did you get a rocket launcher?"

"Craigslist."

We saw the bronze pickup at the end of the road. I said, "Not this asshole again. This guy's been following us for days."

Mike eased up to the truck. We could see that the tires had been shot out and the engine was steaming. Our stalker sat at the wheel, crying. Mike rolled down his window. The driver said, "I was parked here bothering no one, waiting for your friends in the backseat to come by, when these maniacs just opened fire. I took a bullet in the leg and one that grazed my skull and blew my hat off." We saw the hole in the door that may have been the entry for the bullet in the leg. One lens of his glasses was shattered.

"I don't even own a gun," the driver said.

Mike and I helped him down from the cab and into the back-seat of our vehicle. Mike got out his substantial first-aid kit and cleaned and dressed our stalker's wound. Our stalker thanked him profusely, wondered if we might have something for the pain. Mike said, "Name it." Our stalker thanked Mike, swallowed a Percocet, and introduced himself as Lawson Scott, PI.

He said, "The Kurlanskys hired me to find your friend Char-lotte Edge. Said she murdered their beloved son and brother. And I found her with you, but then I lost you in Tonopah. Got stuck behind a jackknifed tractor-trailer for an hour and a half. And then I found you two again in Lovelock, but not Charlotte, and I was hoping you would lead me back to her."

I said, "We won't."

Bay said, "Find her and what?"

"Call them with her whereabouts and punch the clock."

Patience said, "So you're not very good at your job?"

"I'm terrible at it, but I was the best the Kurlanskys could afford. I get two hundred dollars a day plus expenses, and I'm going to lose a bundle on this assignment. I mean, how do I explain a lost truck to Hertz?"

"Explain it *stolen*," Mike said.

"Usually I'm spying on cheating husbands in Mendocino County. Steady work."

I said, "What's that like?"

"One: they are always cheating. Two: they are always cheating with women from work. Three: they never leave their wives. Four: they never leave their girlfriends."

"So the wives leave them?" Patience said.

"About half the time."

I said, "We thought you might be a bad guy."

"Just a working stiff."

Patience said, "Have you thought about another line of work?"

"This is all I'm suited for."

Bay said, "Where are you from, Lawson Scott?"

He smiled. "I usually tell people I'm from Alaska. Petersburg. Tell them I grew up swimming with seals and sledding down glaciers. But it's all a made-up story."

"Why make it up?" I said.

"Because the truth is trite and tedious."

I tried to imagine the horror that Patience had endured and hoped that, for now, in her confusion, she might assume that this was all an appalling dream.

Once we were back on the road, those of us in the backseat—Lawson, Patience, and me—fell asleep one by one. When Bay woke us up, the eastern sky was lightening, and we were turning into a hospital parking lot in Tonopah. Mike parked the car near the ER and helped Lawson out of the Hummer. He said, "I'm glad you like making up stories, Lawson, because very shortly you're going to have to explain this gunshot wound." He leaned Lawson against an Audi. He called the hospital and told them where to find a seriously injured man. We said our goodbyes and drove away.

Patience said, "What about the girls?"

"We have their location."

# 14

MIKE WAS READY to go shopping for our upcoming rescue mission. Deep shopping. What he needed you couldn't buy off the shelf. He said he was promoting a free market economy by circumventing needless governmental regulations. And then he laughed, slipped a Fat Elvis doughnut into his coat pocket, and headed out. Bay, Mercedes, Patience, and I ordered pizza, made cocktails, and sat in the living room talking. Patience said she kept seeing Grady's miserable face everywhere she looked. Her sadness and grief at her assault had evolved to rage. She'd need to see a therapist to talk her way toward meaning and a degree of serenity, but that therapist could not be me. I squeezed her hand; she put her head on my shoulder.

Mercedes told us about her new short story, inspired by the flood of prostitution that had been deluging our lives recently. She was calling the story "Firefly," which was the central character's stage name. It's about a young woman who kills herself after an exboyfriend outs her on Facebook as a porn star. It was not the porn business that killed her, not the dirtbags who inhabit that debased world, but the friends at school she would have to face, their smirks, insults, and corrosive laughter, those who were spreading the juicy news, and the church ladies, her mother's friends she would see on Sundays, the shame and the humiliation of the public revelation. Mercedes said she thought she'd been writing the story of a woman debased by men and by the sex industry, but then the story changed directions without her knowing how or why, and she followed the accidental plot and now she couldn't get Firefly out of her head.

When Kit arrived with our pizza—two Hang Tens and a Popeye and Olive Oil—Bay set the boxes on the counter, explained our situation, mentioned the kidnapped young women now being defiled at the House of Mirth, and said he'd pay for her evening's salary, tips, and then some, if she'd come in for a while and talk with us. And eat, of course, Bay said. And drink. Kit called work and told her manager that her car had broken down and she was waiting for the tow truck. She louched her Pernod with water till it was milky and drank it with her pizza. Django snuggled into Patience's lap, sniffed the aromatic molecules in the air, and closed his eyes.

Bay told Kit that the young girls he'd mentioned to her were being held as sex slaves—there was no other way to say it—at the place she had called the House of Mirth. He told her that we'd called the police tip line several times, but nothing was done. We called the homeowner's association. Got an assessment-of-violations notice as an answer. We had violated the community's rules by having three cars parked in a two-car driveway.

Kit said, "You don't want the cops involved. The two sleazebags who work the night shift over there are off-duty Metro cops."

I said, "One of them built like a brick shithouse?"

"They call him Filthy Luka. The smaller one's Nicky Slots."

"Anyone else inside besides the girls?"

"The madam who calls herself the concierge. Tulin something-or-other."

Bay said, "We have a job opportunity for someone cunning, playful, and quick."

Kit smiled.

"We need to get you inside the house, and I know that's against your company's very sensible policy, and I don't want you to lose your job."

"I can't be delivering pizza all my life. Get in and then what?"

"You'll wear a tiny camera. We just need to know what we're getting into."

"I'll complain of female troubles and ask to use the bathroom."

"Get lost if possible and walk through all the rooms you can."

"They have a standing order every Sunday at seven: two Blondes on the Beach, two Manhattan Men, two Del Reys, one BBQ Chicken, one box of Parmesan Pull-Aparts, and a case of Red Bull."

"Tomorrow it is."

I said, "How well do you know this Tulin?"

"Not at all. Catch a glimpse of her once in a while. But she's on the website."

"Website?"

"Tulinsgirls.com."

Bay got out the computer. I called Elwood. We needed a fourth. I told him the plan, and he agreed. Bay made appointments for a party of three randy fellows looking for nubile girlfriends, Saturday night at seven. "I paid a premium for a private party. We'll have the joint to ourselves."

MONDAY MORNING BRIGHT and early, Kit arrived with the camera and a box of cinnamon torpedo doughnuts. Everything had gone well at the neighborhood brothel except that she'd only made it halfway up the stairs before Madame Tulin told her about the downstairs bathroom. Kit was still able to see that there were two bedrooms to the left of the stairs and one to the right. Mike got the strawberry jam out of the fridge. Bay attached the camera to his laptop. Elwood poured our coffees, and we all watched Kit's eight-minute reconnaissance video.

In the video, Filthy Luka took the pizzas and drinks from Kit, paid her, opened the door, and consulted with Tulin before letting Kit inside. Tulin sat at a desk staring at a computer. She wore a white open-sided blouse, black leotards, black ballet slippers, and reading glasses. The bathroom was off the kitchen, where Nicky Slots sat at the table playing solitaire. He stood when he saw Kit and flexed his knees so his white flared linen slacks fell adroitly over his black-and-white Spectator shoes. He asked her if she was here for a job interview. He wore his blue dress shirt untucked, with the sleeves rolled up in the Italian style to show the contrasting red color of the cuffs. The large living room was uncluttered, tastefully simple, and clean. There was a Modigliani print of a reclining nude on the wall above Tulin's desk.

Mike spread jam on his doughnut. "Piece of cake," he said.

I said, "You know it's kidnapping, right?"


THE RESCUE MISSION went without a hitch. We arrived shortly before seven. Luka, our greeter, asked for our names.

Bay said, "James, party of three."

"Right this way, gentlemen."

Tulin said, "Welcome. Shall I bring the girls down?"

"We like a surprise," I said.

Tulin asked Elwood if they had ever met. He told her they hadn't. She said, "You look awfully familiar."

Elwood said, "I've got one of those faces."

Bay said, "The girls are young, correct?"

Tulin said, "Three unblemished virgins right off the banana boat from Belize. And they're the only ladies in the house right now."

Elwood clapped his hands. "Let's get the show on the road."

Tulin said, "Nicky, would you show the gentlemen upstairs?"

Bay said, "We'll find our way."

Tulin pointed to the three bedrooms in turn. "Blonde. Brown. Blue."


I ASKED BLUE what her name was. Brenda. I said, "Brenda, get dressed."

"You mean un-."

"We're leaving."

"I know you."

"I'm one of the people who tried to rescue you from the bordello up in Pesadilla."

"Your eye looks better."

"Get dressed. Put all of your essentials in a bag. We've got fifteen minutes."

"What the fuck is going on?"

"We're getting you to a safe place."

"I've heard that before."

"As we speak, one of my colleagues is disabling the three bottom-feeders downstairs."

"Who is he, Batman?"

"He's good at what he does."

"I hope you do a better job this time." She took off her heels and put on some turquoise and yellow sneakers with Hello Kitty's face on them. She slipped on sweatpants and a very large Dallas Cowboys T-shirt. She looked around, opened the dresser drawers.

My phone buzzed: the coast-is-clear from Mike. We heard a bedroom door open across the hall.

While we were all busy upstairs, Mike had walked up the front steps wearing a NO BED BUGS: ACE PEST CONTROL T-shirt and a full facepiece respirator around his neck, carrying a leather tool bag. He set the bag down and told Luka, "The exterminator's here."

"We don't need one."

"Until you do."

"What?"

"I got a call about a cock-a-roach infestation."

Luka shook his head. "I'll need to see your business card."

Mike knelt on one knee, unzipped his bag, removed an aerosol can, slipped his respirator over his face, and sprayed Luka in the face with Kolokol-1, an incapacitating agent developed by Soviet scientists and used by the KGB, which takes effect immediately and renders the recipient unconscious for two to six hours if it doesn't kill him. Then he knocked on the door, told Tulin there was a sick man on her porch. When she answered the knock, she, too, was summarily incapacitated. That left Nicky. Mike walked through the living room to the kitchen, and heard Nicky say, "Is it my shift already?" And then Nicky went to sleep. By the time we all assembled in the living room, Mike had dragged the three senseless stooges to the pool and duct-taped them to three chaise longues.

Elwood and Kit drove the girls to the Mustard Seed, a Catholic Worker House of Hospitality, across the border in California near Mono Lake, a place run by friends of Kit. Elwood interviewed the girls, Donna, Lourdes, and Brenda—who told him that her *real* real name was Christy—on the way for the story he'd write for the *Wingo Star* and maybe also place in a national outlet. The girls would stay at the Seed until they could be reunited with their families, if that was wise, or placed in the homes of families who'd been providing sanctuary for illegal immigrants. The best we could do for now was get the girls out of harm's way. And probably get our own asses out of Vegas.

WE DIDN'T GET our asses out soon enough. I woke late the day after the rescue to find that Django had unrolled the toilet paper in the half bath off the hall, had unrolled the paper towels on the kitchen counter, had knocked over the vase of calla lilies on the dining room table, pushed the magazines off the coffee table, and was now lounging on his side in the litter box watching me. His bowl was empty. He was used to and expected a twenty-four-hour Vegas buffet. I apologized, and to make it up to him, I opened a can of flaked fish and shrimp, and he wept for joy.

"You spoil him," Mike said.

"Good morning, Mr. Lynch. Can I fix you breakfast?"

"You making doughnuts?"

"Eggs?"

"I'll bring home a dozen assorted. I'm driving by the House of Mirth—see what's cooking."

I said nothing about the wisdom of returning to the scene of a crime. I got the coffee started, went to wake Patience. She was already in the shower. I peeked in and said good morning. I retrieved the mail, poured myself a coffee, and at the kitchen table sifted through the circulars and bills for people Bay had made up. We got a vintage postcard of C Street in Virginia City from Alice O. She wrote that she found peace and solitude unnerving, tourists amusing, and the night skies glorious.

Bay entered the kitchen and poured himself a coffee. He sat, smiled, and told me that our little friend had chewed through the wire on my phone charger.

"Django!"

Bay said, "I don't know where we're going, but we can't stay here."

"We'll ask Patience. She's the travel agent."

"And we should leave soon."

"Mercedes?"

"She'll join us later. When the class is finished and she can get leave from work." And then Bay said that we all had chipped in to finance the rescue, and he hoped I didn't mind, but he'd tapped into my savings account.

I said, "How much?"

"How much were those three lives worth?"

"You're not going to answer me, are you?"

"Mike will recoup our losses."

"How?"

"You buy arms, you sell arms. And *you* don't want to know."

"I do and I don't."

"We'll leave first thing in the morning."

"Where are we going?" Patience said. She kissed me on the cheek and sat down. I poured her a coffee.

"That's up to you," Bay said.

We had read online that the Shoshone County Sheriff's Department was investigating an explosion in a mobile home apparently caused by a propane gas leak that left two men dead. They did not suspect foul play. No mention that one of the victims died with his leg caught in a spring-loaded trap. Nothing about a bordello in ruins; nothing about a missing county treasurer or an injured deputy, not to mention a slew of bodies in the ruined bordello The tentacles of Invisible Empire's PR department had a long reach, indeed.

We were down to the one vehicle, Mike's disposable Hummer. The plan was for me to drive Bay to Mercedes's, then drop Patience off for her doctor's appointment and Mike at the City of Dreams, where he'd be spending the day and night at the sports book. I'd swing by Elwood's to say goodbye, then fetch Patience at the doctor's, drive her home so she could arrange our travel, buy kitty Ambien at Petland, get the Hummer detailed, retrieve Bay, drive the car to the Caesars Palace parking lot, and leave it. Bay and I would catch a cab home, pack, clean, get some sleep, rise early, and take a cab to the airport if we were flying, to Hertz if we were driving, to Amtrak if we were training. Mike would meet us at whichever.

Mike came back with the Hummer thankfully empty of weapons and ammo and with a box of doughnuts. He told us it smelled like rain outside. Bay told him he was dreaming. I was reminded to check my savings account on my bank app, and I was pretty sure I had more money now than I had before.

Mike opened the box, and all I could think of was a busload of ladies in crazy hats. Bay picked one up. "What the hell is this?" Here was an orange flower on a featherbed of whipped cream on top of a glazed pillbox doughnut.

"Pumpkin cheesecake," Mike said. He himself preferred the one with what looked like palmetto bugs on top that were actually dates.

Patience said we were all going to have heart attacks. I gave her a bite of my maple bacon bar, and she said her teeth hurt. She asked Mike if he'd brought any fruit, and he took the slice of banana off the top of a Fat Elvis. Patience laughed so hard she started to cry.

•    •    •

ELWOOD SAT TYPING at his computer and listening to the Handsome Family sing about Nikola Tesla's last days of wonder. His Chekhov cocktail stood beside the voice recorder, the memo pads, and the iPhone. I made myself a negroni. I told him we were leaving.

"Who am I going to play with?"

"How's the piece going?"

"I've got photos of the girls at the house and of the three criminals downstairs. No one's going to rattle any cages. I may have to lie low after this gets posted. But I can write anywhere."

"You can't post our photos."

"Faces pixilated."

"You don't have to mention the Kolokol, do you? Call it chloroform."

"I'm a journalist, not a fiction writer. I write the facts."

"As you see them."

"I don't fabricate."

"It's all fiction, Elwood."

"I won't use your names, of course."

PATIENCE SAID THE DOCTOR'S visit went as expected, said she'd be worried until the test results were in, would be distressed for a very long time, and would be angry forever. "And I'm not letting go of that anger. It's empowering."

"Just as long as you use that power for good."

Patience smiled and punched my shoulder. "I'm glad you're around."

I said, "Do you want to talk about it?"

"The assault, you mean?"

"Yes."

"No."

•    •    •

I BACKED THE HUMMER into a parking space in the rear of the Caesars Palace parking lot. It seemed a shame to leave all the new toys—the self-balancing luggage system that Mike used for packing weapons; the auto rescue kit with its flashlight, seat-belt cutter, and glass-shattering window hammer; the first-aid kit; and the Igloo beer cooler—in a car we were abandoning. We stepped out of the car. Bay said the air had a sweet and pungent zing. Eddie Fisher sang "Oh! My Papa" on Bay's phone—a call from Little Bob. Bay put him on speaker.

Bay said, "Hey, Dad."

Little Bob said, "Lorena's in labor."

"Congratulations."

"Her water broke just now."

"As it should."

"What's that about?"

"Your baby wants to get born."

"Doesn't taste like water."

Bay put his arm on the window of the Hummer and his head in his arm. "No, you didn't."

"What do we do now?"

"Call the doctor."

"Which one?"

"The ob-gyn."

"What's that spell?"

*"Baby doctor."*

"Don't have one."

"There's no hospital in Flaubert, is there?"

"There's no pharmacy in Flaubert."

"Call 911."

"Nine-one-one. I'm writing it down."

"Or boil some water and get ready for some screaming."

"Will do."

"Call it now."

"Roger that."

"Call me later."

"Affirmative."

Bay hung up.

I said, "I'm worried about that baby."

Bay said we should get a drink or two before catching a cab home. One for the baby, one for our bon voyage. "To the Luxor, where our misadventure began and where it will end."

I said, "The Ronan pharaohs might be there."

Bay said, "Ouch."

On our walk down the Strip, Bay and I noticed flashes of lightning in the southern sky. Bay inhaled and said, "Petrichor?"

"Ozone," I said. "Petrichor comes *with* the rain."

"We may get some."

I said, "Some parts of the Atacama Desert in Chile haven't had rain in four hundred years."

"They should schedule a picnic."

Dozens of men in modest black suits, white shirts, and silk ties, a few of them sporting fedoras, stood separately along the sidewalk, a half dozen or so on every block. They all looked noticeably interested in, but resolutely unengaged with, the working girls out for their promenade. And they all sported high and tight Soviet Bloc vintage haircuts. I asked one of them, a man with an aquiline nose, a dimpled chin, and silvery blue eyes, what was going on.

He said, "You are free and that is why you are lost," and then he opened his hand to show us a cockroach on its back, waving its antennae, and shaking its six sturdy legs. The man said of the insect, "He's late for work." He closed his fingers around the roach and told us that the North American Kafka Society was having its annual convention at Circus Circus.

At the Luxor we quite literally bumped into Loomis, the blunt and burly security guard who had ushered us out of the casino on the day that Layla died. Bay had his eyes on his cell phone, reading a text from Little Bob: *Water boiling. What now?* and walked right into Loomis. Bay apologized. Loomis adjusted his uniform jacket and said, "You two." He flared his nostrils like he was oxygenating for action.

I said, "Hello, Loomis."

He leaned his head back and looked down his nose at me. "Did you boys ever identify that woman?"

I said, "What woman?"

Bay stooped and picked up a trifold camouflage wallet, opened it, and we all saw a photo of Loomis dressed in a Jedi warrior uniform, a raven perched on his shoulder. Bay said, "I believe this belongs to you, Mr. Truman Loomis."

Loomis patted his back pocket and then took the wallet from Bay. We excused ourselves and made our way across the lobby toward the Aurora, a bar that featured exotic drinks and fake northern lights on its ceiling.

Xena, our waitress, told us she'd been in Vegas four months, loved it, came here from Saugus, Mass. She was slim as a minute, fair as marble, had a splash of exuberant freckles on her cheeks, and tight curls in her wild red hair. She aspired to be a singer, she told us. Well, she *was* a singer. She aspired to sing onstage, professionally. She admired Edith Piaf and Billie Holiday. When Xena returned with our hibiscus martinis, Bay passed his hand over his linen napkin, lifted the napkin to reveal a single long-stemmed orange rose, and handed it to Xena, who blushed, thanked him, and hurried back to her station to slip it into a wine bottle.

I said, "How did you do that?"

"Magic."

"Do you have a florist on retainer?"

He smiled and said, "I took Loomis's phone to check out his contacts, see if he knows any of our nasty friends." He took out Loomis's phone in its Darth Vader case and put it on the table.

"You took his phone? He's going to be looking for us, you know that."

"I'll make it disappear."

"Our work here is done."

Bay's phone chimed. A text from Little Bob. *The deputies have arrived. So has the baby.* Before Bay could respond, Loomis's phone wailed like a siren. Bay read the text to me. *Bang! Bang!*

I said, "We should be going."

We hurried out of Aurora and had made it as far as the reception desk before I realized we hadn't paid our tab. Bay waited by the guest check-in while I hustled back to settle up with Xena. And then suddenly Bay appeared beside us. He showed me a texted photo taken just now from one of the upper floors of the Lux of him standing by check-in. Xena said sure, she could get us out through the kitchen. She led; we followed. She opened the swinging doors and yelled out that we were not the INS. "Mis amigos," she yelled. Xena brought us to a service door. Pointed to the right, and from there we found our way to an exit.

I said, "I knew we should have just gone home."

Bay said, "Chill. Lose your head, lose your chips."

And then Loomis's phone lit up and we saw ourselves right where we were—walking down East Reno.

I said, "What do they have—drones?"

"They're tracking us."

"How?"

"The phone!"

And then a text: *Nothing personal. This is business.*

We crossed Las Vegas Boulevard along with a clutch of Kafka impersonators. One of them told me, "Guilt is never to be doubted." Bay slipped Loomis's phone into Franz's coat pocket. Guilt is the way we punish ourselves for our sins. We walked into, through, and out of the Tropicana, crossed Trop Ave. to the Grand, and made our way to the monorail station. I chose to hope that we had finally lost the bad guys. As we boarded the train, Bay pointed out the cameras. And then we saw K-Dirt and Bleak standing at the other end of the car staring at us. They were, predictably, dressed alike in white polo shirts, green slacks, blue suede loafers, and Google glasses. At the Paris Station, an assembly of swaggering young Asian men in rockabilly suits, cowboy boots, and Oakley shades got on and stood between us and the ruthless twins. No beekeeper among them.

Bay said, "Next stop: we go."

I couldn't see our stalkers through the great wall of Asians, so I assumed they couldn't see me. But then I thought that their smart eyewear might be linked with the monorail's surveillance cameras, or maybe they'd gotten some app for X-ray vision. When the train eased into Flamingo Station, we made for the door. The sea of Asians parted, and the towheaded Jack Mormons followed us, and a wave of Asians followed them. K-Dirt caught my eye and grinned. One of the Asians stood between the train's doors and prevented them from closing with an iron bar. One Asian who looked like Gram Parsons in his *Grievous Angel* phase spun Bleak around and dropped him with a sucker punch to the throat. Bleak lay writhing on the platform, gasping for air, clutching his throat. He would not be rising soon. The man between the doors lobbed the iron bar to Gram and blocked the doors with his slim body. When K-Dirt lunged for the nearest Asian, he was clubbed in the face with the bar. The Asians hopped back onto the train and departed.

I looked at the Google glasses in the pool of blood by K-Dirt's rearranged face, and I coveted them as if I knew what I could do with them. Bay saw the lust in my limpid eyes, and said, "You can't walk into a casino wearing those."

We heard what sounded like thunder and saw that it was raining. I said, "Looks like the Asians got bored with home invasions."

As we walked down the ramp to the Flamingo, a column of uniformed security guards ran past us toward the station. Bay said, "We must be the luckiest guys in town."

"Or not," I said, and as if to prove me right, on the large TV screen above our heads, which should have been displaying an ad for Burlesque University or a promo for the holographic Michael Jackson/Elvis Presley/Frank Sinatra extravaganza coming to the Flamingo in August, displayed instead Eli's saurian face.

I said, "He wants us to know he's following us."

"And now we know that Loomis's phone was not the only tracking device."

"Maybe he's hooked up to some municipal surveillance grid or something."

Eli's transmitted image shivered and vanished from the screen and was replaced by Donnie and Marie onstage genuflecting, acknowledging the adulation of their cheering fans. So Eli's employer's IT team had hacked into the Flamingo's computer system. Heads would roll.

I said, "They can track us anywhere."

"And we don't know how."

"We don't want to lead them back to the house."

"More than likely we won't get that chance. The next ambush is now being choreographed."

"I know a place where there are no cameras and there's no chance of getting a GPS signal."

"Let's go."

# 15

WE WALKED OUTSIDE into a monsoon. Sheets of rain blew down the Strip. The boulevard was nearly empty of pedestrians, the exception being a few somber Kafkas ambling along, damp as rescued burlap-enshrouded kittens.

We turned more than a few heads as we tramped through Caesars, leaving our wet footprints in the grotesque carpet. We found the Hummer laughably hemmed in by an unmanned golf cart. All we needed was the flashlight from the auto rescue kit in the backseat. We got it, scooted down the parking lot's embankment, and entered the flood tunnels. I said, "Maybe Mario will have a change of shirts for us."

Bay said, "Goddamn, they're good."

"Who?"

And then we saw the figure running for the embankment, headed our way. Exeunt, both, pursued by a Ronan.

The water in the tunnel rose above our inappropriate footwear—sneakers and canvas slip-ons—as it trickled its way toward Lake Mead. All we needed to do was follow a tunnel to another outlet. I didn't know how far that would be or how long it would take, but the tunnels would all surface somewhere. When we got to Mario's chthonic home, we'd ask for directions. I used the almost alarmingly bright flashlight beam to show Bay the gallery of graffiti that some artist had tagged The Satanical Gardens. Bay said none of this was doing his claustrophobia any good. I shouted ahead to alert Mario that we were coming. Elwood's friend and the friend's friend, I yelled.

Bay said the air down here was stinging his nose and burning his throat. I saw Mario's camp ahead, flicked my flashlight on and off, but got no answer to my hello and heard no jazz playing on the CD player. Mario and Carolyn, still in her red scrubs, lay dead on the cardboard floor. The camp stove had been knocked over. The bed was made, sheets tucked, and pillows fluffed. Zoë the cat was nowhere to be seen. A hypodermic syringe lay beside Mario's body. They must have died recently but long enough ago for some critters to have chewed through the soft meat of Carolyn's left forearm. We heard dogs howling in the distance. Bay looked unnerved. I told him I'd read that in canine language, a howl was a summons to pack members in the vicinity. Bay said that all depended on the tail. The position of the tail is a mark of punctuation. "It's like the difference between, 'Let's eat, guys,' and 'Let's eat guys.'" And then he tapped my shoulder and pointed behind to approaching flashlights.

We had walked about a quarter mile without putting any distance between ourselves and our pursuers when we came to a fork in the tunnel. We listened for the howls and chose the tunnel less clamorous. We chose wrong.

So what are the odds, I said, that we'd walk right into the den of the ravenous feral dogs? Bay the gambler said evidently pretty good, given the unsettling sound of things—the yelping, barking, howling, and whining—all of it, by the way, getting louder. And the odds that our pursuers would choose the appropriate tunnel? Fifty-fifty, Bay said. So why, then, did they all—there seemed to be about six of them now—make the correct turn into our tunnel? And now all of their flashlight beams melded into one glaring beacon like the phosphorescent eye of the Hound of the Baskervilles. And then a gunshot rang out, and the bullet ricocheted along the walls of the tunnel.

Sometimes you get lucky. We came to a ladder in the form of iron rungs bolted into the tunnel wall and leading up to a manhole cover under some Vegas street. Bay boosted me up onto a pipe running across the tunnel a foot under the roof. He took the flashlight. I lay flat on my stomach in my sopping clothes and wrapped my arms and legs around the pipe. Bay leaped to the bottom iron rung and pulled himself up to the ladder. He stood on the bottom rung and pushed up at the manhole cover. It did not budge, but it did clang when run over by an occasional automobile. And then our hellhounds arrived, barking like mad, snarling, and biting one another's necks. The howling was over; the prey had been treed; the killing would commence momentarily. My pipe, a foot in circumference, was getting slippery. I said, "I hope we're in a movie, not a book."

Bay said, "What are you talking about?"

"In a movie you can kill dogs with glee and impunity, the grislier the better. But you can't kill a dog in a book. You get letters."

Bay pulled himself up the ladder and set his feet on the second rung, just out of reach of a maliciously crossbred mongrel, part Rottweiler, part wolf, the alpha male of the pack. We heard the approaching felons sloshing their way to us. The dogs' ears perked up, and they turned as one to the darkened tunnel. Easier prey, they may have thought. They bounded away toward the hoodlums. Bay tried the cover again, managed to raise it an inch or two, and we dared to hope we might soon be free, but the cover was slammed shut by a passing automobile.

We heard a barrage of gunshots, and then several of the hideous dogs ran past us. The dogs were followed by a pair of gun-toting thugs, having the time of their lives firing at the dogs. I said, Bay, make us disappear. This was all so surreal that I expected one of the Kafkas, pants rolled to his knees, to stroll through the tunnel walking a Cesky terrier on a leash. I closed my eyes and imagined I was back home in Melancholy, where I feared I would never be again, and I was on the beach with a drink and a book, reading and listening to the surf, and then I could actually feel the ocean breeze and hear the surf, and it was getting louder as if the waves were all breaking at once, and then I saw the goon squad come running by us, followed by the panicked dogs and a wall of raging floodwater.

Bay took this moment to tell me that he didn't know how to swim. I said no one could swim in this. On the other hand, he said, his claustrophobia was now a thing of the past. The water was four feet high and rising. A dog hurtled by, just his muzzle above the raging river of detritus. These were Class IV rapids. Bay and I clung to our perches, and I thought that we might be okay after all, but now a rolling surge of water washed over me. I told Bay to keep his feet ahead of himself if he fell in. That way he could kick away any dangerous flotsam. And try to stay on your back, I said, but I doubted he could hear me over the din of the resounding torrent. The flashlight was swept out of his hand, and I fell into the drink, blind as a cave fish.

I shot down the rapids, rolling, tumbling, scraping against the tunnel walls, and bouncing along the floor, which was the only way I could tell up from down in the dark. I tried to right myself in the position I had suggested to Bay, but without much success.

I tried not to swallow the filthy water when I did manage to take a quick breath. I hoped not to be knocked out by a forklift pallet or by someone's chest of drawers, and I prayed that my terrifying journey would be blessedly short.

I wasn't worried as much about going under, staying under, drowning—water is an anti-gravity machine; just ask any whale— as I was about getting slammed into the wall at the inevitable fork in the tunnel somewhere ahead of me. When I did hit the wall my impact was softened by a mattress or cushion of some kind, pinned against the wall by the flood. The agglomeration of debris had allowed the formation of an eddy behind it, and I was able, briefly, to stand, inhale, and press my back against the mattress, but then I was bumped and carried away to the left fork, and I hoped Bay would be driven the same way. And then, finally, the current seemed to slow, and I knew I would be okay. I caught a glimmer of crepuscular light and saw an outlet, and then I was spit out of the tunnel onto a gravel wash. I saw a pair of haggard dogs loping away toward I didn't know where.

Just when you think the worst is over, it isn't. I wanted to sleep where I had dropped on a stony bed in several inches of water, but then I remembered Bay, and I got to my hands and knees, but couldn't manage to stand, so I sat, and that's when I noticed I had no shoes and my jeans were torn, but I looked better than the Ronan standing unsteadily fifteen away. His ridiculous mask was around his neck. His face had been scraped along the tunnel wall, which had shredded his skin and left the face a raw and bloody pulp. He raised his pistol.

I said, "We both just went through hell, friend. Why don't we call it even and go home. What do you have to gain by shooting me?"

"I'm doing my job."

"You fire that gun and the cops will be on us like buzzards on a shit wagon. And you're in no shape to make a getaway."

He aimed the pistol but had a coughing fit. If I'd had any energy, I would have charged him, I suppose. I like to think I would have, anyway. I said, "What's your name, Ronan?"

He re-aimed the pistol and squeezed the trigger, but the water-logged gun didn't fire. Clearly not Ronan's day. He got furious with himself and his uncooperative weapon, slammed the gun against his thigh, and shot himself in the foot. He dropped to the ground.

I said, "You're a goddamn mess. Time to cut your losses, bub."

He shot again, but his eyes were shut, and he missed. But that got my attention and kindled my drowsy adrenal glands, and I was up and able to avoid the next erratic shot as well. I picked up a hefty boulder, about a foot wide and three inches thick, and while the reprobate writhed on his back in agony, I dropped the stone rather emphatically on his face, and I didn't hear from him again in the hour I sat there against the concrete abutment, waiting for Bay.

The skies had cleared; the rain had stopped; the voluminous moon was glistening. The gravel wasteland beside me was littered with dozens of plastic milk crates, assorted scraps of busted furniture, a rusted oil drum, strewn garbage, agitated crawfish, two dog carcasses, tattered clothing, and a wire birdcage sans canary. I walked to the tunnel entrance and called Bay's name.

I climbed up the abutment to an empty street, not knowing if Bay was dead or alive, and if alive, was he wandering lost and alone in the pitch-black tunnels? I would have walked to Caesars if I had known where I was. My cell phone was kaput. I walked toward the distant light of the Luxor's blue beam and wondered if they would let my bruised blue and contused barefoot self on the bus should I see one. I had a pocketful of damp bills in my sopping wallet. I saw a young woman on the corner in front of a Laundromat. She wore a lacy white summer shift, drop earrings, and platform boots. I kept my discreet distance and asked her where we were. Where in Vegas? I knew that much.

She said we were a few blocks from Boulder Highway near Duck Creek, where, apparently, I had taken a bath. I asked her if I could please use her phone to make a brief call. I'd give her ten bucks. She said I could make the call free for nothing. I called Patience's number, and Bay answered and said how happy he was to hear my croaky voice. He had feared that I might have become an ex-therapist. His own phone was dead, he told me, so he borrowed Patience's and came looking for me.

He told me that right after I had floated off, he'd opened the manhole cover and climbed out. None of the passing motorists paid him any notice. "I could have been a zombie rising from my tomb, for all they knew." He took a cab home and tipped the cabbie well for the aesthetic damage to the seats and the foul-smelling air in the cab. He said he was driving west on East Sahara. Where was I? I told him, and he told me to sit tight. He would call Patience and tell her I was alive and kicking. I gave the phone back to my benefactor. I heard the sizzle of tires on wet pavement. A car pulled to the curb, and my new friend poked her head in the window, turned, and waved goodbye to me, whistled, said, "It's off to work we go," got in the car, and away she went.

Bay and Mercedes pulled up in her car. I collapsed in the backseat. Bay handed me a bottle of cognac, a towel, and a UNLV sweatshirt. He showed me a photo of a baby and said, "It's a girl."

The pink baby, swaddled in a white blanket, wore a purple knit hat. Her eyes were shut, her brow lifted. The vermilion border of her upper lip rose to an adorable piquito, like a tiny peak of cherry icing. I said, "What's this sweetie's name?"

"Emma Grace. Seven pounds, two ounces. All the requisite fingers and toes."

BACK HOME AT LAST, I showered and threw out the rank clothing I'd been wearing. I wouldn't realize this for months, but I also threw away my father's broken pocket watch with the jeans. I had kept the watch as a memento and a good-luck charm. And you see how well that turned out. The watch was correct twice a day at 11:20. I would tell you that my father died at 11:20 P.M. AKST, but you wouldn't believe me.

Patience had cooked up a pot of green chili stew and a pan of jalapeño corn bread. We sat at the kitchen table and ate. Mike said we should eat all of the food in the fridge since we were leaving tomorrow.

I said, "I thought you were staying overnight at the City of Dreams."

"I ran into someone."

"Who?"

"I saw Eli. He did not see me. And then the power went out."

"What happened?"

"Security locked the doors so that none of the losers could run off with someone else's chips or the casino's loot. When the emergency's generator kicked in and restored power, Eli was lying facedown on a busted blackjack table, and guards were shooing people away from the scattered chips. Most people were too busy gambling or cheering the restoration of light to pay much attention. He had apparently taken a tumble over the side of the Stairway to Heaven escalator. I smell a lawsuit."

The table went quiet. Django the spy jumped down from the top of the fridge onto the counter, sniffed at the stew, and sneezed.

Patience suggested we talk about something a bit more cheerful and less scandalous. Something amusing.

Mike said, "My mother was a clown."

Mercedes said that wasn't a very nice thing to say about the woman who raised him.

He said, "No, she really was a professional clown. She was a member of Clowns without Borders."

Bay said, "You're making this up."

"Called herself Dumpling the Hospital Clown. She loved visiting sick kids at the cancer hospital. Wore this big orange fright wig, a green bow tie, red foam nose, a frilled shirt with pom-poms for buttons, baggy blue pants, and these oversized polka-dot shoes. An Irish clown, for God's sake. Who ever heard of such a thing? And, of course, she wasn't even funny. She was terrifying to most people. She made horrifying balloon animals for kids. All her dogs looked like Cerberus; all her butterflies looked like sausage flowers. Whenever she wore her clown costume, she was in character, even when we were all home at supper. Dumpling didn't speak. She honked her *yes* and *no* horns and she whistled her sentences."

Mercedes said, "That's great and I'm putting it in a story."

"Put this in, then. She was a two-hundred-and-fifty-pound narcoleptic with asthma and ulcerated lips, and she scared the shit out of those little kids. My brother Danny tried to feed her clown poison—blood sausage with freezer burn. He mixed it into her corned beef. When she tasted it, she whistled that she was going to kick his fat ass to Kingdom Come."

Patience said, "Well, that was fun."

Bay said he had packing to do.

I said, "Where are we going?"

# Epilogue

We flew to Phoenix and then to the Twin Cities and arrived at last in Sioux Falls the next morning, where we rented a Dodge Grand Caravan with my actual credit card. We drove three hours to Aberdeen and checked into the TownePlace Suites, the closest motel to Flaubert, still seventy miles away to the southwest. On our way, Django nestled between Bay's shoulder and the headrest, and Patience read Elwood's post about our rescue mission and the vicious and moronic public comments that followed, until we couldn't stand it anymore. When Patience texted Elwood our congratulations, he responded with a note saying that Jory Teague, director of Refuge House, had been arrested along with several of his associates, that Helen Lozoraitis had resigned her position at the Crisis Center, and that the T-Shirt vendors on the strip had cleaned up their act and their grammar and now advertised PIZZA! PIZZA! PIZZA! DIRECT TO YOU IN 20 MINUTES OR FEWER!

JULIE WADE CALLED BAY and told him that Kit had arrived in Memphis, found herself a studio apartment near Beale Street, and would start work for the Wade Detective Agency on Monday. Julie thanked Bay for filling her assistant's position with such a bright young woman. Julie had driven down to see Layla and Blythe's aunt Rita Davis in Monroe to deliver some of Layla's effects. Ms. Davis asked if either of her nieces might have left a car behind. They had not. She held Layla's microwave on her lap, stroked it like a pet, and rocked in her chair. She told Julie that her brother, the girls' daddy, had been killed by his cat, Twinkie, an orange tabby, over in Carthage. Alton got up in the middle of the night to fetch a bottle of Dr Pepper from the fridge downstairs. To settle his stomach. Twinkie was lounging there on the top step, just where Alton set his slippered foot. Alton's feet came out from under him. He went ass over teakettle and cracked the back of his head against the top tread, and that was all she wrote.

For some reason, as I stared out the window from the backseat, stared at the green fields, the cattle ponds, and a distant farmhouse outside of Waubay, I remembered the Little Miss and Mr. Nevada Glitz Pageant and wondered how Mylie and Colt had fared. Patience read us an online account of the pageant that included brief bios of the celebrity-impersonating judges—a male Cher, a female Wayne Newton, and an anorexic Roy Orbison. Mylie won Miss Supreme Personality, which, the somewhat snarky reporter noted, she was not at all happy with. A bubbly eight-year-old bleached blonde from Butte, named Destiny, won Grand Supreme.

In the morning I checked Django into Noah's Ark Critter Center for an overnight stay and a kitty spa treatment: the posh wash and fluff dry, but hold the spritz of cologne and the pet-a-cure. When I left him with the attendant, he gave me one of those soundless kitty meows that just breaks your heart. I met the others for breakfast at Francie's Bacon & Eggs, but I couldn't eat.

•     •     •

FLAUBERT, SOUTH DAKOTA, consisted of five numbered, quarter-mile-long streets running east and west, and four named streets running north and south for the same distance: West, Church, Main, and East. On the south side, Main Street became County Road 221A, which connected the hamlet to State Road 20. The couple of dozen houses were built in a plain, vernacular style and most were painted thunderhead-gray. Mike said, "Kill me now!"

Little Bob and Lorena lived at 11 Fourth Street in an austere side-gabled house. An unpainted railing, missing a few balusters, ran the length of the front porch. A satellite dish was attached with duct tape to a porch column. Someone had fastened a celebratory red balloon to the railing cap; someone had planted a bed of splashy pink tulips in the repurposed bathtub by the front steps, a someone who loved us all, a someone unvanquished by what I had, unfairly, seen as desolation.

And then the screen door opened and Little Bob and Lorena, cradling Emma Grace on her arm, emerged from the darkness as we piled out of the Caravan. Little Bob was trim, just this side of gaunt, grizzled, balding, and smiling to beat the band. Lorena was compact, blonde, and unadorned. Her eyes were cornflower-blue, her cheeks dimpled, and her face freckled. She wore a V-neck floral print housedress and white sneakers. Patience couldn't get her hands on that baby fast enough. Bay made the introductions, and we all went inside, where Lorena's sister Ophelia was telling no one present that she could summon UFOs at will and that the aliens from the planet Aetheria were here to save us from ourselves.

The main room of the house served as kitchen, living room, and dining room, was flanked by the two bedrooms and furnished with an oyster-gray bistro table and three Windsor dining chairs, a green upholstered sofa, and a somewhat exhausted Ultrasuede La-Z-Boy recliner by the potbellied woodstove. A mahogany bureau had been moved to a corner of the main room to make way for the baby's crib.

Out in the yard, the caterer, Dot Lutz, and her affable husband, Ernst, were preparing the food for Emma Grace's coming out party. The folding tables and chairs were set up, the tables covered with paper tablecloths. The air was so still that the laminated paper plates and the napkins lay undisturbed.

All thirty-six of the residents arrived and so did the Dischlers, a farm family of ten from nearby. Five of the guests, three men and two women, were easily identifiable as crystal meth addicts: baggy eyes, open facial sores, fractured teeth, periodically agitated, but in their particular cases, easily mollified.

Lorena said, "Bless their hearts for coming. Life is all trial and tribulations for these suffering souls." The two of us were sitting with Patience, who was nuzzling Emma Grace's neck.

Mike had set up a bar and was making vodka martinis for the guests. Lorena introduced me to the eager young Methodist minister, Kyle Kline, who was here to baptize Emma Grace by water and the Spirit. Kyle said what a blessed day it was. The Lord had shone down His glory on Lorena and Little Bob. Lorena told me that the woman getting all the manful attention was Zandra Schine, the village philanderess. Her husband, Sonny, had gone off to work the oil fields in North Dakota. Lived with about a thousand other men in a modular housing settlement up there.

I said, "The wives haven't ridden her out of town?"

"The wives are quietly grateful. If you didn't notice, we haven't exactly fielded the first-string here."

Ophelia came back outside dressed in a golden choir robe and a blue-and-gold-striped Egyptian headdress, looking like a lady of the pharaonic court of Akhenaten. Reverend Kline called for us to gather around the unheated bain-marie, which would serve as the baptismal font. Emma Grace was sprinkled, not immersed. Bay held her up for all of us to see and then handed her to Ophelia, who whispered into the baby's ear. Bay then lit the candles on the baby cake with a snap of his fingers. We all cheered for Emma Grace Linkletter-Lettique.

I sat next to Little Bob, who had hardly touched his food and who couldn't take his eyes off Lorena and the baby. I asked him how it felt to be a daddy again. He said he was happy and he was sad.

I said, "Why sad?"

"I won't see her grow up."

Lorena asked Little Bob to go inside and fetch a blanket for the baby. I became aware of the sudden change in the weather. It seemed to have dropped ten degrees in five minutes. A breeze from the southwest picked up and scattered some of the napkins, which I hurried to pick up and dispose of. I saw Mike and Zandra slip around the side of the house and head for East Street.

Lorena handed the baby to her sister and went inside to see what was taking Little Bob so long. Ophelia dandled Emma Grace on her lap. Patience sat beside me and said the predicted nasty weather was on its way. Dot felt a headache coming on. When Patience tried to get the weather forecast, we realized for the first time that we did not have phone service in Flaubert.

Reverend Kline said, "Tornado weather."

Ernst tied a knot in the green garbage bag and said, "There's a mobile home park over by Glenham. Any tornado will probably head right for it."

The Dischlers were mumbling a collective prayer, heads bowed, hands folded. Dot said she didn't see a funnel cloud, and weren't we all getting riled up for no good reason? Little Bob came out to tell us the power was out. I asked Little Bob if he had a storm cellar.

He said, "We got a ditch yonder."

The gathered clouds were billowing and brown, and then what had looked like a comma at the bottom of a cloud dropped to the earth as a funnel, and Patience said, "Goddamn it, Wylie, this is getting biblical." And as if to prove her right, it began to hail, and we all took shelter in the house, which itself was rattling on its foundation, and it seemed as if the whole of the lowering sky, and not just the spinning funnel itself, was turning slowly counterclockwise, as if trying to twist the very earth loose from its purchase and lift it into the chaotic heavens. The rubber duck in the baby's crib began to squeak, and we saw a cottonwood spiral up into the whirlwind. Reverend Kline shouted that we should all run to the church and get down into the cellar, but the church was three blocks away, and the tornado was considerably closer and bearing down on us.

Bay said, "Get the baby, pile into the van, and we'll drive to the church."

Little Bob turned in a circle, clapped his hands on his pockets. He said, "Where's the baby at?" Lorena screamed. Patience, Bay, and I ran outside, where the rain and the hail had stopped. The baby's carriage was being pushed along by the wind at a vigorous clip toward the ditch. When I caught up with it, I discovered that Emma Grace was not inside. The funnel was now a hundred yards away, and debris was swirling around and, for the most part, above us. And then I saw Ophelia, untethered in body and mind, walking resolutely toward the tornado. The funnel was now the solid brown of accumulated soil and as thick at the bottom as at the top. The wind thundered and whined. I turned and saw Ophelia holding Emma Grace, whose innocent heart was as light as a feather, saw Ophelia holding Emma Grace above her head as if offering a sacrifice to the cyclone Ammit, the Bone-Eater, the Swallower of the Dead, and Ophelia's resplendent robe was torn from her naked body and born aloft into the maelstrom, and, just like that, the bludgeon that was the whirlwind stopped and spun in place before the woman and child, and then it quieted and diminished and became, at first, lank and ropy, and then ascended back into the matrix of clouds from which it had dropped.

Bay reached Ophelia and took the baby from her arms. Lorena wrapped her sister in a blanket and took the baby from Bay, and then there was silence in Flaubert. And then we all went to church, Christians and nullifidians both, and we all sang praise to whatever force it was that had stilled the storm and saved the town, and the Reverend Kline spoke of Elijah taken up to heaven in a whirlwind and said how at times we need the storm, the whirlwind, the earthquake. "When the whirlwind passes," he said, "the wicked is no more."

The power was back on at Little Bob's house thanks to his gasoline generator. Lorena put the baby to bed, and we all sedated ourselves with vodka and listened for news on the radio. The National Guard, we learned, was on its way to help with the search for survivors. The mobile home park in Glenham had been leveled. Bay said he'd been thinking about following Zandra's husband to North Dakota, finding a private poker game, and getting himself some of that oil shale money. Mike walked in the door with a thousand-yard smile and dropped onto the love seat beside Bay and said, "What's new?"

I said, "Where have you been?"

"Girding up my loins, I think they call it."

"And how did that go?"

"Knocked it out of the park."

I said, "Now what?"

Patience said we were all going home to Florida. She'd bought the tickets when she purchased the Dakota tickets. "Nothing in

Everglades County could be as bad as what we've been through already."

Bay looked at Little Bob and said, "Why don't you three—you four—come with us."

Little Bob said, "Home is where the baby is."

Bay said, "Where's the nearest pediatrician?"

Lorena said, "Dr. Gadbois over in Glenham, but he drinks a bit."

Ophelia said, "*This* baby will take care of *us*."

And I was reminded of Eric back in Battle Mountain. *Not all there, but sweet as honey.*

Zandra kicked the door open, stepped inside, and leveled a pistol at Mike. I suppose I should have known no good would come of the carnal misalliance of Mike Lynch and Zandra Schine.

Lorena said, "What the hell is going on?"

Mike said, "The lady asked for a gratuity, and I politely declined."

Little Bob said, "Don't shoot, you'll wake the baby!"

And Zandra said, "The beautiful baby," and it was as if the vital flame in her face was extinguished, and she lowered her pistol and cried, and I knew then that Zandra had been denied a child in her own life, and that the emptiness that followed, and the grief that was its consequence, had driven Zandra into the greedy and plundering arms of goat-drunk men who were the unworthy but fortunate recipients of her aimless yearning and her aching hunger.

Little Bob said, "Sit your glorious ass down, Zandra, and have a drink."

And on that day of Emma Grace's baptism we all told stories late into the Dakota night so that we forgot all about moving on, and we sustained one another with laughter and sadness, and we thought that we understood, for the moment at least, the varieties of human experience, and on that night the legend was born of the woman of true voice, clothed in the sun, and the bright and lavish child, who together tamed the whirlwind and delivered us all to the Land of Vindication. And on that night, out on the porch, I drew Patience close and smelled the sweet clover scent of Emma Grace on her neck and inhaled her own savory fragrance laced with those odorless but intoxicating pheromones, and we heard the stirring baby cry, and in the succeeding stillness I proposed to Patience once again. I said, "Marriage?" She said, "Family." I smiled. Done!

# Acknowledgments

As always, thanks to Jill Bialosky for finding the story in the manuscript. And to Dave Cole, artist, poet, copy editor, and face-saver. Thanks to Maria Rogers for her generous feedback and incisive reading of the manuscript. To John Bond, who taught me what I know about poker. To Django and Zoë, who hung out with me on the writing desk and sometimes on the writing paper, and who managed to insinuate themselves into the book. Thanks to Bill Clegg for his faith and enthusiasm, and to Richard McDonough, without whom none of my books would have happened. Thanks to my colleague and walking partner, Julie Marie Wade, who also has a role in the book. Thanks to Florida International University's English Department and to my inspiring students. Thanks to Cindy, of course, and to Tristan. Thanks to my sweet family, Paula and Denis, Cyndi and Conrad, Mark and Lucy, Madelyn, Missy, Hiedi, Kristine and Roger, and my mom, Dot. And thanks to our extended family, Liz and Bruce, Kimberly and Jeremy, and Theo, my best pal, the boy who keeps me smiling, makes me happier than I may deserve to be, and who invented the Game of Pens.